PUSHING UP
DAISIES

Amanda Glenn

ISBN:1530818079

ISBN-13:9781530818075

For Chantall who taught me to edit and all four of my wonderful children who are always there when I need them and continually make me proud.

Cover photo: Margaret Eacker

Author photo: Karen Praxel

CHAPTER 1

Teddy Stanley pushed down with her sneaker-clad foot and the shovel slid easily into the earth, freeing a large clump of seedling-encrusted soil. Shovel after careful shovel full she lifted away the tiny plants. It was the second time in a week she'd taken them from their bed beside the garden path. Last Wednesday she'd been looking for the septic tank. It hadn't been pumped out since long before she'd inherited the house twelve years earlier, (if ever), and the drains had been very sluggish of late. She'd always known about where the septic was, just not precisely. A little poking with an old curtain rod paid off and a half-hour's shovel work revealed the secret under the purple daisy patch. After the pumping she'd carefully replaced the seedlings. Today the digging went quickly, she had the plants moved, the plastic pulled back, and was sitting on her top step enjoying a cup of coffee in the warm morning air when Kevin Bates arrived.

"I saved you the best part," she gave him a cheery smile, "you can pull off the old lid."

"No problem." A largish young man in his late twenties, he'd worked for Sam's Septic since high school, in a way he actually enjoyed his job. You met a lot of nice people, they were always grateful to see you, you were outside, more or less your own boss, and the pay was good. He reached down with gloved hands and, grasping the rim, removed the lid, meaning to lean it on the old stump at the edge of the grass.

"What the hell!" Kevin froze, his face gone pale. "It looks like Ben Raymond!"

Confused, Teddy stood to get a better look. Then she gulped, turned just a little pale herself, and agreed. "It is Ben Raymond. But what's he doing in my septic tank?"

An hour later Jefferson Adams Hubbard, the County Sheriff, known as "Sonny" to anyone who didn't have to call him Sir, wanted to know the same thing.

"What's he doing in there?" He rubbed a large hand through what was left of his once sandy-colored hair and eyed the very dead Ben Raymond as if somehow he was going to come up with an explanation.

"That's what I want to know and I want him out of there!" In the beginning Teddy had felt shocked – confused - her stomach churning as she tried to explain to herself the unexplainable. Now what she was feeling was more than a little put upon.

"Just as soon as the coroner gets here and the sergeant there gets through taking pictures," Sonny said. "I don't suppose you noticed anything strange or out of place before you dug up them daisies and made a mess of any possible footprints?"

"Before I dug up the daisies I didn't know there was any reason to check for footprints. Close as I can remember it looked pretty much the way it did last week when Kevin and Leroy finished pumping out the tank and I put them back. It rained some last night and the plants looked like they'd taken hold again real well, which is more than I'll be able to hope for if I don't get them planted back pretty quick now."

"Now Teddy, this is a murder scene and it may be awhile before you can do that." Sonny fixed her with his best "Me big smart man you dumb little woman," smile.

Teddy was having none of it.

"You take your pictures and you take Ben Raymond and you go play detective and find out what happened to him. I want that tank covered so I can get my purple daisies replanted and flush my toilet without it being a media event." She waved her hand in the direction of Sid Chapman, publisher (and, with his brother, owner and complete staff) of the local newspaper who was coming toward them, camera in hand.

Sid lifted the camera and snapped a quick shot of the two of them and then turned to stare into the gaping septic tank.

"What's Ben doing in there?" he asked, as he raised the camera again and began to document Ben Raymond's current situation for posterity.

"Not enjoying the privacy somebody expected he'd have, obviously," Teddy responded. "Between you and the sergeant I'll bet you've taken more pictures of Ben than he's had taken in the last twenty years. You print that picture of me, Sid, and you're a dead man."

"I'm going to put you on the front page Teddy, this is news." Sid grinned at her. "I figure I'm safe enough, you already have one body more than you can explain."

"Hummphh!" Teddy snorted, turned on her heels, and went back into the house for another cup of coffee.

Not overly tall, a shade over five-four, Teddy was compact and sturdy from years of waitressing. She'd worked in greasy-spoon-type places for the most part, with a tavern or two thrown in, and once when nothing else was available the kind of restaurant where she'd had to wear black skirts and white shirts and nylons. Teddy had hated the "uniform" wearing and stuck thereafter to the places where a clean pair of jeans, a little cotton shirt, and sneakers was the drill.

Married at sixteen, she now had two children in their forties and three grandchildren in their teens. Widowed twice and divorced once, Teddy had spent the last twelve years discovering how nice it was not to have to consider anybody's needs and desires but her own. She liked her independence, she liked her privacy, and right now she didn't like the threat to that privacy posed by the yard full of law and press that seemed to be swelling by the minute. She most particularly did not like the idea of her uninvited guest.

Teddy stood at the counter, sipping her coffee, watching through the kitchen window as a youngish man pulled on some kind of plastic coveralls and boots and then got Sonny and the sergeant to lower him into the septic tank. She felt her stomach flip-flop and wondered if she were going to be ill. She topped up her cup with what was left in the pot and made another one. That young man was going to need some when he came out of there.

A long two hours later the ambulance pulled away slowly through the crowd that covered the grassy slope up to the street and slopped over into the graveled dirt road. In addition to the local press and police officials there were neighbors, some of whom Teddy hadn't seen out of their own yards in months and even a few curiosity seekers from town. The grapevine was in good working order. By now the whole town knew at least as much as would be printed in the paper.

"Why can't I cover it up? What am I supposed to do, leave it open in case somebody wants to stick another body in there?" Teddy argued. "Some animal or a kid could fall in that hole and get hurt." Not to mention that it stank and after all that coffee she was going to need to flush the toilet eventually, and sooner rather than later. She was going to mention it, but Kevin spoke up.

"For pete's sake, Sonny, let us cover it up. We can all see it's empty now, that lab guy damn near strained what's left in there, there's nothing more to find. I got to go, I got people waiting on me."

Sonny stiffened, about to tell Kevin exactly where he could go and what he could do when he got there, but sagged suddenly. "Hell, go ahead. But do it quick. I want to see those damn daisies all back before I leave here and I don't ever want them moved again, hear."

Kevin didn't wait to be told twice. In minutes the new lid was on, the plastic replaced, and he and

Teddy were shoveling the dirt and daisies back in place.

The crowd began to thin, bodies and police and ambulances were exciting, two people covering up a septic tank ranked rather low in entertainment value, even around here.

A money-green pickup truck scrunched to a stop behind Sonny's patrol car just as Teddy patted the last of the daisies in place.

Rob Greene, tall, lean, and boyish, albeit about to turn fifty, slid his long Levi-clad legs off the seat and landed his size eleven, mud-encrusted cowboy boots on the gravel with a thud. "Hey, Sonny, "he called, "what's this they're saying about Ben?"

Rob was Ben's junior partner. Ben had hired and trained him over twenty years ago. Lots of other salespeople had come and gone from Ben's little real estate office since, but Rob had stayed and prospered.

"Well, if you heard he was dead, you heard right," Sonny answered, "and not from natural causes."

"An accident?" Rob asked. "How?"

"Don't know how yet. But no accident neither. You don't just go set yourself down in somebody's septic tank for a quiet rest and accidentally pull a lid and a bunch of dirt and daisies over you," Sonny said.

"Murder?!!" Rob looked at Teddy for confirmation.

"That's the way it looks," Teddy nodded.

"Who?" Rob asked, turning back to Sonny.

"Well now if I knew that, I'd be off arresting them instead of standing here watching Kevin and Teddy shoveling dirt around," Sonny barked. "I got some questions to ask Teddy and Kevin here and then I want to talk to you. Stick around."

Rob nodded his assent, solemn faced, and crossed the yard to give Teddy a hug.

"You had a rough morning looks like," he said, leaving an arm comfortably around her shoulders.

"I've certainly had better," she agreed.

"Sonny, I have to get going," Kevin protested. "The Tiddley's can't flush or anything and I've two stops after that."

"Kevin, you just come on down here to Teddy's picnic table and answer a couple of questions. Then you can be on your way," Sonny insisted, leading the way down the garden path.

"Want a beer?" Teddy offered Rob.

"It's only just after eleven," he answered, looking at his watch and then over at the limp daisies. "On second thought it's a great idea."

Teddy's tiny kitchen was spotlessly clean. She opened the door of the RV-sized refrigerator and extracted two beers, handing one to Rob.

"Let's go upstairs, I need to sit down," Teddy said.

"How'd Ben get in your septic tank?" Rob asked, following her.

The first floor of the little house was kitchen, bathroom, and bedroom. Upstairs was the living room. The roof slanted down steeply so that at the road end, over the kitchen, the living room headway was only five feet. The view on the ocean end was

11

spectacular. The Pacific Ocean rolled ceaselessly in on a wide, long beach, a fringe of spruce and pines stunted by the wind edged the view far to the south. Behind the trees a forested ridge rose, a spine of the coast range thrust forward to the sea. To the north the beach seemed to run on interminably. About half a mile up you could see where the highway bent west and ran along next to the sand. Below them on the patio, Sonny and Kevin sat talking at a weathered wooden picnic table. Below the patio was Teddy's garden, shades of green now, but Rob knew that soon it would be a marvelous maze of wildflowers, rosemary, lavender, and honeysuckle. A half-dozen spruce giants dotted about the yard, their green skirts spread high above the roof's level impeded neither sunshine nor view. At the bottom of the garden, on the left, three young spruce, maybe all of six-or seven-feet tall spread their boughs against the wind. Beyond the trees and a small low belt of wild vegetation was an undulating sand dune that only occasionally tried to enter the garden, beyond that, the beach and the sea.

Rob always found the view mesmerizing.

"I've been thinking," Teddy said, "I uncovered the septic tank last Wednesday, Kevin and Leroy pumped it out and put the old lid back on that afternoon. But I didn't cover it back up, put the dirt and flowers back, until Thursday morning. It has to have been Wednesday night. It was windy and raining some. I went to bed early with a book. I wouldn't have been able to see or hear anyone out there short of a brass band. The question is why. Why kill Ben? And why put him in my septic tank?"

CHAPTER 2

Teddy stared down at the tops of the heads below, Sonny's thinning, sandy-gray hair wisping in the breeze, Rob's dark brown hair, thicker and heavier, lifting only slightly in the playful early spring gusts off the Pacific.

Kevin had gone off to get the Tiddley's back in working order and she'd answered Sonny's questions, mostly about why she'd dug up the septic tank in the first place, and why again today.

It had been a hard decision, deciding on getting it pumped. She had tried everything she could think of first, Drano'd all the drains, used the stuff advertised to eat roots, grease etc., even snaked the line. The sink had still drained slowly, and the shower continued to back up. Last Wednesday she'd finally given up, accepted the inevitable, and made the call. Teddy knew the guys from Sam's Septic would have uncovered it for her, but they would have charged her for it, too, and besides she hadn't been sure where it was. As it was, she had just finished brushing the last bit of dirt from the tank's very rusty, four-foot-diameter lid when the large pumper truck arrived. The lid really did look in pretty sad shape and she wondered how much it was going to cost to get it repaired. In the end it simply would have cost too much. The tank was too old and they didn't make them any more so it would have had to be special made, at a probable cost of $200 plus. Teddy's social security check and small savings did not stretch to such luxuries. The old lid with the addition of some heavy plastic would have to suffice. What had really irked was that the tank was in fine working order, the pumping not really necessary, it was the leach lines that were clogged and, if she couldn't unclog them, would need to be replaced. That meant finding them, digging them up... well it was not going to be fun but it was work she could do herself. Last night, Monday night it was, Kevin had called - he and Leroy had just replaced a failed tank with a whole new system. The lid on the tank they removed had been replaced just two years ago and was in great shape and would fit her tank, would she like to have it for $40 - installation free? Would she ever. Kevin said he'd bring it by in the morning.

If Kevin had not been enterprising enough to think of recycling that cover Ben would never have been found, at least not until the tank failed or was pumped again, but that would have been years. Teddy shuddered.

Sonny and Rob were still talking. Sonny seemed to have more questions for Rob than he'd had for her or Kevin. Was it stuffy in here she wondered.

Yes, it is stuffy.

If she slid open the side window she might get a little fresh air and, just possibly, a clue as to what was taking so long out there.

"...no, I'll call Ben's daughter. Her number is bound to be at the office somewhere," Rob said.

"Thanks, appreciate that. I'm better at telling people they can pick up the family heavy drinker in the morning than at letting people know about family dead in automobile accidents or..., well we haven't had a murder around here, not one where we didn't know exactly who did it, in years. Last murder I had to deal with was three years ago when Jenny Harker shot her husband to keep him from beating up on her and the kids one more time." Sonny paused, "I may need to go through Ben's things, at his house and the office, too. Wouldn't be a good idea if anyone went messing around with his stuff until we get this all straightened out. You explain that to Trix, she might be a bit anxious to get her hands on her dad's assets and I don't want her fouling up my investigation."

"I'll tell her. I'll have to check on anything he has pending but otherwise we'll just lock up his office."

"Well, while you're looking, keep an eye out for anything could have made someone mad enough to kill him. It don't seem to me Ben had any more enemies than anyone else, certainly none pushed out of shape bad enough to kill him. But someone sure as hell went and did it. He threaten to toss out any renters lately? I ain't seen no paperwork for eviction since that bunch in the mobile home up Piney Lane before Thanksgiving."

Teddy heard the sound of the bench grating on the cement and dared a peek to confirm that they were rising.

Sonny was still talking. "You sure Ben said he was going fishing alone."

"Made a point of it. Said he'd had enough of people for a while and would be back when he could stand the sight of them again." Rob chuckled, "it generally took him three to four weeks to get tired of eating fish and biscuits and wanting a hot bath."

Sonny turned and paused on the path. "He didn't mention any particular person or group of people I suppose?"

"There's his own rental properties of course, but he'd pretty much retired, hadn't worked any new clients for more than a year now. I'm overseeing the on-going projects and joint ventures. Only people I know for sure he's been seeing are his poker pals. You know better than I who they are."

Teddy hurried down to the door hoping to flag Rob down for a little additional conversation. Sonny drove off immediately, Rob turned and started back toward her.

"Got another beer?" Rob made a face, "I have to call the witch - Ben's daughter - and I think I need fortification first."

"Beer, and soup and a sandwich?" Teddy asked. "It's past lunch time."

"Great," Rob said, coming up the steps. "It's just beginning to dawn on me how much worse it's going to get before it gets better." He accepted the beer she held out to him. "I am now in partnership with "Tricky Trix". That woman now owns fifty-or-more percent of damn near everything I've got."

"Sounds like a bad divorce," Teddy teased.

"Any divorce from Trix would be a good one, ask any of her ex-husbands. Though I want you to know I'm insulted by even the suggestion that I would ever have slept with her." Rob smiled and the glazed look that had come over his blue eyes in the last couple of hours turned back into a sparkle. He sat down in one of the chairs at the little drop-leaf table tucked against the wall between the door and the bottom of the stairs.

"Old Sonny was really working at you out there," Teddy said, her back to him as she busied herself turning a potato, a can of cream corn, and another of non-fat evaporated milk into corn chowder. A single slice of thick-cut bacon, diced, sautéed while she chopped scallions and peeled and diced the potato.

"He wanted to know when I saw Ben last - saw was about it. Monday of last week, he came in when I had some people in my office. I saw him go up the hall to his office and then he left again in just a few minutes, waved on his way out. That was early, before ten anyway. The last time I talked to him was the Saturday before. We had breakfast at Petal's and went over a couple of things on the Windward House and the Harbor Court projects and he told me he was going fishing - said he'd probably be gone a good while." Rob took a deep breath and shook his head. "Sonny wanted to know if he seemed worried about anything. We'd been having some trouble convincing Dave and the others to come to me for decisions and leave Ben out of it. I think Ben was going fishing so they wouldn't have a choice, but I don't think it was really worrying him. Worried me more, irritated really. Every time I tell them something they either ignore me and do just as they jolly well please or they call - called - Ben up and got him to agree it should be done their way. Teddy, they want to keep building cheap, sub-standard housing, doing bare necessity fix-ups, like they've been doing for the last half-century, and the market has changed. There are newer and better ways to do things and in many instances it really doesn't cost any more. They just don't want to learn."

It was a familiar theme, Rob had spent more than one lunch at the little table moaning over the effort it was taking to pull the local contractors out of their 50's – 60's mindset and into even the near present, technologically.

"Onions?" Teddy asked, her hand poised over a stack of thick slices of ham, lettuce, and pickles on dark rye from the local bakery.

"Of course. And lots of that dark mustard," Rob grinned then his face went sober. "Teddy, the last time I talked to Ben we fought. I mean, the man who took a chance on me, helped and trusted me, and the last time I see him before he dies we fight."

"About changing your orders with his pals?" Teddy asked, giving the soup a stir with a wooden spoon and fishing out a piece of potato to check for doneness.

"MMMmm," Rob nodded in the affirmative. "Dave changed my siding order and had it half installed before I discovered it. It'd cost too much to tear it off and start over, so one more time I'm stuck with it. Then when I told Ben, he said Dave had talked to him about it and he'd agreed there was nothing wrong with using the same stuff they always had. Teddy he just won't... wouldn't let go of the reins and tell Dave, or any of them, that it is my decision and to talk to me if they have a problem."

"I'd say that the 'good ole' boys' are going to have to take orders now." Teddy added a shake of pepper to the soup pot. "You really all that worried about dealing with Ben's daughter?"

"Ben said Trix has mellowed out, sure couldn't tell by the last time I saw her. Last Christmas she was in the office trying to convince Ben to sell his house. He's been gifting her a $10,000 portion of the title every year now for years, she wanted him to sell the house and give her 'her share' of the cash. She was really working on him to move into something smaller, kept up about how she worried about him alone out there on his mountain. If she was so damn worried she could have tried calling him more than two or three times a year. Ben once said it was a good thing she got married and divorced so much - only time he heard from her, when she needed money for a wedding or a divorce. Anyway it ended up in a shouting match. He wouldn't give in and she said she hoped he'd die up there all alone."

Teddy set a bowl of steaming soup and a plate with two of the three big chunks of the sandwich and some chips down on the rough-textured blue placemat in front of him and went back for hers. "So if she wants to liquidate everything can you buy her out?"

"Don't I just wish. But that wouldn't be as bad as trying to do business with her. I don't think she's had more than two or three civil words for me in the almost twenty years I've known her. I think she's jealous. You know, Ben always treated me like a son and her like an obligation."

"You said she was ten when Ben remarried and sent her away to boarding school. She never had much of a relationship with him after that. I could see being jealous of the closeness you and Ben had. Don't borrow trouble, maybe she'll just keep out of the way and let you take care of keeping the money rolling in."

They ate in companionable silence, each lost in their own thoughts about the morning.

"Teddy, Sonny asked me about you," Rob said, scooping the last mouthful of soup from his bowl.

"What about me?" she stopped, sandwich half way to her mouth and lay it back on the plate.

"About whether you and Ben were ever... well, you know." Rob had the good graces to blush slightly behind the grin spreading across his face.

Teddy shook her head, not sure whether to be indignant or find it funny. "Ben was a married man when I moved here, which I guess in today's world doesn't mean diddley but it does to me, presuming I'd have ever been interested in the first place. And he was old. I don't mean just the years, ten - fifteen years one way or the other isn't all that much. Ben was old acting, old thinking - him and his gaggle of good ole' boys." Teddy laughed, softening the edge of her words, "Bunch of big spenders. They used to sit there all morning drinking coffee, cracking bad jokes, expecting you to laugh at their lewd suggestions and flirting and then leave a giant fifty-cent tip and I don't mean apiece either. Just two lone little quarters sitting there on the table, half the time they forgot that."

Until this time last year Teddy had worked the breakfast shift at Petal's, Monday through Friday.

Teddy'd worked one or two other places in town before becoming a fixture at Petal's, but she liked the morning shift. She liked that it was less than a three-mile drive from her house, and she had found a kindred spirit of a sort in Rene (she pronounced it Reen), the woman who worked the morning shifts on weekends and backed her up weekdays in the summer months. The four hours, five days a week provided just enough income to keep her head above water. The extra tips from the town's influx of tourist types in the summer provided enough to pay her car insurance, property taxes, and utilities for the winter and swell her modest savings. A trip over the garden hose last spring had sent her tumbling down the hill and left her bruised all over, with a severe sprain to her left ankle. That was when she let her daughter talk her into checking out the possibility of receiving social security benefits based on the earnings of her second husband. It had surprised her no end to find out that she was indeed eligible. She and Phillip Stanley had been married more than twenty years when he died but that was well over twenty years ago. It had surprised her more that the income would just about match what she'd been earning. There was no advantage at all for her to wait until she was sixty-five. Teddy'd stopped worrying about how soon she could manage to get around well enough to go back to work and tendered her resignation - quit.

"I went to dinner and dancing at the Elks a couple of times with Keith before Liza hooked him, but he's the only one of that crowd I ever went out with."

"More fool Keith," Rob said loyally.

21

"Lucky me, I'd say. I can't even begin to imagine putting up with that pompous drunk. It's a wonder he hasn't managed to electrocute himself after one of his liquid lunches."

"Mmmm," Rob nodded agreement. "Keith is also on my shit list right now, I told him I didn't want light fixtures in the bedroom ceilings at Windward, to wire the nightstand plugs to the switches, but he seems to have forgotten and now the wallboard has been hung, it's too late to change it. Probably too drunk to remember." Rob looked at his watch. "I've got to go. I have to call Trix and then I guess I better see what needs to be done about arrangements, too. I'd bet you anything Trix is going to leave that in my lap." He folded his napkin and stood up.

Teddy stood, too. "Call me if you hear anything, I'm a little out of the gossip loop out here." She stepped forward into his open arms for a hug and let her head rest against his chest for a heartbeat thinking, as always, how good a man could smell. "I don't want to have to go to Petal's for coffee every day just to keep up on the excitement."

CHAPTER 3

Teddy spent the rest of Tuesday in conversation. On the phone with acquaintances, some she hadn't spoken to in months who just had to call and get the inside info on Ben's murder, or standing in her yard with assorted neighbors all of whom were "just out walking" (some for the second time today) and stopped by to say hello.

The neighborhood was not exactly urban. Arlington "Avenue" was an unsurfaced road - dirt and whatever gravel the residents cared to add to make it passable - a block long, between two equally unpaved streets that ran down from the coast highway. There were three houses on the ocean side of the street with a minimum of one vacant lot between them. Teddy's house was the middle one, the oldest and smallest. There was only one house on the other side, at the north end of the block. Both of the side streets had several houses, "new" construction, one or two years old, huge modern glass palaces almost on the beach, made to look all the bigger by their perch on the pillars required by the current building codes to keep them above storm surge. By comparison, Teddy's little shingled house looked like a detached woodshed.

The vacant lots were all pretty well wooded, a mixture of spruce, skinny shore pines and shy hemlock with an occasional cedar and here and there a thicket of pussy willow or swale ash. Wild rhodies and fuchsia would turn the street into a garden path in another couple of months. Right now it was a hundred shades of green and normally deserted, most walkers preferring the wide beach.

The other two houses on Teddy's side of the street were second homes. The one to her south used as a short-term rental with a different family there every weekend. The house to the north with just one semi-cleared lot in between belonged to the Bensons, Lon and Minna. They lived in the valley and had been weekend residents on Arlington Avenue for going on thirty years. Furst Hanby, a retired wheat farmer and his wife Anna, lived in the house across the street and a lot or two beyond the Bensons. Furst was a pleasant, sweet-tempered man. Anna was a bitch-and-a-half, and didn't like Teddy. But even she was willing to overlook that today and came walking down the street just as the Lynches, from across the highway, were finally leaving. Anna stood on the garden path, stared at the wilted daisies atop Teddy's septic, and asked all the same questions.

"How did he get in there? Didn't you hear anything? Who do you suppose did it? When did it happen?" Then came what was becoming the usual observations. "A man that rich must have a lot of enemies." "Must have been quite a shock." After that the conversations had generally turned to the sad state of affairs in today's world, etc. Finally, the phone would ring or another walker would stroll casually by, and the whole thing would go on instant replay.

About five, the gathering dusk was darkened by a potential rainstorm and the curious on foot or otherwise seemed to be taking a dinner break. Teddy decided to leave the phone calls to the answering machine and pull her shades.

She put a chicken breast in the oven to roast atop a bed of chopped carrot, celery, and onion and went up to watch the evening news.

The phone was ringing. What time was it? Teddy opened an eye to peep at the clock, 6:30, not too early to get up but to early to be calling. She lay still and listened for the answering machine to pick up.

"Come on Teddy, if you're not awake you should be. I gotta work for Doris this morning. Come on down and have breakfast, I want to hear all about it."

"Damn you Rene, I was sleeping good. Had a real nice dream going," Teddy said, having swung her feet to the floor and lurched to the kitchen to pick up the receiver.

"I been up two hours and I don't want to hear about you all warm and cozy and dreaming. We got fresh biscuits coming out of the oven in the next half hour, get moving," Rene instructed and hung up.

Teddy showered, dressed, applied lipstick, eyeliner, and mascara, made the bed, and was out the door in just over twenty minutes. At five after seven she stirred cream into her coffee and lifted the cup, breathing in the pungent steam to savor the bouquet before taking her first sip.

"So tell me all about it," Rene demanded.

Teddy was sitting, back to the door, to the rear of the narrow cafe, away from the popular front booths and the ears of the curious. There were only two of the regulars in thus far but more were inevitable and Teddy knew they would not be shy.

"You put in my order?" Teddy asked.

"When you walked through the door. You'll get your bacon when the biscuits come out of the oven. Talk." Rene knew what all the regulars and most of the semi-regulars ate, how they liked their eggs, and how they took their coffee. Once in a while someone surprised her with a sudden desire to vary their diet, but not often. She delivered the cream with the coffee and would bring the butter and honey for the biscuits on her next pass with the coffeepot. The two in the front booth were digging into their pancakes and Rene stood waiting for Teddy to confirm the details of the wild story the cook had told her when she arrived.

Rene lived up river, half an hour from town, and only came in when she worked. She'd lost her husband and her teenage son in a car accident years ago and moved home to live with her parents. They raised goats and made cheese, most of which got shipped to a big deli in Portland, and eked out a living on land Rene's grandfather or great-grandfather, Teddy couldn't remember which, had settled as a pioneer. Rene provided better than good service, a friendly smile, and a tolerant ear to the kibitzers and flirts. She had never dated, not a customer, not anyone. She wasn't interested. It wasn't just that her parents, now in their eighties, needed her, she was content with her life just the way it was. A good gossip with Teddy every now and again was all the socializing she was interested in.

Teddy relayed the now all-too-familiar story in bits and snatches as Rene moved back and forth taking care of arriving, eating, and departing patrons.

"There can't be too many people know I had my septic pumped," Teddy observed as Rene paused to top up her cup.

"I heard Leroy talking about being out at your place one morning last week. He was having coffee with that bunch he runs with. They were getting set to go clear a lot somewhere. He was talking about how you left some trees and the wild rhodies and myrtles."

A bell dinged signaling plates ready for service and Rene moved off toward the kitchen window. She delivered the plates, rang up a tab, and poured more decaf for a regular at the counter before returning.

"Last time I saw Ben he came in for breakfast Saturday with Rob. Boy, the two of them were sure grumbling at each other. Then Rob left and Dave, Keith, and Jamie showed up and they all grumbled at Ben some, too. Ben didn't seem to be on anybody's good side." Rene went off to see that her customers were content, filling a cup here, getting extra jelly there and then, after making a fresh pot of coffee, returned to pick up the conversation. "Same morning both the Paileys lit into him, something about some investment Ben had handled for them."

The little dining room was suddenly very full and Teddy sat and munched her crisp bacon and enjoyed the hot-from-the-oven biscuits and honey while she mulled what Rene had told her.

So, any number of people could have known her septic tank to be empty and ready for visitors. Kevin and Leroy must pump two or three every day, why hers? The isolation? Convenient to where he had been killed? How had he been killed? Mentally she began a list of things to find out when she talked to Rob next, adding immediately an inquiry about the nature of the Paileys' investment and the reason for their unhappiness.

"Hey girl, what you doing hiding back here."

"Well, hello to you, too. How's Pete the pest today?" Teddy replied. Pete Metler, the newest of the regulars having been in town barely three years now, slid in across from her, his lanky legs seeming to fill up the space under the table. A solid built man, tallish, lots of white wavy hair, and kind brown eyes, he had moved here permanently after his wife died. Before then they had been weekend people. Pete had begun to "court" Teddy right off, coming in for breakfast everyday, talking her up and hinting they should "get together". Even after Teddy had quit work, Pete had used his friendship with the Bensons as an excuse to drop in.

"Just checking to see if they were down," he'd say, "thought I might as well say hello while I was in the neighborhood." They would talk for a while, generally out on the patio or sitting on the steps. Teddy always felt an invitation up to her living room seemed to offer more intimacy than she wanted. Once or twice when it had been raining she'd asked him into the kitchen for coffee, but few men besides Rob ever made it up the stairs. Rob didn't count.

"I hear you had some excitement at your place yesterday," Pete said, and then looked up with a smile at Rene as she delivered his coffee.

"I want two eggs over easy, bacon and hashbrowns, crisp, and..."

"...a short stack with syrup, unheated." Rene finished for him. She smiled and went to drop the order.

"One of these days I'm going to order something else and really surprise her," Pete laughed.

He went on to ask "the questions" and Teddy found herself feeling put out. She gave him "the answers" short form and when Rene came with his breakfast refused a refill, paid up, and left.

Two people hailed her before she got to her car and when she'd answered their queries, Teddy headed for the post office, glad it was still early and would be deserted. Today's mail would not be up for another hour. She hadn't been to the post office for several days so she knew there would be something in the box, junk mail if nothing else. Junk mail was exactly what she got, the box was stuffed solid with it. Teddy piled it into her tote to separate and burn in her little stove at her leisure and headed home.

As she passed Rob's office she saw him standing in the doorway talking with an animated Marrianne Pailey. Rob looked up, waved, and flashed Teddy a smile. Teddy waved back and caught daggers from the eyes of the disapproving Marrianne.

Marrianne Pailey was not the only one in town who disapproved, or did not understand, her friendship with Rob.

CHAPTER 4

When Teddy first inherited the little house she'd had no intentions of keeping it. She and Hal, her husband at the time, had driven to the coast to check it out. Hal declared it an uninhabitable shack, which it pretty much was. No foundation to speak of. A cinder block enclosed workroom at the downhill end offered some stability, but the house was held up for the most part by huge timbers that looked like they might have been beach salvage, planted in cement so that the "basement" looked like the underside of a wharf.

The house itself had no insulation, no wallboard, just the bare studding. Well, not bare really. Edmund Reises had been a maker of stringed instruments, lyres, mandolins, and violins. Instruments in all states of construction hung everywhere. And tools, tools of the oddest and most exotic nature. When they found the key to the basement workroom they found it was stacked with wood, judging from the labels, most of it rare with unpronounceable names. The metal shower in the tiny bathroom made you wish you'd updated your tetanus shot. The quarter-inch plywood walls that closed it off from the rest of the house and more or less provided the separation between the kitchen and the bedroom seemed to amplify the bathroom sounds one normally would prefer to have repressed.

The lot abutted the beach but it was impossible to see the water, though you could hear its roar muted by the thick stand of trees that seemed to have the tiny structure under siege, towering over it, surrounding it, ready to reclaim it given the chance. A barely discernable path wound between the trunks and under the drooping branches. Teddy felt like the flying monkeys from the Wizard of Oz would sweep out of the darkness any second as she and Hal pushed their way through the encroaching salal and suddenly arrived at the dune. It had been a glorious day, the sun warm, the whole Pacific Ocean clear blue-green rushing to shore in lace trimmings.

"Pretty nice huh?" Teddy'd said awed.

"It'll bring the price up some," Hal retorted.

They'd gone to town to find a Realtor and found Rob. Rob came out first thing the next morning and Teddy signed the listing, but it was already too late. She had cooked breakfast on the dangerous looking stove and sat at the old formica table with its mismatched, rusted, chrome and plastic chairs, drunk her coffee and come to understand that this was hers. The very first thing that had ever been hers and hers alone.

It had always been rented - apartments, trailers, houses - always rented. And always where and what someone else had chosen. Married at sixteen to a man ten years her senior, she had been a widow at nineteen with one small child and another on the way. Within a year she had married again, John Stanley had been almost twenty years older.

She'd moved in with her mother when Stan died, and that had not been a good time. Not quite a year later she met Hal. He was five years her junior, had a motorcycle not a car, was a roofer and made good money. He liked to party and made her feel like she was young again. It had been fun at first. Hal didn't save, he smoked too much, drank too much, and he wasn't real keen on the institute of marriage. He sure as hell didn't want to be grandpa. A tug of war developed between Hal and her family.

As long as they did what Hal wanted, as long as there were just the two of them, life was pretty nice. But it left no room for anything that might be Teddy's. Not her children, not her grandchildren, not her aging parent, or her far-flung circle of aging siblings, and they all seemed to have need of her. While Stan had lived, she had been their mainstay, the anchor of reality as they went through life's crises. Things had changed but old habits of dependence clung on and it rubbed an incurable sore that only grew and festered between Hal and herself.

They didn't really fight on the way home from the beach. Teddy was too busy thinking, dreaming. By the time they turned in the driveway she had mentally cut down the majority of the trees, constructed a foundation, put up wallboard, painted, designed a kitchen, and was planting a garden. Her garden, her house, her ocean beach to walk on.

Hal said she was nuts and pretended she'd never mentioned keeping the little house. He started planning the bike trip they would take when they got the money.

Her mother said it was dangerous to live out there in the middle of nowhere, she'd get killed in her bed, she was just being foolish - again.

Her daughters wanted to know what she thought she was going to live on and let her know they thought she was being selfish moving so far away from them and her grandchildren. Teddy accused them (not unjustly) of being worried about where they were going to get another free babysitter.

The more they all harangued, the more they disbelieved, the more determined Teddy became. Stan had been a handyman and a good one. She'd learned a lot over the years about the things she would need to know to turn the shack into a home. She could do it, she knew she could do it. Knew she had to at least try. Three weeks after she first set eyes on her inheritance she packed up her Toyota hatchback and headed for the beach, ostensibly to clear out Edmund's tools and personal things. In her heart she knew she was never coming back.

She sold most of the tools and woods to a violinmaker that had stopped by to visit, unaware of Edmund's death. Reluctant to use the chainsaw she found in the basement she took a small bow saw and removed some of the most offensive branches on the path to the beach. Then she cleaned out, threw out, and rearranged. When the food she'd brought with her ran low, Teddy went to town and stocked up and on the way home she stopped and told Rob she had decided not to sell.

She'd been sure he would be angry with her, everyone else was.

Rob, not only wasn't angry, he offered to come by and show her how to use the chainsaw. They cut down three broken and sad looking pines and let the sunshine back into the front of the house. Working together, they limbed the trees, piling the slash to be burned, stacking the wood to be split to fit her tiny wood-burning stove. Teddy fixed him potato chowder and ham sandwiches and they'd talked, each about their problems and their dreams. They'd been friends ever since.

It was an intimate friendship, emotionally and intellectually, not physically. They'd both been married then, though both marriages were unraveling. By the time they were both free the friendship had gotten too precious to risk by taking it to such a dangerous plain. Teddy needed to find her own life, was too hungry for her independence, too afraid of losing her friend to whatever of life's monsters inevitably took away her lovers. It was the one topic they never discussed. As far as Teddy knew he just didn't feel that way about her and never would. Why would he? That was okay, he was her friend, and she was sure of that. Sure that in that way, he truly loved her.

They talked, on the phone, or Rob would take her to lunch, or she would fix him lunch. They played sounding board for each other, offered suggestions, and never minded if the other didn't take it. It was the laughing together that was best and after a talk with Rob life always seemed to fall back into perspective. Giant problems shrank to manageable proportions and heavy weights were lightened and even discarded.

Teddy'd known a lot of people. Good people some of them. Most of them had seemed to need an awful lot from her, some had demanded more than she could give in return for their friendship. Rob asked for absolutely nothing, except perhaps the dark brown mustard that Teddy didn't personally care for, and he always seemed to be there when she needed him. She wasn't about to try and explain that to anyone. They wouldn't understand. How could they, she didn't really understand it herself but she was eternally grateful for it. The last twelve years had been the happiest of her life.

In a small town people do talk, but after the first five or six years their friendship was just one more of the accepted local anomalies. Now and again someone might speculate, but it just wasn't new gossip any more. As for Marrianne Pailey's disapproval, well she disapproved of everything and everyone west of Philadelphia where, she seemed certain, civilization stopped.

CHAPTER 5

Teddy arrived home to find Sonny parked on the road in front of her house, leaning against his car, talking on his cell phone.

She pulled off into the graveled rectangle that was her "garage to be" and waved a greeting at him.

"Where the hell you been," Sonny demanded, snapping the little phone shut and shoving it in his jacket pocket.

"Petal's, eating breakfast, like I do at least once or twice a week. Why?" And what the hell business is it of yours, she wanted to say but didn't.

"We got us a murder investigation here and I expect a little cooperation," he said unreasonably.

"Sonny, you have a murder investigation - that is not my problem. I just happen to find the body, that's all," Teddy retorted.

"Yes, well, the way I see it there has to be a reason Ben Raymond ended up in your septic tank. I gotta believe you're involved somehow. Could be you killed him. Or could be someone wanted us to think you did," Sonny said, placing his ham fists on his well-padded hips and looking at her hard. "Ben's buddies are all up in arms and wanting answers. Now! I ain't going to let them push me none but I aim to get this cleared up quick-like. There's an election coming up and I don't want to give that bunch supporting Hugh Snow anything to go on about."

"And a solved murder will be a feather in your cap," Teddy said, with a bit of a smirk.

"Right," Sonny agreed. "So why don't you invite me in and we can get down to brass tacks."

Teddy sighed. This was not the way she'd envisioned spending the morning.

They sat at the kitchen table.

"So, she asked, "What more do you think I can tell you?"

"You said you went to bed early Wednesday night," he consulted a twisted little notebook that appeared to be about half full already with page after page of Sonny's angular scrawl. "About 8:30 - you always go to bed that early?"

"I have a TV in the bedroom. If it's chilly, sometimes I go to bed to read or watch TV in the evening rather than try to keep the fire going." Teddy felt invaded, her personal habits were none of his business.

"You got a good motion light out there over the door. Anyone coming into the yard would set it off. And it ain't broke, I tested it while I was waiting," Sonny accused.

Teddy just looked at him waiting for him to make his point.

"Teddy, shouldn't you have noticed that light going on?" He said with eyebrows raised quizzically.

She looked at him puzzled.

"You trying to tell me you didn't know someone was out there fooling around in your yard?" He was almost triumphant.

"I told you yesterday, I didn't see or hear a thing."

Teddy was astounded, Sonny was implying she had somehow been involved in the murder. "The only window on this floor on that side of the house is the frosted one in the bathroom. See for yourself." She got up and led the way first to the door of the bathroom. The compact little room contained a stacked washer and dryer as well as the shower stall, the sink and the commode. A small, 6-X-18-inch, horizontal frosted-glass window, the kind that crank out, was high on the outside wall. It would certainly pick up little to no glow from the motion light.

Teddy didn't say a word but, grim-lipped, led him into the bedroom. The south wall was all closets, the only window a nine-foot, insulated, double pane of glass looking west, toward the beach.

"Great view," Sonny said grudgingly.

"When I go to bed I shut the drapes." She lifted the edge of the navy blue drape lined with heavy white material. "They pretty much cut out any light even in the day." She yanked the cord and the heavy drapes slid shut completely darkening the room and then yanked the cord so that daylight flooded back in making them both blink.

Sonny looked around at the position of the bed and the door.

"Sonny, even with the door open, which it was, I couldn't have seen a light shining in that bathroom window if you were standing out there with a flashlight shining it in on purpose. Like I told you I did not see or hear a thing. And even if I had been able to see the light was on, that thing comes on for every deer, rabbit, or stray cat, even a hail storm or heavy rain sometimes, I'd have ignored it like always." She had a sudden thought. "There were renters in next door. At least one of those bedrooms has a window that might have caught the light. Why don't you go ask David at the rental place if he has their name and phone number?"

Sonny, whose face had been getting more and more glum as it became apparent that Teddy could not possibly have seen the light if it had gone on, brightened.

"I was going to do that anyway. And just because you couldn't have seen the light if you were in bed like you say, it don't mean you couldn't have been the one out there putting Ben in that hole or helping someone to do it." Sonny's face brightened further.

"Sure and then I forgot all about his being there and invited Kevin to come uncover him." Teddy was furious. "That is the stupidest idea I ever heard. I'm not that dumb, though you may be to have come up with it."

"Now Teddy, don't go getting all upset," Sonny soothed.

"And I am not going to stand here in my bedroom arguing with you about it. Why in heaven's name would I kill Ben?" Teddy strode quickly back to the kitchen and opened the door. "Unless you have anymore questions I have work to do."

Sonny was not to be put off. He followed her down the hall but plopped himself back on the chair at the table. "Only a couple more," he said, checking his notebook. "You talk to Rob last Wednesday?"

"Rob?" Teddy saw where Sonny was leading. She didn't have any plausible reason to kill Ben but Rob might have and she might have been willing to help him. Well that was a lot of nonsense, too. "You mean did I tell Rob I was getting my septic pumped? As a matter of fact I don't recall that I did. It was sort of a decision at the last minute. I don't think I talked to him Wednesday at all." The minute she said it she knew she was wrong, she had talked to him late that afternoon. She had called him, frustrated with the needless cost of the pumping, the need for the unaffordable new lid and the backbreaking task before her of digging up and cleaning out the damned drain field. She had even told him she had not finished putting back the daisies. She willed Sonny not to ask again, if he did she would have to tell him the truth. Rob hadn't, wouldn't have, killed Ben. Rob was incapable of hurting, let alone killing anyone. She believed that without question, still, no sense giving Sonny ideas. Sonny seemed out to find a killer, not necessarily the killer.

"He ever complain to you about Ben?" Sonny asked.

"Sure, though not as badly as you grouse about the county board and you haven't killed any of them yet, though I do remember you saying a time or two you'd take pleasure in wringing their collective throats."

"I mean specifically. Recently," Sonny insisted in a tone of voice he reserved for speaking to children, small dogs, and women when they seemed not to understand what was expected of them.

"Specifically, no," Teddy equivocated. Generally speaking Rob had been very unhappy with Ben's inability to let go of the controls with one hand while pushing the responsibility on him with the other. Ben had taken all the legal steps to give Rob full control over the business months ago. Rob had not been willing to remind him and his buddies of that, the town was too small not to make every effort for a smooth transfer of power. He had resisted her urgings, and she knew the urgings of others, to just lay it on the line and tell Ben and the rest of the good ole' boys in no uncertain terms to straighten up or he would begin working with other contractors for the services they provided. No, Teddy thought, Rob already held the trump card, there was no reasonable argument for the case Sonny was trying to make. She smiled at the thought as a cold chill tickled down her spine. Since when had Sonny ever felt the need to be reasonable?

You look kind of green," Sonny observed. "Want to tell me about it?" he asked hopefully.

"Just a woman thing," Teddy said, taking a deep breath and giving him a smile that just dared him to make some kind of remark about her being too old for PMS or hot flashes.

Sonny apparently found the statement too much to deal with, he cleared his throat several times and backed toward the door.

"You don't go nowhere out of town until we get this all wrapped, right?" He ended the admonishment with a plea.

"Didn't have any plans to," Teddy replied.

"Yeah, well just let me know if your plans change. I might have some more questions." Sonny clomped down the steps and up the grassy slope to the street pulling his cell phone from his pocket as he went. He sat in his car several minutes talking animatedly and then roared off down the street spitting gravel.

Teddy stood in the door, staring, but not seeing the band of blue sky above the trees across the road, or the fresh green tips on the spruce trees, or the hard swollen buds on the wild rhodies. She wished she had asked Rene a few more questions about what Dave, Keith, and Jamie'd had to discuss with Ben that last morning. And about the Paileys, too, for that matter. Teddy stepped back across her threshold determined to ask Rene to come out for lunch after work. Rene always seemed to enjoy it and it had been a while.

Her hand was stretched for the phone when it rang and made her jump.

"Hello?"

"Want to hear a good one?" Rob's voice was light and unworried.

"You have a good new joke?" Teddy asked.

"More like an old bad one. It seems two weeks ago Ben signed a new will and put everything into a trust. It gives me his remaining interest in the office, clear and clean, and set up for me to cash the trust out of our other partnerships and investments over ten years. Trix is going to have a cow. All she gets is a monthly check, for life. I'm the trustee and to manage all the property and I'm the residual beneficiary if she has no - and I quote - natural born children."

"But she's never had any and didn't she have..."

"...a hysterectomy years ago. Ben always blamed her for not having children, even claimed the surgery was her fault for staying on the pill too long. Guess this was his way of ragging at her one last time. Cruel if you think about it," Rob said. "On the other hand the trust will keep her from running through the money and dying a street person, which is what he always prophesied she'd do. And it leaves me in control just like he said he would."

"It also leaves you taking care of her trust forever. She's not more than a year or so older than you and though she does smoke like a chimney and drink too much, too, I'd say, she looked in relatively good health the few times I've seen her. You will be taking care of Trix's business for a long time."

There was a quiet on the line and Teddy knew she had punctured his balloon. "At least this will crimp Sonny's theory. He's getting all fixed to accuse you of murdering Ben. I think he has me down as accessory."

"You're kidding!" Rob chuckled, "Guess he's worried about the next election and needs a quick answer. Too bad I'm not guilty, going to spoil his plan."

"I got the uncomfortable feeling he was after an easy arrest and wasn't willing to work too hard for it - like in being sure of guilt. I think you better be careful."

"But I have no motive," Rob began to explain then went quiet again. "I guess if I were Sonny, I could see this trust business as a very good motive. I mean now there is no doubt about my position. As long as Ben was alive he could have changed his mind, kept interfering. Damn this is getting complicated."

44

"No kidding." Teddy responded, "And liable to get more so before it gets better. Just think how thrilled Trix is going to be when you tell her about the trust. Bet she tries to get it broken or whatever it is they do."

"No bet, but Ben's lawyer says it's set up to penalize her if she tries. You got plans for lunch tomorrow? I have to go meet with the lawyer this afternoon and in the morning I'm meeting with "Burying Bob" at the funeral home. I'll tell you all the ghoulish legal details and you can tell me all about Sonny's little flight of fantasy."

"Deal, what time you picking me up?"

Teddy called and caught Rene before she left for home.

"Can't today but I'm working for Doris all this week, she's gone east to see her new grandbaby."

"Friday then?" Teddy did not like putting it off so long. She had a sense of urgency about talking to Rene without her being on the constant move, but neither was she going to cancel tomorrow's lunch with Rob. She wanted to convince him that Sonny was out to make him his ticket back into office.

"Great. I can get a look at those purple daisies they hid Ben under. I think you could sell tickets and make your fortune if you were willing to leave your septic tank open. Sure is the major subject of conversation right now."

"My septic tank or the murder?" Teddy asked.

"Take your choice, they seem fairly inseparable."

45

Teddy decided to postpone any thoughts of digging up her leach lines in favor of getting a jump on the burgeoning dandelion crop popping up in her pathways, after a rain they pulled so easily. It was no use, the parade of visitors was continuous. Some only drove down the street, really slow, staring. But, if she knew them, if she'd served them so much as a glass of water, the pushier ones would wave and then park and come tromping down the hill past the daisy patch. It was kind of fun watching them walk as far from the edge of the daisy plot as the narrow path would allow, giving the slight mound nervous looks. But the questions had not improved with the retelling. Even going to the very bottom of the garden, out of sight of the road, where the path curved around a patch of wild lupine and slipped through the salal barrier and onto the dune, was not effective. Working along in the devoted gardener's position - legs slightly apart for good balance and pulling resistance, head down, the widest part of one's backside aimed skyward - she was beginning to accumulate a creditable pile of weeds in the basket she dragged along beside her when a shadow slanted across the path.

A group of people, eight or nine strong, had come up from the beach.

"Is this where the murder was?" a woman with unreal red hair, dressed in resort white with lots of gold jewelry demanded.

"Actually they don't know where the murder was, the body was found in the septic tank." Teddy straightened up and pointed up the hill.

Two of the group pushed through the salal and started across a flower bed where tender fingerling size spikes that given the chance would have grown up to be daffodil, broke and crushed under their feet.

"It would be better if you'd stay on the path. The bulbs are just coming up," Teddy said, speaking up quickly as the remainder of the group made to follow their brave trail breakers.

"Sorry about that," one elderly lady said softly, trailing the others who skirted back around to where the path met the sand and climbed on up the hill.

Teddy gave up and went up after them taking a cross path that wound around and up, climbing the hill to the other side of the house. She went inside, dropped the shades, and after pouring herself a large glass of orange juice went to do the unthinkable - watch daytime TV.

CHAPTER 6

Thursday dawned bright, clear, and cold. One of those days that look so glorious from the inside looking out, the morning sun lighting the spray that flies from the tops of the cresting waves and whitening the roiling surf as it parades to the shore. Teddy stood before the bedroom window, doing her morning stretches to limber up for another assault on the garden paths and recognized the come-on. She decided on a pot of coffee, cereal with a sliced banana, and the newspaper until the house's shadow shrunk and moved off to the north a bit. It would be more comfortable working with the sun on her back.

As the morning progressed, the foot and car traffic picked up, the patch of infant purple daisies had become a shrine - a local must see. Some who had come the day before returned with friends and family. Teddy did her best to ignore them. When they called to her, asking the questions, she waved and kept working, her back to them and the sun. One couple, people she couldn't remember ever seeing before, cameras slung around their necks, tromped on down the path to where Teddy was pulling long tendrils of wild blackberry that snaked in from the lot next door.

"Here you are, we knocked on the door," the woman scolded.

"Up there, above the patio, that's where it happened, right?" the man said. "I told mother that was the spot," he continued, not giving Teddy time to answer. "Boy, I sure bet you were surprised. Too bad you didn't leave it open though, I would have liked to have a shot of that to send to the kids."

Teddy tried to overcome the urge to giggle at the thought of "the kids" reaction to a picture of an open septic tank, but then, she reminded herself, maybe they were as simple-minded as good old mom and dad here.

The man lifted his camera and snapped a picture of Teddy standing there, hands full of berry whips, mouth undoubtedly open.

"Guess they took the body out right away though," he lamented.

Teddy looked at her wrist as if consulting a watch - she hadn't put it on this morning.

"It's getting late, I have an appointment I have to get cleaned up for. Please stick to the paths on your way out, I don't care much for weeds, or people, in my flower beds." Teddy, brandishing her fist full of berry vine, pushed past them up the path. "And I don't much care for having my picture taken either," she said under her breath.

"Don't suppose they know yet who killed him?" the man asked, trailing along behind her.

"Nope," Teddy answered.

"They think you did it?" he asked.

"You'd have to ask the sheriff that," Teddy answered feeling really testy.

"What..." he began.

"I'm just too busy to talk right now," Teddy interrupted, she dropped the berry vine into the fire ring as she passed and hurried on.

"I just wanted to know if..."

Teddy crossed the patio and entered the basement workroom shutting the door firmly in the man's face. There were no inside stairs but mom and dad out there didn't know that. She listened for them to leave, peeking cautiously out the tiny window almost opposite the septic tank to see if she could see them. Two pairs of legs, one in jeans one in orange polyester stood on the path for what seemed to Teddy an eternity. They were talking, but the thick walls of her new cement foundation muffled the words. At last they turned and moved off, then she heard a car pull away.

Teddy emerged from the basement angry at having to hide in her own home to escape the prurient interest of an obviously bored community. She rounded the corner to the front of the house to come face to face with the business end of a large video camera being wielded by a young man with a cap printed with a Channel 11 Logo.

"Do you live here?" he asked, shoving the camera and its attached microphone farther into her face.

"Yes and you're trespassing." Teddy growled, dunking under the camera to bolt up the steps and into the house.

Teddy took a long shower, put on a clean pair of Levi's, a black sweater, and fixed her makeup. Then she returned her youngest daughter's call, knowing she was at work and therefore would only have to talk to her answering machine. Teddy reassured her for the third time in twenty-four hours that all was well. While she talked she pulled a pair of soft blue socks from the drawer and sat on the steps to put on her white leather sneakers. Lastly she fastened a pair of small gold hoops in place on her ears. She was ready - Rob wasn't due for almost an hour.

The van from the TV station that had been sitting there on the road the whole time she was showering and dressing finally pulled away. Teddy made a rush for the basement.

When Rob arrived she was just pounding the sign into place at the road's edge.

NO TRESPASSING !!!

They drove south to one of the big tourist hotels not frequented much by the locals. Even so the waitress who seated them bent low over the table as she handed them menus.

"Some excitement at your place, huh!" she said in hushed tones.

"Some," Teddy answered and opened the menu studying it intently.

Teddy ordered a mixed seafood grill, Rob opted for salmon fettuccini and asked the waitress to bring a half carafe of the house white.

"I thought about going to Petal's for fish and chips but we wouldn't have gotten a moment's peace. You wouldn't believe how pushy people are getting," Rob said.

"Try me. You saw my sign. I feel like a sideshow exhibit. If one more self-important, nosy man comes tromping through my flower beds I may just change my mind about guns in the home and arm myself with something big and dangerous." Teddy took a sip of water and sat back to take in the view. The swells were huge, welling up to crest over a line of big rocks, sending up great feathery plumes of spray. It was almost high tide and there was very little beach showing in the rocky little cove far below them. She felt herself relaxing and grinned at Rob. "We haven't come here in a long while. Last time the crisis was Marlo's pregnancy."

Rob had become a grandfather for the first time almost a year ago. Now he loved it, then he had been appalled at the idea. His only child, a daughter from his first marriage, was in her middle twenties - plenty old enough to be starting a family. Marlo had been married more than three years to a nice, responsible CPA. "But me a grandfather," he had whined.

"I wish I could see how this was going to turn out as well," Rob replied. "I had to shut my office door, have Becky take messages and turn people away. Sure can't get any business done that way."

The waitress came with the wine and he filled the glasses.

"Happy Thursday," Teddy said, lifting her glass.

"And good friends, past and present," Rob added.

"So, when's the funeral?"

"Saturday. The coroner is supposed to release the body this afternoon. Teddy, it's really weird. He said Ben died of a blow to the back of his head."

"You mean somebody hit him," Teddy asked.

"No, he said it was more like he fell, I don't know how they can tell, but he said fell, and wasn't moved for several hours before he got dumped in your septic tank." Rob shook his head as if trying to physically rearrange the idea in his head to make better sense. He sighed. "It's going to take me weeks to get through the rent ledgers and project records I found in his desk. A couple of them appear to be duplicates of the ones I just put on the computer, but the rest are all brand new to me. Looks like I'm going to earn my inheritance. Ben left me a whole lot of power and responsibility. He left Trix the cash."

"That old scoundrel always did get his money's worth out of you," Teddy said.

"I got more than a little out of it over the years. I own a great house, eight rental properties, and a good piece of several of Ben's joint ventures. I barely had a dime to my name or a pocket to put it in when he hired me," Rob reminded her.

"So you've said, more than once. Rob you've worked hard, Ben did not give you those things, you earned them." It was an old argument and Teddy knew now was not the time to rub at it. "But Ben did give you the chance and the support and encouragement you needed," she ceded. "So how's Trix taking all this?"

"About as I expected. The first words out of her mouth after I told her her father was dead were, "I'll need some money for clothes before the funeral." She didn't ask how or anything else about his death. Then she started telling me she would want "her" money out of the business right away." Rob chuckled. "She squawked liked she was laying an egg when I told her about the trust. I gave her the lawyer's phone number. I decided he could earn his money explaining it to her."

The waitress came with their salads and a basket of warm rolls.

When she was again out of earshot Rob continued, grinning, "Trix called just before I left to pick you up, I didn't talk to her. I want to talk to the lawyer again first. Becky said she sounded whiny. That means she wants something. I want to be sure of where I stand before I go any further."

"A very good idea," Teddy nodded. "I suppose she'll want to stay at the house when she comes down."

"Probably. Sonny picked up the keys Tuesday. He was going to search the place. I guess I'll have to get someone out there to clean up before the princess arrives."

"Just you be sure the trust pays for it," Teddy cautioned.

"To be sure," Rob agreed. "And the trust is going to pay for an independent audit of all the books, including the real estate office so that it's really clear and clean exactly where everything stands. I took a quick read of those ledgers I was telling you about and..."

Rob fell silent as the waitress returned with their entrees.

Teddy sipped at her wine and watched the surf sliding in over the rocks and lifting at the giant trunk of a tree, barnacled from long days in the sea which lay lodged sideways behind a largish boulder.

"Can I get you anything else?" the waitress asked.

"No, thanks," Rob answered, "it looks great."

It did look great and Teddy was hungry. The three skewers - shrimp, scallops, and salmon - on a bed of herbed wild rice wafted up an enticing scent and demanded all her attention.

"Oh this is good," Teddy said, with a small smack of the lips after her first bite. "Much better than fish and chips at Petal's. And we couldn't have had wine, either."

"MMmmph," Rob nodded in agreement, his mouth full.

"I suppose the "good ole' boys" are all lined up to play pallbearers?" Teddy asked, after several more bites.

"I haven't seen hide nor hair of them. Bob said he'd call them. Getting that all coordinated is his job. I just gave him the names of who I thought would be most interested," Rob laughed softly. "Good thing Ben isn't heavy, some of those guys aren't in that good of shape."

"You know it's odd, I don't think any of them have been around to see my septic tank, either," Teddy observed. "Of course I've been hiding some of the time so they may have come by, nearly everyone else sure has. Even Anna walked down to chat."

"You're kidding!" Rob stopped, his fork in mid-air.

"Big as life and just as if she had never had a nasty word to say about me," Teddy told him.

Anna and Furst Hanby had been close friends with Edmund Reise for more than twenty years before his death. Theirs had been the second house on Arlington Avenue and Edmund the only person ever to stay constantly in Anna's good graces. When

Edmund's heart began to give him serious problems Anna and Furst had been good and helpful friends. When Edmund died it was learned that he had left his house (his only asset) to the wife of a second cousin that had been dead for almost thirty years - someone he had never met - and as Anna was quick to point out, had never done a thing for Edmund. She went ballistic. Anna's first opinion of Teddy had been gold digger and it had gone down hill from there. Anna never seemed to be angry at Edmund for not leaving her the house, only at Teddy for getting it. Anna'd been outraged that the first thing Teddy'd done was put it up for sale.

"But then what could you expect," she'd said.

When Teddy decided not to sell the house Anna was outraged all over again. It was too much to bear, that woman living here, on her street, in dear Edmund's house.

Furst had been polite, kind, and when Anna wasn't looking, even helpful. It had been Furst that had told Teddy about the probable location of the septic tank and the other underground connections she needed to be aware of when she started digging out under the house in preparation for the forms for the basement. And it had been he that had given her the name of the lumberjack turned arborist capable of removing the trees she wanted down without damaging the ones she wanted to keep. Furst often stopped for a chat during his morning walk. Anna seldom left the house and should she be looking out the window when Teddy passed, on foot or in her car, Anna scowled, lifting her head as if to avoid some unpleasant scent, and turned away. Teddy had been amazed, angered, and finally amused by the whole thing.

"So what did her mouthiness have to say?" Rob asked.

"Oh, she was very cordial, just out for a walk you know. Interested in all the excitement. Come to think of it, Anna's emphysema is so bad and neither of them sleep all that well I wonder if they might have seen something that night," Teddy mused.

"Unlikely. Anna is always more than willing to share anything that might be harmful to someone else. If she had seen anything the world would have heard of it by now." Rob split the last of the wine between the two glasses. "Teddy do you think Trix could have killed him, I mean she was surprised when I told her about the trust but not when I told her Ben was dead. Maybe she killed him because she didn't want to wait any longer to inherit."

"I'd buy it except how did she know about my septic tank? And as far as being surprised about Ben's death, well face it - he's been ill for ages. You wouldn't have been surprised either if it hadn't been murder. Trix have any close friends here in town?"

"Friends that might abet a murder? Honest Teddy, I don't think there's anyone in town she hasn't insulted seriously at least twice. Now if she had been the one you found in the septic tank, Sonny would have no shortage of suspects."

CHAPTER 7

When Rob returned Teddy to her house it did not surprise either of them to find a gawking gaggle of locals standing on the path beside the purple daisy patch. A plaid wool shirt in shades of gray hung jauntily on the no trespassing sign.

"Damn!" Teddy said, not exactly under her breath. It didn't help to see Pete, in the midst of the group, turn and wave at her.

"Any of you guys ever learn to read?" Rob called, getting out of the pickup. He was smiling, which softened his words some. Pete and company took no offense.

"Just who we was looking for." A large man, a workday regular at Petal's, boomed out. "You got something I can put these in," he held up a handful of daisies seedlings, dirt barely clinging to their wispy white roots, "my wife will get a kick out of having these growing on our septic tank."

"I kind of liked them growing on my septic tank," Teddy said, pointedly. She pushed through the group to stare at the pillaged flower patch. He had pulled the plants from the middle, trampling the ones along the path edge to do so. "And they'll grow a whole lot better if everyone will keep their big feet off of them."

Teddy didn't cry often, but she could feel the frustration welling up and, turning her back on the group of men, climbed the steps fumbling with her door keys. Rob took the keys from her and opened the door shutting it firmly in Pete's face.

"Damn! Damn, damn, damn, damn, damn," Teddy said, as the tears began to slide down her cheeks.

"Don't let them get to you," Rob soothed, taking her in his arms.

"I'm not crying over that bunch of idiots," Teddy sniffed. "It's just the daisies..."

And one more crisis to face after a lifetime of crises that had worked at her as ceaselessly as the sea wearing rock to sand. Teddy sniffed again. She could hear Rob's heart beating under her ear and feel his arms warm around her, a large hand patting her back gently. She was not alone. With a deep inhale of breath that seemed to lift her, she squared her shoulders and smiled up at him.

"Thank you. For lunch... and for being here. What would I do without you?"

"That's what friends are for," Rob smiled back. "Want me to shoo away that crowd before I leave?"

"No, never mind. If it isn't them it will just be some other group of lamebrains." Teddy giggled. "Did you see Pete's face when you shut the door?"

"I think that man would like to hang a no trespassing sign on you."

"Not likely," Teddy said, firmly. "I like my life just like it is. I don't need a big strong male blockhead to lean on. Just a good friend every now and then," Teddy said, patting Rob's chest twice with her hand and smiling up at him.

"You can cry on my chest any time, but right now I have to get back to the office. I have an appointment with some folks from Idaho who want to look at ocean view property." Rob bent and gave her a quick kiss on the cheek. "I'll call you tomorrow."

Rob left and Teddy put her grubbies back on, determined not to be confined to another afternoon of daytime TV.

When she opened the door she found Pete sitting on her steps, his shirt still hanging on the sign. He was alone, the entertainment value of a patch of purple daisies growing over a septic tank having proved limited.

"Mad at me?" he asked, looking up at her.

"Pete, what makes you think I like you well enough to get mad at you?" Teddy asked.

"Now Teddy," Pete pleaded, "I just came by to see if the Bensons were down and check on how you were with all this going on. Those guys were all here when I got here, honest."

"Well, I'm just fine, thank you. And the Bensons won't be down this week, they're in Hawaii for the rest of the month." Teddy went down the steps past him, headed for the basement door.

Pete, never quick on getting any hint that didn't fit in with his personal agenda, followed right along. "Don't suppose you'd like to go to Petal's tonight for fish and chips?"

"Don't suppose I would," Teddy answered, gathering her gloves and cutters into her basket.

"Tomorrow night then?" he asked, hopefully.

"Pete I really don't..." Teddy began.

"You seem willing enough to have lunch with Rob Greene at the drop of a hat. What's wrong with having dinner with me?" Pete interrupted.

"Pete there is a great big difference between lunch with Rob and dinner with you, or anybody else, as far as that goes. And I don't feel like having to explain it to you again. I am not interested in dating," she held up a hand to stave off the usual comeback, "I'm not interested in even a little dinner between friends. And I would really appreciate it if you would quit putting the Bensons and me on the spot by suggesting we go out as a foursome. If you want to visit Lon and Minna you go right ahead and visit them. Leave me out of it. Now if you'll excuse me I have weeds waiting."

Teddy left Pete standing openmouthed on the path and headed down the hill.

By 5:30 she had taken all her irritation out on the dandelions and salal and her paths were looking good. Feeling a great deal better, if a little contrite about having ripped poor Pete off so thoroughly, she dumped a last basket full of debris on the burn pile and gave some thought to what she would have for dinner.

By the time she had finished washing up and changed into an old pair of gray leggings and a baggy black sweatshirt with Mickey Mouse on the front, the homemade vegetable soup she'd put in the microwave to defrost was ready for a final heat-up zap. Teddy fixed a tray with the soup, some cheese, crackers, and a large glass of ice water and took it up to watch the evening news and plan what she would fix Rene for lunch the next day.

Just after eight a flash of lightning lit the sky over the ocean and the boom of thunder shook the house then rolled off to the north. Teddy watched as the fast-moving storm alternately split the air above the black sea and rumbled grumpily. In half an hour the show was over, the lightning having moved too far north to be seen, only an occasional rumble reaching her ears. Then the heavens opened and hail followed by a pounding rain hushed out even the sounds of the surf.

Teddy went down and took a small package of crabmeat from the freezer. She would fix Rene crab chowder and fresh cornbread. The sound of a car starting up on the road drew her to the window. Red taillights moved south, somebody looking for the rental perhaps. She leaned closer to the window and looked through the fringe of trees. There were lights on there. She relaxed. Her own motion light was on too, the rain or even the car on the road could have caused that. Teddy shrugged off an uneasy feeling and decided to go to bed and read.

The phone was ringing. Teddy opened one eye and sought out the red glow of the digital clock, trying to make the dots stand still and make sense. 6:37! It couldn't be. She reached for the phone then remembered she had left it in the kitchen. Rolling from the bed her mind flooded with prayers that it only be good news and questions about the possible who and why, she also spared a thought to the idea that early morning phone calls were becoming a really rotten habit in her life lately.

"Hello?" she demanded.

"Teddy, this is Billy. I don't know who else to call. Could you come work this morning?"

"This morning? You mean now? What's happened? Where's Rene?" Teddy fired off, giving him no time to answer.

Billy, of indeterminate age had been the breakfast cook at Petal's since before time began. He arrived every morning at 4 am to make rolls and set batter, opened the doors at 6, and by 11, which is to say before anyone might dare to ask for a non-breakfast item from the menu, disappeared. No one ever saw him during the day, not in the grocery store, not walking on the beach, not anywhere. There was the recurring rumor that he was some kind of mixed up vampire - one who had to get back in his coffin by 12 noon instead of sun up. The clerk at the liquor store would have told you (if she were not the type that considered such information client-privileged) that Billy was an alcoholic whose daily schedule was set in well-cured cement; work, drink, sleep - repeat.

"Billy, what's going on? Where's Rene?" Teddy demanded, the uneasy feeling that had sprung from bed with her growing.

"She's not here. She isn't coming. Her mother just called." Billy sounded as if he were gulping air. "They told her she was dead," he finished in a rush.

"Dead?!! Who said she was dead? How?" It didn't make sense. Teddy struggled to pull her thoughts together. "Who told Rene's mother she was dead?"

"The police - some fellow in a uniform - came to the door, there was an accident. Teddy, that's all she told me. Teddy, please, this place is filling up and I got Donny waiting table but..." he trailed off.

Donny was a good busboy and perfectly capable of handling the regulars on a winter morning but he would have to leave for school at 8:30. Teddy's mind reeled. Rene was never sick, never late, never idle. Rene should have been there at 5:30 filling shakers, making coffee, putting out jelly. Rene couldn't be dead. Not just like that.

"Please Teddy," Billy pleaded, "I got to go, Keith's over-easys are about to be hard fried."

"I'll get there quick as I can," Teddy gave in.

The line clicked and she stood there holding the phone trying to focus. Dressed, she had to get dressed.

"I said I would never serve another cup of coffee," Teddy reminded the image in the mirror, toothbrush in hand.

"Never say never."

She attacked her teeth with the brush. Twenty minutes later, dressed in clean jeans and a blue-and-white striped cotton shirt, she opened her door and tripped over an oblong white box. Irritated, she kicked it to one side and hurried down the steps and up the slope to the car. In another ten minutes she was tying Rene's black apron around her middle.

Billy had looked over his shoulder when she came in the back door and waved his spatula at her with a grim smile.

"Donny, you get to clearing those tables, Teddy'll take care of the customers now," he yelled out the service window as he flipped a long row of the pancakes that were a part of three out of four orders every morning.

"Where's Rene?" was the new, never-ending question. Over and over Teddy had to repeat the all-too-short message Billy had wakened her with.

"We don't know how," she said for the umpteenth time to a demanding foursome of regulars whose curiosity equaled their concern. A movement at the door caught her eye and she looked up to see Sonny crossing to the counter. She returned the empty coffeepot to the machine and set a new pot brewing before she went to talk to him. Teddy felt her stomach knotting. Talking to Sonny would make it official. When he said it, Rene would really be dead. Her feet felt leaden.

"Got you working, huh?" Sonny greeted her sullenly. "Just coffee and one of those cinnamon things Billy makes, if there's any left." He shoved the menu she'd handed him back at her.

Stalling, not wanting to hear the inevitable, she put the pastry in the microwave to heat and brought the coffee before she let herself ask.

"What happened?"

"Missed the curve, went into the river," he said flatly.

"Rene's been driving that road for years, how..."

Teddy wanted to argue.

"Could have been an animal on the road, isolated patch of black ice... Hell, I don't know. It happened. Trucker saw where she left the road and the back end of the car sticking out of the water and called it in. It happened."

Sonny stirred two containers of cream into his coffee and then sat, staring at it.

The small room was quiet. Everyone had been listening. The bell that signaled plates to be picked up sounded like a gong in the quiet. Billy slid two orders of pancakes onto the narrow service shelf.

Teddy whirled at the sound and the room broke out in animated discussion. She worked steadily until the lunch shift arrived. The grapevine was in working order and most of those who came in after Sonny's arrival already knew about the accident, not that that kept them from asking questions. When she hung the apron on the peg, getting ready to leave, it suddenly occurred to her that not one person had said a word about her septic tank.

CHAPTER 8

When Teddy opened Petal's back door to leave a strong gust of wind blew her backward, nearly off her feet. The accompanying rain soaked the heavy navy, zip-front sweatshirt she wore for a jacket. Teddy pulled the hood up over her head and ran for the car. The rain seemed appropriate. Driving home, the tears she'd battled yesterday fell freely.

"I'll cry all damn day if I want to," she declared to the giant splats of water landing on her windshield.

Several times in the short drive wind gusts tugged at the car. Had a strong gust caught Rene unaware and propelled her off the road into the river? It simply hadn't been cold enough for black ice.

Teddy was soaked for a second time making the dash from the car to the house. After stripping off the wet clothes and tugging an old chenille lounge robe over her head, Teddy picked up the phone to call Rene's parents. She'd only met them three or four times. Stoic, hardworking people with a hard life that had just gotten harder. Teddy wasn't sure what she could possibly say but she felt the need to offer whatever comfort she could.

None at all it turned out. Bob Markey, Burying Bob he was called, though never to his face, answered the phone. There would be no service. Rene would be cremated and her ashes spread in the meadow behind the house. Rene's own wishes, same as her mother and father when the time came, same as he had done for Rene's husband and boy when they died. Bob said the Klell's were out tending the stock but he would relay her condolences.

Teddy hung up the phone and felt the chill of the rainy day shudder along her spine. She needed action - start a fire - make some lunch - make the shopping list for the materials needed for her assault on the leach lines - do something, anything, but keep busy. Try not to think how Rene's life, anyone's life, could come to a halt with such a dull thud. A temporary displacement of activities as the chinks were filled, and the living went on. Tomorrow, Alice would be back to work the weekend shift, a new waitress would be hired, breakfast would get served at Petal's. Anything you were going to do, anything you wanted to do, better to do it, better to live in the here and now. Tomorrow was always a day away and sometimes it never came at all.

Teddy's less-than-cheery frame of mind was confirmed by the whomping of the wind as it hit the ocean end of the house and ran along under the eaves. It was only during such storms that Teddy regretted having removed quite so many of the big trees. They had moaned and groaned and swayed so in the wind that first winter, terrorizing her, that she'd turned the majority of them into massive piles of firewood. Now she understood that while trees could fall on houses, without the trees the wind could assault the house directly. You had to place trees strategically and always have new ones growing so that when one over-topped its optimum height or got broken by the wind you didn't have to wait twenty or thirty years for a replacement. As a result there were now trees of a wide assortment of heights placed carefully around the yard to protect without overcoming the view. However, for several years yet her living room windows would rattle and complain when the winds howled in off the sea. Now and again the whole house seemed to strain to keep its hold on the foundation, creaking in protest. It was then that Teddy turned on all the lights, built up the fire, turned up the radio and baked, knitted, cleaned, and read. It was then, too, that she planned next year's garden or concocted some marvelous new soup or stew. If the wind's message was that she was insignificant - fragile - merely human, her reply was one of stubborn survivorship.

Soon, the radio tuned to a local station that tended to country and western mixed with soft rock, the sweet sea smell of crab chowder mixed with the aroma of baking cornbread, Teddy was making endless lists. The things-to-buy list was speculation until she had dug up enough of the existing drain tiles to know if she could merely clean them out or had to replace them. She had marked the connection to the septic tank with the piece of old curtain rod stuck deep in the soft soil. By beginning there, she should be able to discover the placement of the drain field by simply digging up the tiles one at a time. It was a plan anyway, and it would feel good to be doing something constructive. Now if only this storm would blow on past so she could get on with the doing of it.

Teddy made a spicy red crab chowder, not the milk-and-potato-based kind she would have made for Rene. The zesty soup and hot cornbread warmed the last of the chill from her and when a bright sun break presented itself she pulled on her jeans, sweater and rubber boots, preparing for a walk on the beach to see what changes the storm had brought.

Some storms ate sand and uncovered long-buried logs or changed the way the little creeks drained. Other times tons of sand were deposited and built new contours into the dunes. If you were lucky you might find a float, though in recent years it was more often a Styrofoam crabber's float than even the big plastic balls used by the fishermen. The glass floats, used once by the Japanese, were extraordinarily rare. A walk on the beach was a treasure hunt and always an intriguing one. Another pleasure was the finding of a sea-bleached twisted piece of driftwood, beautiful to look at, some demanded to be drug home and displayed as garden sculpture. Teddy was particularly fond of those with crevices or cavities that could be planted or would hold water for the birds.

Today the wind was blowing hard from the southwest making a moonscape of the beach and reshaping the leading edges of the grass-crusted dunes. The surf was running high, the wind carrying tall plumes of spray into the air from the breaker's crests as they plunged shoreward. Teddy noticed that several large logs had moved north and east from where she had last seen them. In one place, where some past storm had deposited several flatish, fist-sized rocks, the drying sand was blowing out from under their edges leaving them standing like surreal golf balls on their sand tees.

She pushed her sunglasses more firmly in place, not because of any glare, but to block the wind-born sand and snugged down the string that gathered the hood of her sweatshirt about her face. She walked to the second creek that crossed the sand close to a mile down the beach. On the return, the wind at her back, pushing, she noted the tire tracks in the sand being erased as the sand filled them. Someone had been driving on the beach. There were several places for a vehicle to get down on the sand. Sometimes it was one of those sand-surfers, this looked more like a real car.

"WOW!"

The idea hit her as she angled up across the dune toward home. The house, the whole upper part of the yard was clearly visible from here, and accessible. Ben's body could have been brought in across the sand and up the hill, anyone walking on the beach the day her septic tank was pumped could have seen.

You're reaching, she told herself. *Seen what? - a septic tank being pumped and thought, 'Oh goodie I can go kill Ben and put him in there'.*

"Overactive imagination," Teddy explained to the wind. Still she watched the pathway carefully as she climbed back toward the house. Anything dropped on the sand would be long since obliterated, but if they had dropped something in the garden, maybe, just maybe, she would find it. The only thing she found was a black lens cap. "Dad's probably," Teddy decided, thinking of the pushy couple with a chuckle. "Face it girl, there have been so many people through here in the last couple of days there

71

is absolutely no way to tell what got stepped on when or dropped by who." Still she stood and pondered for a minute the water-filled footprints across the lavender bed before a sudden darkening of the sky signaled the return of the rain.

Approaching her porch steps she spied the white box she remembered vaguely kicking aside on her way out this morning. It had landed on its side and spilled its contents out on the grass.

"Roses! Where the hell...?" Red, long-stem roses. Teddy had never seen any real ones before. Pictures sure, and plastic ones, even silk ones like her mother kept on her TV, shorter-stemmed real ones even in Mother's Day bouquets over the years. But these were real, truly long-stemmed roses, a whole dozen of them, only slightly the worse for their morning in the rain. She gathered them up and breathed in the heady scent.

They had to cost a fortune!

"Where did you come from?"

Teddy searched the box and the ground for a card and found none. If there had been one it had been blown away by the wind. The box was plain, no florist's name, the tissue the roses had been nestled in was a soggy mass of purple. The rain and wind pushed insistently around the house to grab at her. Clutching the roses and the soggy box of tissue she went inside.

The only thing she had even near tall enough for the roses was an old gallon mayonnaise jar she sometimes kept flour in. Teddy sat the "vase" on the tiny dining table and reached for the phone book.

There was only one florist in town and they not only hadn't sold any long-stemmed roses, they didn't carry them except on special order, even on Valentine's Day - people around here were unwilling to pay the price.

A quick check of the calendar reassured Teddy it was the 23rd of February not the 14th. These were not Valentine roses then. Could they have been meant for someone else, someone at the rental perhaps? It would be impossible to mistake her little house for the rental, even in the dark.

"Thank you whoever − why ever." Teddy said, addressing the bouquet, and went up to add a couple of sticks of wood to the stove.

CHAPTER 9

A little after five Teddy finished the Sue Grafton mystery she'd been reading and decided it was time to check out the refrigerator for dinner ideas. She was halfway down the stairs when she spotted Rob's pickup pulling to a stop on the road. It was unusual for him to make an unannounced visit this time of day but then the whole day had been unusual. Teddy opened the door and watched him stride down the slope.

"You hear about Rene?" she asked.

"Yeah. I'm sorry, I know you were good friends," Rob answered sliding an arm around her and delivering a quick hug. "Been a rough week all round."

"For you, too," Teddy said pulling him inside and closing the door. "What else has happened?" The drawn look on his face said there was more news, and not good news at that.

"Somebody broke into Ben's place, made a hell of a mess. Sonny found it yesterday afternoon when he went back up there to search again for whatever it was he thought he was going to find. Anyhow he called me to come up and see what's missing. It looks like they just went through everything, I mean I'm more or less familiar with the house and I can't see that anything was taken. Then this morning when I got in I discovered someone had been in Ben's office. They came in the back door, forced it with a crow bar it looks like, the only office messed up was Ben's."

"They take anything or just make a mess there too?" Teddy asked, opening the refrigerator and silently offering a beer, holding the can up.

"Thanks," Rob said, accepting the beer from her. "They emptied all the desk drawers and the filing cabinet, smashed the computer. I sure wish I knew for sure what they were looking for. Sonny said it was just kids thinking Ben had money stashed. I'd buy that if it were just the house."

They climbed the stairs to the living room.

"You said you wish you knew for sure. What do you think it might be?" Teddy asked him, settling on the small, overstuffed couch.

Rob took his usual seat in the big bentwood rocker and leaned back, letting its firm back support and rocking motion do their thing. "I think I have to go over those books I took from Ben's office very carefully. Marrianne Pailey was going on about Ben misleading them the other day and I just put it down to her general meanness of spirit, if you know what I mean."

"I know what you mean. Marrianne has a truly barb-wire kind of personality. She looks mean and she is mean, no softness to her except perhaps in the head. You know she once lectured me sharply on the dangers to my reputation if I continued to make such a public fool of myself over a younger man," Teddy laughed.

"Mhhuh?" Rob looked at her quizzically.

"You. She'd been driving by your office a day or two before and seen us and I quote "embracing in public". I think you must have given me a hug or something on the doorstep. Anyhow she did not approve and let me know all about it," Teddy explained.

"Oh," Rob looked amused, "and what did you say?"

"I told her I'd take all the hugs I could get, particularly from younger men, that they made me feel good and sweetened my outlook on life and that she should try it some time," Teddy answered. "I think she took offense."

"She takes offense at the sun coming up. But Teddy, she may be right about Ben. I mean I don't want to believe it, but there's something off about those books I took out of his office the other day. I'm going to have to sit down and do some serious comparing. I hate this. We're going to bury Ben tomorrow and I want to be able to say goodbye and thank you and right this minute I am so full of suspicion." Rob took a long draw on his beer. "Whoever killed Ben must have had a reason. I think they went looking for something that would implement them. The hell of it is it could have been anything, maybe they found it. You know, a business card or a contract or..."

"The books you had with you?" Teddy said slowly.

"Yeah. Could be."

"Who else knows you have those books?" she asked him.

"No one. There was no one in the office when I took them."

"You didn't tell Sonny?" Teddy asked.

Rob shook his head. "Never got a chance to. Every time I've seen him there's been so much else to talk about."

"Maybe you shouldn't, not until you're sure whether or not they have anything to do with Ben's death."

"Teddy, what are you getting at?" Rob looked puzzled.

"If Ben was doing something funny with those books... Rob, isn't Sonny one of Ben's big investors?" she asked.

"Not as big as he makes out but I see what you're getting at. But you don't think..."

"Oh I don't think Sonny would have killed anyone on purpose but you said the coroner said Ben had fallen. What if Marrianne or somebody convinced Sonny that Ben was up to no good and they fought and Ben got knocked down? Isn't Leroy Sonny's nephew? He could have known about my septic tank, thought to hide the body." Teddy was getting into her supposition.

"Teddy I think you've been reading those murder mysteries again. On the other hand, Ben is sure enough dead. I guess there's no need to say anything about the duplicate set of books until I have a chance to go over them and be really sure just what was going on."

Rob finished his beer and set the can on the little side table. "So who's sending you roses?" he asked with a little wiggle of eyebrows. A teasing light added sparkle to his blue eyes.

"Wish I knew. They apparently got delivered last night." Teddy explained about the taillights she had seen and tripping over the box on her way out that morning. "The card is probably stuck in a bush in Anna's yard by now if not all the way to town."

"Gee, should I be jealous?" Rob smirked.

"Won't know that until I know who sent them will I? Want another beer?"

"No thanks. You could call the florist."

"Done that. They didn't get bought locally. I suppose they could have been meant for someone next door but they will just have to come get them if they want them."

Teddy had never been real happy at the idea of an ever-changing set of neighbors. Most of the time it was a quiet family group. Once or twice it had been an "adult party" crowd and gotten noisy. More often they had just been nosy and she'd found strangers wandering around her garden more than once.

"I better get on home and get at those books. I meant to before now but there's been so much to do and, well I guess I know I'm about to discover something about Ben I really don't want to know." He looked at his watch. "Oh rats! I was supposed to pick Trix up ten minutes ago. I've been commandeered to take her to dinner. I think she wants to try and wheedle some instant cash out of me." Rob was halfway down the stairs as he finished the sentence.

"Hey, I get another hug before you go," Teddy said, going after him.

"You bet," Rob turned at the bottom of the stairs and wrapped his arms around her. "I need all the positive reinforcement I can get before I face her.

You should have seen her arrival this morning. Dressed to the nines, black suit, expensive one, black nylons and four-inch heels! And a hat!"

"What no veil?" Teddy asked.

"Probably saving that for tomorrow. You going to come?" he asked, looking down questioningly at her.

"If I do it would only be out of curiosity and I think there will be quite enough thrill seekers there without me." She noted the disappointment in his face. "Unless you would like me to be there?"

"I'd like seeing a friendly face. But I guess I'll be pretty busy with Trix," he bent to kiss her on the cheek. "You stay home and keep the beer cold." Rob hugged her closer for a second and then released her and took the two short steps to the door. "The service is at 10 and then we're all supposed to troop out to the cemetery. The good ole' boy's good ole' gals have arranged for food at the house. Ben would have hated it. I hate it. No need for you to suffer through it too, but can I stop by after?"

"You know you can."

Standing in the open door, the kitchen light casting their shadows onto the slope, Teddy put a hand on his arm and reached up to kiss him softly, quickly.

She watched from the door until the green pickup's taillights disappeared down the dark street to the south. Off to the left she heard a car start up, someone at the Hanby's she thought at first. Then a car backed into the road from what had to be the Benson's driveway and went north.

Teddy opened the drawer next to the door where she kept her flashlight and grabbed her jacket from the back of the chair. She knew the Bensons weren't down and they always let her know if one of their children was going to use the house. They'd been broken into by a bunch of bored teens two summers ago. Teddy picked her phone up and armed with light and communication headed out the door.

CHAPTER 10

It was very dark once she got beyond the halo of her motion light. The glow of the flashlight seemed dimmer than it ought and Teddy made a mental note to replace the batteries soon. The gravel on the road crunched under her feet, despite the ever-present roar of the surf and the gush of the wind, it seemed loud in an otherwise silent dark.

The Benson's yard light that was supposed to operate on a light sensor was not working again. Probably the rain had shorted it out. Maybe, she thought, someone had disabled it.

"They can't be there still, you saw them leave," she assured herself.

Swinging the light back and forth across the drive she could see it was empty and she flashed the light up over the door and windows, everything looked normal. She climbed the steps and tried the door. Locked. Teddy circled the house checking the windows, trying the back door, flashing her light under the deck and down into the forest of spruce, myrtles, and wild rhodies Minna had lovingly clipped and trimmed and turned into a fantasy forest garden. The shadows danced and threatened, the wind causing the trees to wave and sigh. Teddy climbed the steep path up the north side of the brick house back to the street and shined her light up and down the graveled roadway. At the north end she could see the lights of the house that sat opposite the end of the street, to the south, way down, at the rental she was sure, the light reflected off the rear lights of a car parked on the road edge.

She regretted not bringing the Benson's key so she could check inside. A flash of lightning out over the sea lit the sky brightly and was gone followed at once by a crackling boom. Teddy pulled up her hood and made a dash for her own home as the heavens opened.

"Tomorrow is soon enough. If the house has been broken into there's nothing that can be done about it now and Sonny has already had enough problems for one day," Teddy counseled and quickly agreed with herself.

A second flash of lightning lit the sky as she closed and locked the door. Again the thunder crackled out almost as soon as the sky blinked dark.

"The forecast said isolated thunder showers, I wish they'd go isolate themselves somewhere else," Teddy grumbled.

The forecast had also said rain, heavy surf, and high wind warnings for the night, easing about noon on Saturday. She hoped Rob remembered to take an umbrella to the cemetery.

Her stomach growled. It was time to eat. Nothing in the refrigerator appealed. She warmed the left over crab chowder and made garlic toast.

The storm did not fully arrive until after three but the wind had buffeted the house just enough to keep Teddy from sleeping soundly. Shortly after three a particularly strong gust slammed into the southwest corner of the structure and whomped along the eaves, lifting and twisting. A few minutes later what sounded like basketballs hitting the windows and roof brought her wide-awake and on her feet. When she drew the drape she could see the gusts of rain, horizontal and filled with salt and sand pummeling the window and obliterating any possible view out.

"Coffee," she decided, and turned to seek the chenille robe from its hook in the closet. Pulling it over her head she headed for the kitchen and soon had the coffeepot making its comforting slurp-slurp sounds.

"Toast and honey?" she offered and decided to accept.

Teddy went through the little house turning on the lights and when she had carried the toast and coffee up to the living room, turned on the late night radio station that played Big Band era music and gave local weather and news on the half hour. At 3:30 the announcer warned people to stay off the beaches because of the heavy surf warning and predicted sustained winds of 35 to 40 mph gusting to 75 in exposed areas, and rain, heavy at times.

"No kidding! So what else is new?" Teddy wanted to know.

And he told her. "Looks like Sheriff Hubbard has a second homicide on his hands. They pulled Rene Pullman's car from the river late yesterday and the driver's side has scrapes of green paint that Alman Klell, Mrs. Pullman's father, says were not on the car when she left for work yesterday morning. That's two homicides in three days. Sheriff Hubbard was not available for comment."

Teddy sat in stunned silence while the announcer moved on to read the following week's school lunch menu.

Somebody pushed Rene off the road! It was unreal. A drunk driver maybe?

"Yeah at 5 a.m.?"

Teddy couldn't just sit there. She got up and went down to the kitchen to top up her cup.

"Some idiot passing when he shouldn't. Had to be."

Rene had complained before about hot rod drivers zipping past her at high speeds in the early morning hours.

But that was all too convenient, too neat an answer. Teddy tried not to think about it but the idea would not go away. If she had thought Rene might have overheard a less than innocent conversation that could lead to the identity of Ben's killer, maybe the killer had gotten the same idea.

"I won't believe it," she said firmly.

But she did believe it. She was very, very sure of it.

The radio was serenading her with Pennsylvania 6-5000, the wind continued in its effort to peel off the roof, howling in outrage at its failure. Teddy sat curled on the sofa trying to bring back every word Rene had said Wednesday morning.

That Leroy had been talking to his group of buddies about pumping her septic tank.

That Ben had argued with everyone - the good ole' boys, the Paileys, even with Rob.

Who else had Rene seen and heard talking to Ben those last days before he showed up where someone had definitely thought he would never be looked for?

Who else had been there Wednesday morning and seen her talking to Rene? Who had figured out that Rene might have heard or seen something that if passed on might reach the wrong ears and mean trouble for them? Trouble enough to convince them to run Rene off the road into the river.

It seemed impossible but the wind was getting stronger, more aggressive, it had swung around and was coming straight in off the water.

Teddy checked the clock, almost four, it would not be light enough to see what was going on outside for more than two hours, that was presuming she'd be able to see through the dirt and salt plastered to the glass. Now the gusts hammered the big window, straining it inward, the house seemed to blanch under the blows. A particularly heavy gust hit and from the direction of the lot between her and the Bensons she heard the sharp report of breaking wood followed close by a second rending sound and then a thud that had an echoing tremble under her feet. Teddy was not sure whether it had been a tree falling or just another gust of wind that shook the house but either way she was beginning to feel very intimidated by the whole thing. That's when the lights went out.

The lights went out, the radio went off, and several more sharp reports that experience told her were trees and limbs being twisted and broken came to her ears, trailing out across the lot next door and into the woods on the other side of the street like the sounds of an awkward giant passing.

Teddy switched the radio to battery power but received only static for her effort. The station had lost power, too. She felt her way downstairs, telling herself that the storm had not gotten louder - it only seemed that way in the dark, without the music.

Panicked at first because the flashlight was not in the drawer, she remembered she'd left it on the table when she came back from the Bensons. Once she found the flashlight it was easy to find the candles and light them - one short fat one on a saucer for the kitchen table, two utility votives in deep glass holders to take up to the living room. She poured herself the last of the coffee - better to drink it while it was still hot. The trick was carrying the coffee and both candles up to the living room without making two trips. A tray solved that problem. Teddy climbed the stairs with her flickering load, fully expecting that the lights would come back on any second.

"A tisket, a tasket," Ella Fitzgerald's rich voice suddenly issued forth from the radio but the lights stayed off.

"Bet we have a line down somewhere close by," Teddy explained to Ella. The rechargeable batteries in the radio were still good, obviously, and the radio station had regained its power.

It was getting chilly but Teddy was concerned that the wind was so erratic that it could cause a backdraft, forcing smoke back into the house. She did not build up the fire, opting to curl up with a heavy knit throw tucked around her. This was one of those times when Teddy felt most alone. The wind sent another giant walking up from the beach toward the highway, and Teddy clutched the coffee mug and tried to count her blessings.

By 6:30 it was just light enough to see the wild gyrations of the tree limbs. The fellow on the radio was full of all kinds of cheery news; power lines down, trees blocking roads, limbs through roofs, vehicles damaged, even some flooding of the nearly sea level streets of the old town area. In between these uplifting bits of news there was lots of Dorsey, Tommy and Jimmy, and Glen Gray interspersed with Frank Sinatra and Frankie Lane. Teddy went down to the bathroom and on her way back blew out the candle in the kitchen. Half an hour later she was able to blow out the other two. Maybe it was because she could see, but it did seem the storm was lessening.

Below in her garden a tall spruce on the property line sported a broken limb dangling forty feet over the herb beds. The windows were crusted with sand and salt and pine needles. The rain was steady, falling at a steep angle, but no longer horizontal. Teddy curled back on the sofa after her through-the-looking-glass inspection and fell asleep.

CHAPTER 11

Bright sun streamed in across the floor and Teddy blinked her eyes, trying to get the purple-and-blue spots to abate. The lights, she noticed, were on.

"What time is it?" she asked stretching painfully. When her eyes focused at last she was able to see the clock. "Ten! I really zonked out there didn't I?" she stood and stretched some more, the Elvis Presley rendition of "Fools Rush In" coming from the radio concluded and the announcer began the weather.

Teddy listened with one ear, her attention focused on a window tour of her grounds. The broken branch no longer dangled over the herb bed, it lay handily in the path, and would be easy to cut up. There were lots of bits and pieces to gather up but no other major damage to be seen from the big window. Fast-moving clouds on the horizon, dark and tall, sailed an electric blue sky, the sun gilding their tops. The surf was still running high and wild, thick belts of white lace edged a boiling green-brown sea.

"Wind gusts recorded at the Sea Lion Caves of 105 miles per hour," the man on the radio was saying.

Looking out the side window toward the Benson's she could see what appeared to be new damage on several trees and a space where there had been none before. A tree, probably a pine, had gone down. She was startled to note that up near the road a large pine hung horizontal in the boughs of another, its shredded stump end dangling a good thirty feet off the ground. From the south-facing window, Teddy looked down on the path and the garden that surrounded and covered the septic tank. A rivulet of mud ran down the path to the patio, a usual event after a major rainstorm, otherwise all seemed normal enough. Beyond the septic tank, in the vacant lot that separated her from the rental, two skinny spruce and a pine leaned wearily on a sturdier neighbor and the large house was more visible. It would take an on-the-ground survey to figure out what was missing.

Suddenly feeling scruffy and hungry Teddy went to put on coffee and take a shower. An hour later, omelet and toast consumed, dirty dishes consigned to the dishwasher, Teddy pulled a waterproof windbreaker over a sweater and tugged on her boots. She wanted to take a walk while the sun break persisted, knowing all too well that it might not.

First she looped south and then up along the highway, even from her front door she could see that several trees had been broken, if not toppled, by the crushing affect of the wind. The giant had left a trail of destruction. He had also opened the view, it was more obvious from the highway looking west, where glints of the sun off the sea and flashes of white were visible. Coming back past the Hanby's, Teddy waved to Anna sitting in the window. Anna moved a hand as if to return the salute and then, remembering herself, dropped her hand and turned her head.

From the ground the pine sideways in its neighbor was just as startling as it had been from her window. Teddy stood several minutes wondering at the power that could snap the bole of a tree at least ten inches in diameter and deposit the tree top twenty feet away and thirty or more feet in the air. She wondered if "Mom" and "Dad" would be back with their camera. Surely this was a picture the "kids" would be interested in seeing.

A pushy little hail shower hurried her on her way, pelting down with its icy grains the size of the really expensive tiny green peas she liked best. Teddy thought of Rob and Trix and the good ole' boys, probably at the cemetery now, and wished Ben bon voyage. At least this hole in the ground was his own. She stood dripping on her doorstep, really wanting to finish her walk with a quick trip down into the garden and perhaps a peek at the beach. If she went in now she would have to take all her damp stuff off and let it dry out before she came out again. The weather accommodated and as quickly as it had come the hailstorm turned to a sun shower of misty rain and dried up.

It was almost two before Rob arrived.

"Coffee?" he asked hopefully when she opened the door.

"Only take a minute, it's all set up and ready. Have a seat." Teddy turned to the counter and flipped the switch on the coffeemaker. "So, how'd it go?" she asked turning back.

"Not bad if you like circuses," Rob replied, shaking his head. "I think old Burying Bob was trying to drum up business. Jamie Minch and I were the only pallbearers under 60 and Harry Bates, Kevin's dad, and I were the only sober ones."

"Who else'd he get?" Teddy asked, pretty sure of the answer.

"Keith, Dave, and Sonny," Rob said. "I don't know if Sonny and the rest of the good ole' boys had been up all night or met to drink breakfast, but their breath was 80 proof and none of them were steady on their feet. Keith and Jamie looked green and old Dave was paler than Ben."

"Well, they've been a pretty tight little group. I'll bet Ben ate half his meals with them. Breakfast and lunch anyhow. Ben's projects provided them with a lot of work, too."

"Almost full time for years," Rob said grimly.

Teddy knew Ben's continued insistence in using his friends and refusing to even let any others bid on the work had been a source of irritation for Rob. Dave Dexter had built a good third of every building built in the area in the last thirty-five years. Keith Thornwell was a wiring contractor and Jamie Minch a plumber. Rob contended that none of them had had a new idea or updated their methods since the early seventies. And some of their set-in-cement modus operandi had been less than the newest and best even then.

"I guess Ben's death has hit them hard on several fronts then," Teddy commented, pouring the coffee. "I got oatmeal raisin cookies, or would you like a sandwich?" she asked.

"Cookies. I had lunch at Ben's. The good ole' gals outdid themselves. Cold ham and roast beef, pasta and potato salads, some kind of a yellow Jello thing with bananas and whipped cream in it," he made a face, "a big pot of baked beans and half a dozen kinds of pie."

"Ah yes, Liza Thornwell's infamous yellow Jello." Teddy took the lid off the cookie tin and set it on the table. "Glad I wasn't there. I've never had any myself but I have heard tales," Teddy giggled. "I take it the ladies minded their manners?"

Liza Thornwell was a newish addition to the good ole' set. Eight or nine years ago Betty, Keith's wife of nearly thirty years had fixed him his dinner, waved him off to play poker with his cronies, done her dishes, neatened up the house and driven her late-model car into the sea. No note, but witnesses said she smiled and waved when she passed them and then had driven, deliberately, straight through the barricade. The whole town knew Keith had been playing patty cake at least twice a week with Liza, the barmaid at the Sandy Inn where the good ole' boys gathered after a working day (or before, or during it for that matter) to "work out the details".

A year to the day after burying Betty, Keith married Liza. Rumor had it that Liza had added whole new dimensions to the term pussy-whipped. Betty had been a frugal little woman who made do and did without. Liza did without nothing. The rest of the good ole' gals did not talk to her, not even on those occasions - like Ben's funeral - when social obligation demanded their presence at the same function. Liza did not cook, the yellow Jello dish her only kitchen accomplishment and ever present when the societal need to bring a "dish" occurred. The good ole' boys never noticed or at least did not acknowledge either the silent treatment Liza received from the other women nor the omnipresence of the cloudy, lumpy yellow salad/dessert.

For Liza's part she had little to say to the others anyway. They were, as she was fond of pointing out, "all old enough to be my mother." She delighted in wearing the most outrageous outfits she could concoct. If not all spandex and bustiers, most of her wardrobe was equally eye popping. Dressed to warm up the room, she'd simply drape herself around Keith's neck and hang out with the good ole' boys at the opposite side of the room from the sixtyish, polyester-clad women.

"They ignored Liza, kept the food in order, and did themselves proud. Liza acted barmaid, and Trix and the boys made some serious dents in Ben's liquor cabinet. I guess I helped a little too," Rob smiled sheepishly. "There was a pretty big crowd. It's amazing how many 'friends' one has all of a sudden when something like this happens." Rob took one of the big chewy homemade cookies. "Sonny was real quiet, watching like he was expecting someone to make a mistake or maybe suddenly get remorse and confess."

"Did he say anything about Rene? On the radio last night they said there was green paint on her car, like maybe somebody forced her off the road."

"I heard that this morning. Didn't really talk to Sonny. I did see him out looking at all the cars in the parking lot at the mortuary. Half the vehicles in town are some shade of green. It sure is odd though. I mean why kill Rene?"

93

"Could be a really stupid accident, you know somebody passing when they shouldn't and then not stopping when Rene went off the road." Teddy shuddered. "It's so hard to believe. She was supposed to come to lunch yesterday. I was going to ask her about what Ben and the boys had been arguing about, you know last week before..."

Rob tilted his head and looked at her, his face serious. "I want you to be very careful who you talk to about all this. Until Sonny finds out who killed Ben and about Rene there's going to be someone out there who won't be afraid to kill again to protect himself." He emptied his coffee cup and got up to refill it. "When are the Bensons due down again?"

"Not until the middle of next month, which reminds me, I need to go take a look over there." She explained about the taillights she had seen the night before.

"Get the key, we'll go look right now," Rob said, setting his cup down and pushing back from the table.

"Holy Cow look at that!" Rob said on the way over, sighting the horizontal pine. "It must have been some wind here last night." He gave Teddy a sidelong searching look. "You get any sleep?"

"Fitfully till about three, then none at all until this morning. I'll make up for it tonight."

Teddy opened the Benson's front door. It was an upside down house like her own, except the front door entered on the upper level into the large living room. The kitchen, bathroom, and two closet-sized bedrooms were below. Because of the slope, the front door was barely above road level. The house looked smaller, only one story from the road, from the garden side it was two stories, wrapped with a wide deck. There was no sign of a break in. The brick house felt a little chilly and smelled slightly stale, a normal thing for a coast house closed up for more than three or four days let alone several weeks. Downstairs it was dark and musky, the canvas shades blocking the light and the view.

"Everything looks just fine. It was probably just a couple of neckers using a quiet place. I guess I went running around in the dark for nothing."

"Next time you call Sonny and let him or one of his deputies do the running around in the dark, they get paid for it," Rob scolded, a hand rubbing the perpetually tense spot between her shoulders.

"It would have been a waste of my taxpayer dollars," Teddy said, smiling. It was nice to know someone was worried about you.

"So tell me, did Sonny bring his new girlfriend to the funeral?" Teddy asked, as they climbed back up to the living room.

"Uh huh. And the good ole' girls seemed to approve completely," Rob answered. "They had her over in the corner bending her ear."

"Giving her the lowdown on Liza no doubt. And laying down the local rules," Teddy said, nodding her head knowingly.

"Didn't you go out with Sonny a time or two?"

"A friend would not remind me of it," Teddy teased. "He took me to one of the barbecues once. Once was enough. Those old gals really grilled me. I was old enough, just, but I don't think they thought much of my attitude. They also were less than

95

impressed with some of my friends." Teddy wiggled her eyebrows at him as she pulled the door to and locked it.

"So he dropped you?"

"You know very well I dropped him. And then I went out with Keith a time or two but it was real easy to see that Liza was a fixture, I think I was just camouflage for what was really going on. And she is welcome to him, I might add," Teddy said with energy.

"Hard to please, aren't we?" Rob remarked. "Marrianne Pailey thinks Pete Mettler is making a fool of himself over you, you know? She said so today, just loud enough for me to hear, if you know what I mean."

"The Pailey's were at the funeral? I thought they were mad at Ben."

"You think that would keep Marrianne away from a primo social event like a funeral? She was responsible for the pickles and olives I believe. Anyway she did go on about you and Pete, for my benefit I'm sure, knowing it would get back to you. She is the most malicious old bird. Makes you wonder how Howard puts up with it."

"Habit, and it would be just too much work and embarrassment busting up. Or, I suppose, maybe, he really loves her. It's strange the people we choose to love and marry. Nice people seldom seem to marry other nice people. It amazes me how many couples exist in which one or the other is putting up blindly with someone the rest of the world can see plainly is cheating on them, or is an impossible drunk or a royal pain," Teddy reflected, opening her own door. "Though there are some couples that are sane, relatively sober, and nice all at the same time. Look at the Bensons. I don't suppose either of them is perfect but they sure seem to get along well without all the pain some people cause each other. They're good friends as well as lovers. Minna told me once that's what makes the difference."

Teddy sighed, remembering her own marriages, the first lust driven, the second need and convenience, the last, well, she wasn't sure what that had been about. Escape? Protest? Companionship and an attempt to get back to where she'd lost control of her life? Hell, she had never had control of her life, not until she moved here.

Teddy looked at Rob and knew he was also thinking of his failed marriages. He had said once the first time he had been too young, the second time she had been. It had been an extraordinarily hard blow when Rachel had left him ten years ago. He'd wanted it to last, wanted to celebrate a fiftieth wedding anniversary, wanted calm, serene companionship into old age. He'd have settled for a moderately peaceful coexistence. Rachel wanted a bigger city, one with some nightlife, she wanted to party, she wanted more adventure in her life. And to be fair he had too, when they first got married. But somewhere along the way he had grown up and discovered the solid reliable adult within himself. Rachel was a beautiful, spirited woman, a trophy wife some would call her, and he had lost the trophy. It had taken a long time to quit hurting. Rob told Teddy once that he wasn't sure he ever would. Teddy felt he was afraid of getting his fingers burnt again. She knew she was.

"Coffee's still hot," Teddy offered.

"I'm floating now. How about a walk on the beach?"

"Sure," Teddy redid the jacket she had been removing, "let me get my boots on."

CHAPTER 12

They walked down through the garden collecting small branches deposited by the storm, and piled them beside the path when they reached the connection to the dune. It was windy, and they leaned slightly forward to balance.

"Wow! Look at the amount of driftwood. The rain must have scoured out the streams," Rob observed.

Whole trees, some obviously long dead, others with bits of green left to attest to their having been ripped against their will from their hold on a stream bank or hillside, lay like jack straws at the high tide line. Smaller bits and pieces ranging from several feet to scant inches piled in little catches, deposited like so much loose change in the bank to be reclaimed another day. Far north they could see a group of people, a family judging by the two larger and three relatively smaller stick figures, two large black dogs cavorted about them. Rob and Teddy walked south.

"You find out who sent the roses?" Rob yelled.

The wind whipped at their words.

"Not a clue. I wish I knew who to thank," she paused pulling the zipper closing of her jacket higher, "or who to send them back to."

"Why?" Rob asked leaning in to get the word to her.

"Nobody spends that much without expecting something for it."

Teddy knew it sounded super-cynical the second the words were out of her mouth, but the truth was the idea of an unknown admirer, one who bought expensive presents and delivered them in the dark of night, was just a little unsettling.

"Life is getting entirely too complicated." Rob shrugged. "Two weeks ago I wanted nothing more than for Ben to go away and leave me alone to do the work the way we'd agreed upon. I wanted him to enjoy his retirement, go fishing. Not get himself killed. Now I have all the control I wanted and I don't like where it's leading."

Teddy waited not asking questions. She knew Rob would get it all out in his own way.

"You know how put out I've been over Dave and Keith and even Jamie only doing the same old thing the same old way. I've been thinking it was just a matter of redneck stubbornness, not wanting to learn anything new. Teddy, it's going to take a little more digging through that extra set of books Ben was keeping. I'm having to compare them a nail at a time, but it looks like Ben and the boys were working some kind of funny business. Or Ben was working some kind of funny business on them. Or, I don't know... maybe it was just one more of their little time-honored "this is the way we've always done it," things, but it sure isn't adding up right. I haven't figured out yet who was cheating who, if anyone was being cheated at all."

They had come to stand in the lee of a large dune south of Teddy's house perhaps a quarter of a mile. There was a large house on the low bluff behind the dune. New, its tempered-glass facade drinking in all the view possible from its perch on great cement stilts that raised its two-and-a-half-

100

story bulk above its lot by a good fifteen feet. Under the house an assortment of luxury cars and a sand sailer, a go-cart affair rigged with a sail, hovered out of the rain if not out of the wind. Between the house and the beach proper the dune looked flattened and it came to Teddy that they'd "rearranged" the sand to improve their view. It was illegal but people did it. They were nearly always sorry for it, too. The wind and the tide would make an attempt to come visiting. They had, after all, been invited.

"Sometimes people really just cheat themselves. Could be it's all just a way of keeping score, you know, between Ben and his buddies," Teddy said. She was standing close, her faced protected from the wind by Rob's broad shoulders.

"I hope so, Teddy, I really hope so." Rob folded his arms around her and held her close. "I guess I better quit stalling and get back to work. You got any plans for next week?"

"Next week? Why?"

"Trix doesn't want to live in Ben's house and it's too far from the beach to make a good rental. I'm going to sell it and buy something, maybe on the beach, that will provide a good income for the trust. Trix says she never wants to see this place or the Pacific Ocean again unless it's from a condo in Hawaii." Rob took her hand and started back up the beach. "I'm not sure Hawaii is far enough away, but we shall have to count our blessings. Anyway, I could use some help sorting out Ben's stuff. Trix says burn it. I figure the high school could use a lot of it for their rummage sale."

"Sure, I'll help. But Ben lived there a long time, it's going to take a while. I'll fix us a picnic just let me know when," Teddy answered. It was unlikely they would find anything more interesting than a stash of old dishes, surely whoever broke in had taken away any possible clues to Ben's mysterious death, but then you never could tell.

"Monday probably. The sooner the better. I want that house on the market as soon as possible. We always seem to get a little mini-boom in sales first thing each spring."

They climbed back up across the dunes to the foot of Teddy's garden and started up the path to the house. Teddy was surprised but not worried to see Sonny's patrol car parked on the road.

"What do you suppose he wants now?" she wondered aloud.

"Maybe he has some news for us," Rob said hopefully.

As they came up the path past the purple daisy patch they could see that Sonny was on the passenger side of Rob's pickup, apparently examining the front fender area.

"What you looking for Sonny?" Rob asked warily.

"You got a few new scratches here," Sonny observed, a glint in his eye that made Teddy uneasy.

"Got into some bushes the other day showing some folks undeveloped lots," Rob answered evenly.

Teddy felt an icy chill encompass her. Sonny was suggesting Rob had something to do with Rene's death.

"You wouldn't mind if I took just a bit more off, just for comparison's sake?" Sonny asked, his pocketknife already at work.

"Well strictly speaking I guess I could make you get a warrant for that, but sure, go ahead," Rob said.

Teddy and Rob stood just where they had when the ominous conversation began, side by side at the corner of the house. Teddy moved even closer to Rob's side. Her hand reached out seeking his. He took the hand and squeezed it gently.

"Anything else we can do for you, Sonny?" Rob asked.

"Nope, I got me a heap of green vehicles to visit yet today. You two have a good evening now." Sonny smiled with one eyebrow arched as if he were the first to hint at some more intimate relationship between the two friends. He pocketed the small plastic bag he'd dropped his scrapings into and left, pulling away leisurely.

"Do you believe that?" Teddy was angry. "Just where does he get off."

"He's just doing his job. But it's going to take him more than one day to get a sample from all the scraped-up green pickups around here, there are more than a few green cars out there, too." Rob gave her hand another reassuring squeeze. "I better get on back to my bookwork. I'll call you tomorrow about Monday."

He leaned down and gave her a peck on the cheek and then strode on up the slope.

"Remember what I said about not telling anybody about those books yet," Teddy called after

103

him and then felt the need to look around and be sure that there was no one within earshot. The street was empty, the wind whipping up the hill making sky dancers of the tall spruce and almost erasing the sound of Rob's voice as he answered her.

"Who would I tell?"

He smiled, got in the pickup, and with a wave drove off.

The wind made the garden uncomfortable and Teddy made short work of cleaning up, cutting up and stacking the downed limb. After raking up the twigs and small branches that littered the rest of the garden she went in to stoke up the fire and spend the remainder of the fast-disappearing afternoon doing inside stuff. A little laundry, cleaning the bathroom, a quick vacuum, she even cleaned the windows on the inside. The whole time she was working, her mind was trying to get a grip on the events of the past two weeks starting with the day she had decided to dig up the septic tank the first time.

It was getting dark, the sun making a splashy show of going down, spreading first a gold and then a rose glow over the wet sand that seemed to color even the air under the trees and across the garden. Teddy poured herself a glass of wine from the bottle of her favorite red, and went to stand at the living room window to watch the show.

The more she thought about it, the more she wished she'd had the chance to ask Rene a few questions about the bits and pieces of discussions she had overheard between Ben and all those people he had apparently been on the outs with. It was obvious someone else, the killer, had thought she might have heard something that would be a problem if she repeated it.

"Fantasy! Pure fantasy!" Teddy scolded her reflection in the window. "It was just some hot-rodder, some idiot driving too fast and too scared to stop and take the consequences when Rene's car went out of control and into the river."

The rose/purple-tinted-Teddy looking back at her wasn't buying. *Whoever killed Ben killed Rene,* she insisted.

"Maybe," Teddy conceded, sipping at her wine.

The crowd in the rental house was a noisy one. Teddy had counted five cars. Couples with kids and dogs. The dogs were allowed, but theoretically the house was only to have an occupancy of six. Some of them could be staying elsewhere she supposed, and just come over to party, but she'd take bets on it. During the evening as the wind eventually died down the sounds of music and an occasional whoop of laughter filtered across the vacant lot. In a way she was kind of glad of the "company" in her quiet little neighborhood.

Sunday dawned an end of February wonder of bright blue sky, clear aqua water with immaculate white lines of breakers decorating its chest, with the sun warming the air wonderfully in the almost total absence of wind. A great morning to do away with her storm inflated burn pile. Teddy downed a quick breakfast of coffee and toast and took her second cup of coffee and a handful of newspaper out with her to start the fire.

It didn't take more than an hour for the dead twigs, branches, and berry whips to be reduced to a low pile of fine ash. She didn't like to leave a fire unwatched and worked around the garden, pulling a weed here, finding another small branch stuck in a bush there, feeding the fire bits and pieces as it slowly diminished and went out. When she was satisfied it had burned about as much as she could hope, Teddy watered the remaining ashes, raked them over good and watered again.

Up by the house, twice, Teddy had spied people gathered on the street staring down into her yard, something that happened often during the late spring and summer when her yard was a mass of blooms. Now, as then, she ignored them. They were standing behind the no trespassing sign and she was careful not to wave or recognize their presence in any way that might encourage them to come farther into her garden.

"Maybe I'm becoming anti-social," Teddy expressed to a large salal root she was stringing up from a bed filled with low mounds of gray-and-green foliage that would become waving, knee-high mounds of catmint and tall heads of monks hood. "But I really do find these ghouls irritating." The root quit coming and she reached down with her cutters and nipped it off.

Across the path, the fat heads of the giant white hyacinth, barely up through the soil, were swelling and about to bloom. Soon this part of the path would be fragrant with their perfume. The honeysuckle on the stump behind the hyacinths was still clutching tight its spring bounty of new leaves and buds, but another couple of weeks would see it relaxing and putting out with a mass of new green decorated with the fluttery pink and yellow blooms. Spring was so satisfying. Teddy looked up to watch a seagull arcing across the sky out over the dune, unbelievably white against the clear blue, and silently thanked Edmund Reise, as she often did, for the blessing of her home.

It was after lunch when Rob called. Teddy was working on ridding the flowerbeds that edged the patio of volunteer grasses when she heard the phone ring. The extension in the basement had a loud brinnnggg to it that could summon her from almost anywhere in the garden. Teddy took her time getting off her knees and removing her gloves as she walked, not ran, to answer. Anyone she wanted to talk to knew to let it ring, anyone else - oh well.

"Hello."

"You must have been down in the back forty," Rob teased.

"No, only the patio, but I was down on my knees trying to get the grass out of the borders."

"Okay if I pick you up about nine-thirty tomorrow? I've got to make sure the office is open and someone is there before we head up to Ben's."

"Fine by me. I'll do up lunch and be waiting. You spend any more time on those books?" Teddy asked.

"Er... Yeah. I'll tell you all about it tomorrow. So far it's still pretty confusing," his voice was suddenly dull and nervous.

"Tuna sandwiches and potato salad okay?" Teddy asked, accepting that he didn't want to talk about Ben's private set of books or the murder just now.

"Sounds great." In the background she could hear a phone ringing. "Gotta go, see you in the morning."

"Bye," Teddy got in just before the line went dead.

She had an uneasy feeling in her chest. Something was wrong that Rob didn't want to talk about in the office.

"He'll tell you tomorrow," she assured herself, returning to her weeding.

CHAPTER 13

Teddy was ready at 9:25, just in case, but knew from experience that Rob would be anywhere from 30 minutes to an hour late. When Rob pulled to a stop at a little after ten she gathered the hamper, her canvas tote and her jacket and paused only long enough to twist the doorknob to be sure it had locked.

"Boy, you look like somebody stole your lollipop," she observed, as she slid on to the seat and reached for the seat belt.

"Good morning to you, too," Rob said, with an effort at a smile. "Actually I feel just about as bad as I look. I spent all last evening on Ben's rental ledgers."

"And?" Teddy asked, watching his face closely.

"And, the rental part is pretty straight forward. But the maintenance and repair records are..." Rob trailed off, nodding his head to one side when he found the right word, "inflated. Not much, I mean basically just hedging on what he would be reporting on taxes but," Rob sighed heavily, "there's something funny about his payment records, too, you know to Keith, Dave, and Jamie for work they did for him. I'm no expert on these things. It's going to take a while for me to finish figuring it out, but Teddy, I..."

"He was your friend and you don't like finding out he was less than honest. But isn't it just a game he liked to play, they all like to play, thinking they're getting away with something. He didn't make that much out of it did he?" Teddy asked, wanting to ease Rob's pain.

"Not much per rental, but there are 27 properties, Teddy, it added up to a tidy sum and," Rob took another deep breath, "I think he was working some kind of game with the costs on the projects, too," he got out in a rush.

"How?" Teddy asked

"I want to be really sure before I say anything more. I mean everyone keeps books differently and these old-time guys had their little tricks, ways that made sense to them but maybe didn't have a real effect."

He sounds like he's trying to convince himself, Teddy thought.

They had passed through town and were climbing into the foothills on a winding road. Teddy'd never been out to Ben's house but she knew that his drive was about 12 miles up the river road and wound up several more miles into and through a heavily wooded area. She wondered if Rene's car had gone off the road beyond Ben's drive or if they would pass the spot. A renewed sense of loss washed over her.

"...so I will know more after I finish comparing Ben's books with my computer records," Rob was saying.

They rounded a sharp curve and before them on the right, they could see yellow plastic ribbon laced between the trees. Rob slowed and they both peered over the steep bank at the crushed greenery and the rushing water of the river below.

"That's where...?" Teddy asked.

"Mmmhuh," Rob nodded. He reached out a hand and patted her knee. "I know you really liked her."

"She was a good-hearted and gentle person and she'd been so hurt... when her husband and son died. It's not fair. Life's not fair is it?"

"Damn straight it's not." Rob patted her knee again. "But all we can do is the best we can. And maybe try and be sure we don't leave anybody feeling sorry we were here."

"Did I ever tell you how glad I am you're my friend? I'm not sure I ever told Rene. You don't think about having to say those things until it's too late to say them."

Teddy put her hand over his and gave it a squeeze.

"Likewise. I mean, who else would volunteer to help me clean out Ben's closets." Rob flipped on his turn signal and slowed. A gravel road, not much more than a car wide, angled up the hillside to the left. "This is a pretty drive, especially in the fall."

Teddy could see the deciduous trees sprinkled among the spruce and hemlocks, their gray branches adorned with just visible nubbins of green that promised a mass of foliage soon and come fall would provide a riot of color. On one sunny curve a brave early dogwood sported its first few white blooms. It took another ten minutes before they pulled to a stop before a large, rambling, ranch-style house. It was painted with the same pale-gray paint that Ben used on all his properties, and trimmed in white. The door was blood red with an ornate black knocker.

"It's huge!" Teddy exclaimed, "no way are we going to get it sorted out in one day."

"It's even bigger than it looks, because of the hill, there's a full walkout basement. About a third of the basement is garage but the rest is a tangle of rooms Ben used for storage," Rob said, stopping the pickup. "Basically everything goes, I'm just going to have them back up a truck and take it away. But I figure I should remove any bits of personal or business stuff, records, notes, that kind of thing. And the garbage of course."

They started in the kitchen, with a box to put any records or other items Rob did not wish to give to the rummage sale, and a big plastic garbage bag for the items that simply needed tossed. There wasn't much in the keeper category, when they finished the room there were three bags of garbage and seven big boxes of rummage.

"Those dishes are original Fiestaware, somebody will be tickled to get them," Teddy noted, shutting the last cupboard. They had thrown out the blackened and dented pots and pans, cleaned out the refrigerator, the pantry and sorted through the three drawers of "junk" screws, rubber bands, match books, lids, gadgets with unknown uses, flashlights etc.

Rob went to get more boxes from his pickup and Teddy started on the laundry room.

"Ugh!" she exclaimed opening the first cupboard. "Why do people do that?"

The shelves were stacked with coffee cans of cooking grease. Teddy piled them into a garbage bag. The cleaning products from the next cupboard she left on top of the washer. In the dryer was a load of sheets and towels. She folded them into a box and opened the door of the small closet to find an electric broom, three paper sacks of newspapers and one filled with more bags.

The closet shelf held shoe polish, a can of cleaning fluid, and one of lighter fluid. Teddy put the shoe polish in the garbage bag and the two cans of flammable fluid on top of the washer with the cleaning products. Then she moved on to the living room.

By one-thirty they had finished upstairs and stopped for lunch before tackling the basement.

"You still haven't even half filled that box," Teddy said, nodding at the half-dozen brown envelopes, a green ledger Rob had found tucked down between Ben's bed and the nightstand, and several inches of loose papers that barely covered the bottom of the big box. "Were you expecting to find a lot?"

"I don't know what I was expecting to find. Something to help me understand the ledgers I found in the office, I guess. Those sandwiches look good I hope you made me two."

They were seated in the living room where a card table placed in front of the big bay window showed signs of being a favorite eating spot. Rob brought a second chair from the dining room and Teddy set the lunch out on the lone placemat. The view was spectacular, looking down across a wide mowed expanse edged in wild rhodies and fuchsias and some other deciduous trees with bright red blossoms just emerging that Teddy determined to get a start of before leaving.

"I can see why he loved it up here. His wife must have loved it too, she next to never came to town, according to Rene."

"They both loved it. She fed the birds and cultivated her forest garden. There are paths everywhere with marvelous surprises tucked along the way: benches, picnic tables, special plants. There's a whole bank of daffodils that's breathtaking about this time of year. You come out from a tunnel of dark green overhanging branches and see this mass of sunlit yellow across a little stream." Rob looked around the clean, almost sterile-looking room. "It used to look cozy in here, a fire in the fireplace, fresh flowers and plants. After she died Ben forgot to water the plants. Said a fire was too much trouble, just turned up the heat when it was cold. But he wouldn't move down into town."

A bald eagle made a dramatic swoop across the far end of the open space, wheeled and swooped back. Teddy reached for the binoculars on the window ledge.

"Did you see that, what a beauty," she exclaimed, raising the glasses and trying to focus in on the huge bird.

"Ben said there was a pair that nested regularly off to the right there somewhere," Rob said.

Teddy was having trouble getting the range and scanned the glasses across the tree line. They were powerful and the far ridge leapt forward as she twisted the focus. Lowering her aim to bring in the nearer tree line Teddy glimpsed what looked like a green pickup, it quickly disappeared in the trees. "Are there any other houses up here?"

"Nope, it's all state forest. This place is almost completely surrounded with public land. There are a couple of vacant lots down near the highway. Why?"

"I think I saw a pickup through the trees. That is the road down there isn't it?"

"The forestry people may be checking on one of their test patches. They've replanted several spots on the next ridge using a variety of sizes and methods to develop a quicker restart for clear-cut or burned slopes," Rob explained. "Any more of those cookies?"

The garage was a nightmare of old tools, ladders, paint cans, Ben's shiny new red Explorer and his ancient blue pickup. Teddy stood and stared at the cars.

"Did Ben have another vehicle?" she demanded more than asked.

"No. Why?" Rob looked at her curious.

"Because if both his vehicles are here, then doesn't it follow that he was killed here?"

"Sonny must have thought of that," Rob said. "But he sure never said a word about it. I mean you're right. If Ben wasn't killed here, then the killer would have had to have driven his car back, or have picked him up and taken him somewhere else to..." Rob grimaced and left the sentence unfinished.

"But if Sonny thought Ben was killed here he would have this place all taped off with that yellow ribbon wouldn't he? I mean he wouldn't have let you have it cleaned."

"Probably," Rob said, "but who knows what Sonny is thinking. Maybe he never even came down to the garage, I didn't. He should of, but.... Let's check on the storerooms." He picked his way back to the foot of the stairs and opened a door into a dark hall. "The light is here somewhere," he mumbled.

Even when the light went on, the hall was dark and uninviting. There were five doors spaced unevenly along its length. The first turned out to be a bathroom, grimy and dust-covered with a definite locker-room smell.

"Ben only used this to clean up when he worked on the pickup. I didn't bother to have it cleaned before Trix came, I knew she wouldn't come down here," Rob explained.

The second door on the left proved to be a storehouse for empty terra-cotta pots and other garden errata. There was a set of plaster-cast elephants, several trellises, two wheelbarrows, and three benches, and that was only the top layer near the door. The last door on the left opened on a short hall with two more doors. One of the rooms was locked, the third key Rob tried from a ring of ten opened the door. The room, about nine by nine feet square, was stacked from floor to ceiling with cardboard boxes, nearly every one of them marked "Tax Records".

"This what you've been looking for?" Teddy asked.

"Maybe, but God, it looks like he saved every piece of paper he ever received and every return he ever filed," Rob moaned.

Across the tiny hall a slightly larger room contained a huge old rolltop desk, a scarred-wooden table ringed with five sturdy chairs and four, five-drawer filing cabinets.

"Ah ha," Rob exclaimed, "I'll bet our answer is in here if there is one."

"Well at least we know this room has been used recently," Teddy observed. "See, it's been dusted not too long ago. Or at least the table and filing cabinets have been," she corrected herself, as a finger run across the desk came away with a major amount of dirt. Teddy opened a drawer of the nearest filing cabinet to reveal several bottles of liquor. The drawer below contained glasses.

Rob began to examine the contents of the other cabinets.

"Every bill for every project back to the very beginning it looks like. Teddy I think there is a dolly somewhere in the garage, he used to have one, I know. I'm going to take these out of here and back to my place." He started out the door. "See what else you can find in the desk. Ben must have put the walls up around it, we'll never get it out of here.

Teddy obediently began to rummage through the desk. The only thing of note besides all the regular office staples were two more ledgers that matched the one Rob had found upstairs, Both with all but a few blank pages ripped out. On the floor under the desk, Teddy spied a single sheet of green ledger paper with a torn edge. As she bent to pick it up the lights went out. She'd heard a grating sound like a reluctant garage-door opener in operation and then blackness and silence.

"Rob," Teddy called out, trying to orient herself in the pitch black room. This room was on the inside of the hill with no windows and no light penetrated down the two halls from the window in the garage. "Rob," she called again louder, "What's happened?" Teddy stuffed the piece of ledger paper in her pocket and felt her way along the wall toward where she remembered the door to be. "Rob! This is not funny. Where are you?" Teddy could hear the panic in her voice as it echoed off the walls. Her hand found the doorframe and she moved out into the hall feeling her way slowly along the wall in search of the door into the large hall.

"Ah!" she felt relieved to have found another door. "Dummy, this hall is only four or five feet long, how lost could you get?" Teddy laughed at herself. Moving forward she stumbled over a stack of what her body told her were boxes, dusty, musty, boxes.

"Wrong door," she decided, and backed up, colliding with the door, which pushed shut behind her. "Damn!" Teddy muttered and felt for the handle. It turned but the door didn't open. "Hey! Rob! Hey! I'm stuck in here. Rob!" Rob did not answer. It was dark, and the musty smell from the old papers was threatening to make her sneeze. Teddy pounded on the door. "Rob, get me out of here. Achoo! Achoo, achoo, aaachooo!"

CHAPTER 14

"ACHOO!" Teddy could not stop sneezing. "Think damn it, this door has to be blocked or something." She began to feel around the doorframe and finally her fingers came to a good, old fashioned, box dead bolt. The kind with an automatic spring - shut the door and it's locked. You had to use a key on the outside but there was a knob on the inside. Teddy turned the knob and sighed with relief between sneezes.

"Now turn right," she instructed herself. "Then right again at the end of the hall and the stairs are just past the ladders, on the right." She came to a door, "garden stuff," she counted off. "Bathroom," Teddy named the next door. "Only a couple of steps more and there will be daylight in the garage. Boy, am I going to give Rob what for for leaving me alone in there."

Her hands encountered the door at the end and she lowered her right hand, seeking the doorknob. It was hot, really hot!

"Fire?" Teddy questioned aloud sniffing the air. Only a faint aroma, sort of a bacony smell, came to her. "Smoke rises, if the house is on fire you wouldn't smell it right away down here," she reasoned. She touched the door handle lightly again and laid her left hand flat on the door itself. The handle was hot, the door was very warm.

Teddy took two steps back into the blackness of the hallway.

"Think, don't panic," she instructed, "There has to be a way out. Rob where are you?" she called as loud as she could.

Teddy continued to back down the hall, watching fascinated as fingers of flame licked from under the door to the garage. She trailed a hand on the wall on either side to keep track of where she was.

The other two rooms! "Of course, they're on the downhill side, they'll have windows!" Teddy concentrated on the wall to her left. There had been a door, beyond the bathroom but before, no, across from the garden room. She continued backing, unable to turn her back on the flame that sent its eerie red glow dancing up the door. Her hand found a doorframe. Elated, Teddy turned to it and felt for the knob, praying it wasn't locked. The door opened effortlessly into a space just large enough to allow the door to swing in. It was a large room, with two windows, French doors it looked like, but between Teddy and the windows with their ragged white drapes was at least three households full of furniture; beds, mattresses, tables, chairs, sofas, piled to the ceiling in a mind boggling tangle. She would never be able to get across it.

Teddy swallowed the panic swelling in her throat and backed into the hall once more. There would be a window in the next room, too, there had to be. She left the door open for the bit of light that might penetrate as far as the hall.

Now she could smell the smoke, no mistake. The red-orange flames burning up under the door reminded Teddy of the flame from a gas log. She turned away from the fire and in the smoky gloom sought the last door. It was square at the end of the hall. Teddy grabbed the knob and twisted, it was open, but her heart sank.

At first glance it appeared to be a closet. There was a blank wall four feet away, directly in front of her. Then her eye caught the sense, more than the real knowledge, of light off to the right. Sticking her head around the corner she could see that it was a large room with its own tiny vestibule elled off at one end where the door was, and with the exception of three refrigerators and four stoves it was empty. Bamboo roll-down shades covered the two sets of French doors blocking the sun so that only a thin glow of daylight emanated from them.

Teddy was only halfway across the room toward the windows when a whoosh and a blast of hot air from behind her signaled the fire's encroachment into the hall. She lost no time in finding the pull and raising the shade on the nearest set of doors. They were locked!

"Of course they're locked, you ninny," Teddy said, looking furiously to identify the kind of locking mechanism. Even after she undid the long bolts that slid up and down into the doorframe the door would not budge. Teddy re-examined the doors themselves. Wood framed with a double line of small glass panes in each door. She looked around for something, a tool to pry or smash her way out? At first she didn't see anything, then in desperation she opened the oven of the nearest stove and pulled out a metal rack. It was getting smokier and she was beginning to sneeze again.

Whack!

Teddy hit the line of small panes in the nearest door with all her might, two broke and the narrow band of wood between them splintered.

WHACK! WHACK WHACK!

She hit the growing gap again and again, feeling the fire, drawn to the fresh air, warming her back. Using the rack she knocked the majority of the glass and wood from the frame and, counting the blessings of a reasonably slight build, squeezed out into the bright afternoon. Teddy ran across the brick-paved terrace toward the driveway.

"Rob, Rob, where are you?" she yelled as loud as she could.

Rob's pickup was backed up to the closed garage door, the driver-side door was open. He was nowhere in sight. The first floor of the house was completely involved, flames shooting skyward from every window.

"Rob!" Teddy called. *Where are you?* She wondered. *Did you go back in there looking for me?*

Through the garage window Teddy could see the red glow of the fire consuming the garage walls. Teddy got as close to the window as she could and tried to see inside knowing she should get back.

Those cars could blow up.

The thought registered and she raced for Rob's pickup, if she didn't move it now it would soon be too late. Teddy had always chided him for what she thought was a careless habit of leaving his keys on the floor under the driver's seat, now as her hand found the keys she blessed him for his consistency. She fumbled with the release that would let her slide the seat forward enough to touch the pedals, started the engine, and slammed the pickup into gear. She shot across the wide gravel turn around, hitting the brakes just in time to stop the back tires from following the front into the soft earth of the flower border.

The garage door seemed to be following her. At first Teddy thought the fire had caused one of the cars to explode blowing the door outward, then she realized the wooden garage door was being splintered and born outward by Ben's old blue pickup. The pieces of the garage door fell away as the pickup skidded sideways into the flowerbed beside her and stopped.

"I always wanted to do that," Rob said, getting out.

Teddy scrambled to get to the ground, and to Rob. Blood was flowing freely down the right side of his face and he looked awful.

"What happened?" Teddy cried, hugging him.

"I was so afraid you were still in there," Rob said, hugging back, "I couldn't get to you, the stairs and that end of the garage were too hot." Rob put a hand up to the bloody side of his head. "Someone hit me. I opened the garage door and walked in, to get the dolly, and next thing I know I'm on the floor by the door and everything is burning. I couldn't get to you," he repeated hugging her closer. "Oh Teddy, I was so scared."

"Me too. I got lost in the dark and then I broke a window."

They stood there together for several minutes watching the fire, shock immobilizing them.

123

"Teddy, somebody tried to kill us," Rob said at last.

"Well, they didn't succeed," Teddy said firmly. "What do we do now?"

"Get the fire department I suppose, though it seems like a lost cause. By the time they get up here there isn't going to be much left but ashes."

"At least they're not our ashes," she said with a shudder. "But whatever evidence might have been in those filing cabinets or the house is certainly gone."

"That's for sure. Come on let's get these rigs out of here," Rob said, nodding his head in the direction of the two pickups. "We're still way too close. Follow me on down the hill and we'll use the phone in the guesthouse. Cell phone won't pick up out here."

"Guest house?" Teddy questioned.

"Ben built it for Trix, right after she got married the first time, to give her privacy when she visited. Trix never cared for it, too rustic for her tastes." Rob grimaced.

"Your head hurting?" Teddy asked. "It really looks like you could use a couple of stitches."

"Hurts some, what I could really use is a strong drink and some Advil." He attempted a smile. "You okay to drive?"

"Lead on," Teddy answered, turning to get back in the green pickup.

Half a mile back down the drive Rob turned off on a grassy trace that was more of a wide path than a road. They passed through a rambling hedge of myrtle and wild rhodies and climbed slightly across a spruce-edged glade. At the far edge, tucked into the trees, was a log cabin with a dark-green metal roof and dark-green trim around its multi-paned windows. A patch of early daffodils bloomed beside the small, railless wooden deck that served as a porch.

It was utterly charming, Teddy thought. Rob took the key from the top of the trim over the left window and opened the door.

Inside, an entire wall was occupied with a stone fireplace. An efficiency kitchen lined the back wall under the overhang of a loft reached by a steep, narrow stair that wound over what Teddy discovered to be the bathroom.

"Trix didn't like this?" Teddy questioned, shaking her head.

Rob crossed at once to the kitchen and lifted the telephone from its wall bracket, smiled as he heard the dial tone, and punched 911.

It took only seconds to give the alarm, directions, and request Sonny's presence as well.

In the bathroom, Teddy found washcloths and a half-full bottle of hydrogen peroxide. There didn't seem to be any hot water and the cold ran rusty at first, but by the time Rob was off the phone, she had a couple of wet washcloths ready to provide first aid clean-up to his head.

"Ouch! That hurts," Rob yelped, as she wiped away the blood from the gash.

"And this is going to hurt more," Teddy said, as she doused the wound liberally with the hydrogen peroxide and then clamped a wrung-out cloth over it. "Just hold on to that for a while."

"Geeze woman, I'm already hurt. Damn, that stuff stings."

"Kills the germs," Teddy explained, wiping at the blood on his forehead. "I really ought to get you down to the hospital and get that stitched up."

"As soon as Sonny and the fire department get here. Right now we should get on back to the house. Not much we can do but watch the fire but..." Rob winced and put his hand to his head. "Let's leave Ben's pickup here, I don't think I feel much like driving right now."

CHAPTER 15

It was twenty minutes before they could hear the sirens and another ten after that before the three big red vehicles, two of them pumper trucks, followed by Sonny's patrol car, followed by Sid Chapman's "press" car slid to a stop amongst much spraying of gravel and mud. Chief Watkins began shouting orders to his well-trained volunteers. Sid began taking pictures of the fire and anything else that moved. Sonny steamed down upon Teddy and Rob, red-faced and bug eyed.

"Just what the hell is going on out here?"

"It's burning," Rob answered flatly.

They were standing well down the drive, the blaze too far out of hand for the firefighters to do much more than watch and maybe prevent the fire from spreading to the nearby trees and thus to the forest.

"I can see that, how'd it get started?" Sonny demanded, "And what happened to your head?"

"Somebody tried to kill us," Teddy said angrily. "What are you going to do about it?"

"Now Teddy," Sonny soothed, "what makes you say that. It could have been wiring or..."

"Faulty wiring doesn't hit people over the head, Sonny," Rob said, quietly.

"What you two doing out here anyway?" Sonny shouted. The fire was getting louder, hotter, and they backed up several more paces to stand beside Rob's pickup, parked in a wide spot beside the drive.

Teddy found her throat was dry and her voice cracked as she tried to answer.

"Packing things up for the high school rummage sale."

"Well I hope Ben's fire insurance was paid up," Sonny observed dryly.

"It was," Rob said. "Look, there's nothing we can do here. The house is gone, that's all there is to it. My head is really beginning to hurt."

"Sure." Sonny looked at Rob hard and noticed for the first time just how injured he was. "You two go on down, and Teddy, see that he gets some stitches and looked at by a doctor. I'll come by and talk to you both later. Where you going to be?"

"At my place, I don't think he should be alone tonight." Teddy answered before Rob could say anything.

"Oh?" Sonny's raised eyebrows spoke volumes.

"Won't be the first time I've slept on that couch," Teddy said pointedly. "You keep your mind out of the gutter, Sonny Hubbard."

"What I don't understand is how you let the fire get so far out of control. Ben has a good water supply up here and hoses." Sonny caught sight of Sid headed toward them, "I'll talk to you two later, you better get now. I want to hear this story before Sid prints it on the front page."

Rob was being very quiet and looked pale.

"Let's go," Teddy said, reaching for the driver's side door handle.

Sonny hustled Rob around to the other side and pushed more than helped him in, thumping the door after he closed it as a signal for Teddy to take off. With a quick look at Rob slumped in the passenger seat Teddy started the engine and slid it in gear, immediately cutting a tight left turn into the gravel drive headed downhill. She got a brief glance at Sid waving at her to stop and saw him again in the rear-view mirror, hands on hips, as he stood beside Sonny.

"Put your seat belt on," Teddy ordered fastening her own with one hand.

"Yes ma'am," Rob replied, reaching wearily for the buckle. "You sure got bossy all of a sudden."

"You doing okay?"

"I'm fine, just a little tired and a whole lot confused. He... they... whoever, were trying to kill us. Or at least they didn't care if they did. Whatever they were looking for when they broke into the house before, I don't think they found it. Teddy, I think they burnt the house down so we wouldn't find it either."

"So, now all we have to do is figure out what `it' is, or was. Terrific."

Teddy had shifted quickly through the gears and they were pelting downhill and around the curves just as fast as she could go and still keep more or less on the road. Twice before they got to the highway Teddy caught her breath and gripped the wheel hard as they swung about a tight corner and the pickup seemed to lean over precariously, the back end skittering sideways. She let out a big sigh as they came out onto the blacktop.

"I don't suppose you'd mind driving carefully enough to get us there in one piece?" Rob asked.

129

Out of the corner of her eye, Teddy could see he was leaning back in the seat, pale, but smiling at her.

"I mean I'd hate it if you wrecked my pretty new pickup," he teased.

"Everybody's a critic. I'll have you know I was driving when you were still in kindergarten. The only car I ever wrecked was because of some black ice and a tree that got in the way."

Teddy felt Rob's hand pat her knee.

"You just watch out for those aggressive trees, I'm going to be just fine. I promise," he said. "I sure could use an Advil, got any in your purse?"

"My purse? My purse was by the window - where we ate lunch. Damn! I'm going to have to get my driver's license replaced, and my Visa card and..." Teddy mentally inventoried the contents of her purse. "My favorite lipstick was in there. About forty bucks, too. And my house keys!"

"In the glove compartment," Rob said.

"What?"

"Your spare set of keys, the ones you gave me for emergencies, they're in the glove compartment." Rob said, then groaned.

"Hurting?"

"No, I just remembered, that ledger I found, it was in that box with those other things. I left it down there with you when I went to find the dolly. I sure wish I knew what Ben had been up to. If someone is going to kill me I'd like to know why."

Teddy nodded her head in agreement. "Maybe we can figure it out before they try again."

"Now there is a cheery thought."

Rob slid lower in the seat and closed his eyes.

It had taken forty-five minutes to get to the emergency room. Twenty minutes for them to give Rob a tetanus shot and put five stitches in his head and another twenty for the pharmacy to fill the prescriptions for painkillers and antibiotic creams for the burns that were beginning to blister on his arms and shoulders. It was already dark when Teddy pulled to a stop behind Sonny's patrol car parked in front of her house.

Chapter 16

"Now really, why were you up there?" Sonny asked, stirring a second spoon of sugar into the mug of coffee that sat steaming in front of him on the dining table.

"I was going to give all Ben's furniture and household things - pots and pans, linens - you know, to the rummage sale. Teddy was helping me sort out the garbage and personal stuff." Rob lifted his mug with two hands and breathed in the heady aroma before taking a hefty draught. "Trix didn't want any of Ben's things and she didn't want the house, so I was going to sell it. Will still sell the acreage." Rob set his mug on the table hands still cupping its warmth, his eyes drifted shut.

"You okay?" Teddy asked. She hadn't yet sat down and now came to stand beside Rob's chair a hand on his shoulder.

"Tired. I think those pills the doctor gave me are kicking in. The throbbing is slowing down, I feel really tired." Rob put a hand up to touch Teddy's and smiled up at her. "I'm just fine, only tired."

Between the bandage wrapped around his head to secure the patch of white gauze covering his stitches, the red blotches where hot embers had seared his skin and a definite paleness under his tan, he did not look fine.

"I can tell Sonny all about what happened. Why don't you go on back to the bedroom and get a nap. I'll fix some dinner later," Teddy urged.

"Teddy, I am fine. And I want Sonny to get busy and find out just who's going around doing his level best to do us in and why. I mean, just what makes you or me a threat to whoever killed Ben?"

"Now, we don't know for sure it's all connected," Sonny started then held up his hands to stop the protests both Teddy and Rob had stiffened to deliver. "It could have been vandals, kids who started the fire accidentally maybe, and hit Rob to keep from getting caught; or someone who was out to rip off a house they thought was empty and hide the evidence by burning the place down or..."

"Nonsense!" Teddy spit the words at him angrily. "You know better than that Sonny. You don't set the place afire before you take the stuff out if you're `ripping it off' like you said. And kids out to spray graffiti, or mess around, don't go hitting people on the head. They'd have just run. Hell, Rob's pickup was out front, they wouldn't even have come in the house. Make sense."

"Now Teddy," Sonny whined.

"She's right, you know," Rob said softly. "Whoever lit that fire knew we were in there. I think they didn't want us to find whatever it is they hadn't been able to find themselves. And they didn't much care if Teddy and I ended up dead in the process." He put his hand to his head and shut his eyes again momentarily. When he opened them Rob made eye contact with Sonny and held it. "I got hit because I almost discovered him, or them, could have been more than one. And they shut the garage door, locked me in, with a fire already going upstairs. I suppose they may not have known Teddy was with me, but they sure knew they were leaving me to fry."

133

"All right, let's take it from the beginning. Tell me everything you did or saw after you got up there." Sonny took a big gulp of his coffee, put his cup down, and took out his twisted little notebook.

"Sonny!" Teddy protested, looking from Rob's pale face to Sonny's expectant one with real alarm.

"We got up there about ten," Rob began patiently, and then proceeded to explain all their movements until he had left Teddy alone in the basement office.

"I went up the stairs and out the front door, if there was someone in the laundry room or the kitchen I didn't hear or see them. But I would guess, by the way the fire was burning overhead and down the stairs that's where it was started. Anyway, I went out the front door like I said and drove my pickup around to the garage door. I wanted to load up those filing cabinets and take them back to my place to read over the contents. Sonny, I think the answer was staring me in the face if I could only figure it out." He paused and took a drink of his coffee. "I used Ben's keys to open the garage door, the one on the left where Ben always parked his old pickup, and went in to find the dolly. He generally kept it in that back corner. Anyway I didn't get far, that's when I got hit," Rob swayed slightly in his chair as if saying the words had brought back the physical reality of the moment. "The next thing I know I'm waking up on the floor and there's smoke and I can see fire on the stairs and all that part of the wall and ceiling. I couldn't get to the door to the hallway where Teddy was. I tried, and then I saw her face at the window. When I heard her start up my rig, to pull it away from

134

the building, I just gunned Ben's old rig right through the door after her." Rob took a drink of his coffee and sagged deeper in his chair.

"Now you are going to go get some rest," Teddy insisted. "Come on Sonny, help me get him into the bedroom."

"I can walk," Rob said, started to rise, wobbled, and then sagged back grasping the table to help himself stand.

"Sure you can, but we all need a little help now and again," Sonny said, moving quickly for all his bulk. He motioned Teddy aside and slipped a big arm around Rob, under his shoulders, taking on his weight. Teddy scurried down the short hall and pulled the covers back on the bed.

Sonny eased Rob into the bed and pulled off his boots.

"Thanks," Rob mumbled, "I just need to sleep."

Teddy pulled the covers up over him and followed Sonny back to the kitchen.

"So, what were you doing while Rob was getting himself hit over the head?" Sonny asked, his coffee cup held out for a refill.

"Playing Blindman's Bluff all by myself." Teddy poured them both more coffee, sat down and told Sonny everything that had happened after Rob left her alone in Ben's basement office. She'd gone through it all for Rob while they waited for the fire trucks, it had been the single most frightening experience of her life and even in the second telling she felt her tension growing, her heart thumping wildly.

"Man you two sure had yourselves a time." Sonny sat back in his chair and clapped his big hands on his thick thighs. "Sounds just like one of them adventure stories."

"Sonny if you think we're making this up..."

"Now, I didn't say that. I'm sure it all happened just like you said. But it's my job to look at things from all sides. I mean there's some as is going to say Rob could'a lit that fire."

"Why for Pete sakes? Why would he do that?" Teddy was standing, her voice rising.

"He said it himself Teddy, somewhere in that house there well might've been evidence that would point out just who murdered old Ben and dumped him in your septic tank. Maybe Rob gave up on finding it and decided to burn the place down just to be on the safe side."

"And burn me down right along with it! Sonny you've had one beer too many and pickled any brains you ever did have." Teddy was shaking with anger. "Rob did not kill Ben, and he didn't light that fire. Rob would never hurt me, never. What about that car or truck, whatever it was, I saw while we were eating? Who was that? You go find out about that green truck."

"I intend to. Could be it was the forestry people like Rob thought. Teddy I ain't saying Rob did nothing, I just have to look at all the possibilities that's all."

"Well that's not one of them as far as I'm concerned. I mean, if he had, why would he lock himself in like that. And how'd he get his head

136

bashed in? It just doesn't wash Sonny, even if I were willing to consider the possibility."

Teddy was suddenly very tired as well as angry. She wanted to curl up under a warm blanket and let the sound of the surf erase all the confusion and irritation that filled her.

Sonny stood up and closed his notebook. He looked tired himself, and unhappy.

"I got to go back up to Ben's place and see if the Chief can tell me anymore about how the fire got started. They got ways now to pinpoint such things. They can tell right where the match was lit and set to it, or so he tells me. I'll get back to you in the morning. Tell Rob to take it easy," he added, turning to the door.

Teddy stood in the doorway and watched him go.

There was a fine mist of a rain falling and a damp chill crept in the open door and made her shudder. Sonny's taillights faded down the road, soon hidden completely by the trees and still Teddy stared out into the night. It felt like a million years ago now that she had been so pleased to be getting the lid for the septic tank. It had seemed like such a stroke of good fortune. So much had happened since, ugly, frightening, horrible things. Murder. Ben. Rene. And this afternoon it had very nearly been her and Rob. Who could have that much anger - or need - or fear? Just what did it take to start a person killing? Make them keep killing? Serial killers appeared to do it for the rush, a compulsion, victims connected by some common trait or physical aspect that attracted the killer to them. This was different than that. The connection centered on Ben and the killer, something Ben had done to or knew about his killer. She was sure of it. And whoever killed Ben killed Rene because of something she might have heard that would help identify the motive for Ben's death, not because they liked the killing, but because of fear of discovery. There was no longer any shred of doubt in her mind that Rene had been murdered. She felt sure the fire was meant to destroy evidence, and maybe to destroy the people who would understand that evidence. It was a chain, each action requiring the next. The damp chill and the dark night it came from were suddenly too threatening. Teddy hurriedly shut the door and locked it.

Her stomach growled.

"I need to eat and I'll bet Rob is going to wake up hungry after a while," Teddy decided aloud.

She opened the refrigerator door and studied the contents.

"Comfort food" won out. Teddy buttered two slices of bread, and then heated up her black cast-iron frying pan. When it was good and hot she lay one piece of bread, butter down, in the pan and quickly covered it with slices of cheddar cheese, the cheese with a slice of ham, topping the sandwich with the remaining bread, butter up. The butter sizzled and Teddy lifted a corner with a spatula to check the browning. Impatient, she checked twice more before it was ready to be turned. Then she flipped it expertly and turned the stove off, knowing the residual heat would finish the job. Teddy poured herself a glass of diet Coke, set the glass on a tray covered with a place mat to keep things from sliding as she carried it upstairs. She removed the perfectly done grilled-cheese sandwich to a plate and cut it diagonally, just the way her mother had always done.

Teddy watched an old movie while she ate, trying to put the day completely out of her mind so she could return to it later with more perspective. She and Rob would talk it over when he woke up, until then "I will not let it overwhelm me," she explained to John Wayne. John seemed to understand. He leveled his best blue-eyed stare at the bad guy and whomped him one on the jaw, sending him sprawling across the bar.

CHAPTER 17

At first the sounds of someone moving about in the bedroom below her was alarming. Used to falling asleep in front of the television she was also used to being quite alone in her house. Pulling herself into wide-eyed wakefulness, her mind sorted rapidly through events to get up to speed on where she was and what was going on. She spared a glance at the screen to note that John Wayne had ridden once more into the sunset and Cary Grant and Irene Dunne were now indulging in a brawl of a different nature. The clock on the wall said 12:05.

"Teddy?" Rob's voice seemed as tentative as she felt.

"I'm here. Are you okay?" Teddy answered, struggling to her feet and coming close to tripping over the blanket that was still wrapped around her.

"Hungry mostly. And a bit of a headache."

Teddy heard the refrigerator door open. She untangled herself from the blanket and started down the stairs. "I'll fix you some eggs, you sit down," she scolded.

Four eggs, six pieces of bacon, four pieces of toast, some apricot jam, a large glass of milk, and two Advil later Rob seemed to be feeling much better.

"I smell like smoke and so does your bed I'm afraid."

Teddy lifted a shoulder and sniffed at her shirt. "We are both a little reminiscent of a burn barrel. I guess I was too tired or too het-up to notice before. I can wash your clothes but I don't see how you can take a shower without getting all your bandages wet."

"Emphuh," Rob nodded, his mouth full of the last bite of toast and jam. "What I really want to do is get home. Teddy, I think whoever started that fire is desperate to destroy any evidence that might exist to connect them to Ben's death. Sooner or later it's going to occur to them that I might have taken whatever it is out of Ben's office before they ransacked it the other night and that I have it at home. I better finish comparing those ledgers with my computer records and get them in a safe place."

"Just where do you think that is? I mean," Teddy did not want to say what was tugging at the edges of her mind. Sonny was, after all, one of the good ole' boys, not outside the inner circle of mutual back scratchers. The local fraternity of beer-drinking, back-slapping, narrow-minded, and devotedly chauvinistic gray hairs had been instrumental in his getting elected in the first place, and certainly of prime importance in keeping him in office. Still she didn't want to say, right out loud, he would subvert the truth. She wasn't entirely sure why she felt so positive the good ole' boy network was more than a little involved in all that had been going on.

"Sonny might shine a parking ticket or look the other way over some of the smaller stuff where his poker pals are concerned, but I can't see him covering up for murder or even the break-ins." He had read her mind. "You know one may not be directly connected to the other."

141

"Huh?" Teddy tilted her head and tried to take in the implication of his words. "You mean whoever broke into Ben's, your office, maybe even started the fire, might have done it because Ben was dead but didn't kill Ben?"

"It's possible," Rob nodded his head slowly. "And I don't think whoever it was that broke into the office was very computer literate, you can't erase information by smashing a screen or breaking a keyboard. You have to call up a file and delete it or cause the system to crash though even that may not always be final."

"Well not a whole lot of local folks are that up on computers. Not the ones over thirty anyway," Teddy said, thinking of her youngest grandson and the way he had whizzed through his "homework" on the computer the last time she had visited. "If you'd been broken into by a thirteen-year-old the information would be gone for sure."

"I just wish I knew exactly what the `information' was. The only thing I have left to work with are the set of books I took out of Ben's office and the project records I've got entered on my computer. I've made a set of back-up disks; did that before Ben was killed. Mostly because of the way the power goes down around here every time some idiot runs into a power pole or digs up an underground line, then the surge when it comes back on. That surge can wipe out a computer's memory and even destroy the equipment, keeping copies just made sense. The real problem is I still don't know what it is I'm looking for. I didn't get but a glance at those records we found at Ben's but I'd swear Ben was up to something more than a little padding for IRS purposes," Rob laid his napkin on the table. "I think I need to get home and go over what I have until I can figure out what."

"It could wait until morning. You've had a pretty rough day, you know. And I'm not sure you should be alone, or driving for that matter."

"And just what would your good neighbors say if my pickup was here in the morning?" He teased with a grin.

"That I'd finally caught you at a weak moment and had my wicked way with you just as they were always sure I would," Teddy grinned. "You afraid for your reputation?"

"Seldom hurts a man's reputation to fool around. Enhances it in some circles," Rob said, "only neither one of us travels in those circles and I think it would be grossly unfair for the locals to be convinced we were having more fun than we actually are."

"I doubt many of them could ever understand how good a real friendship can be. We're already having great `fun' of a kind they couldn't possibly comprehend. But if you are determined to save my good name I want you to call me the minute you get home please."

"Yes ma'am." Rob leaned forward and planted a kiss on her forehead. "And I want you to lock up good and make sure you know where your phone is. Okay?"

"Yes daddy," Teddy said and made a face at him.

Teddy woke several times during the night. First it was the smoky smell that persisted despite the fact that she had stripped the bed and taken a shower. She got up and started the washer, adding extra soap and color-safe bleach. The surf woke her when the tide changed, the rumbling roar identified at once in her groggy mind and she drifted back to sleep. Soon after that, squabbling raccoons had pulled her from dreams of being lost in endless dark corridors with doors that opened into flames. Finally, exhausted, she had slept soundly, dreamlessly until the phone on the nightstand jangled her into disgruntled awareness.

"Hello," Teddy growled.

"Aren't you little Mary Sunshine," Pete's deep voice drawled. "I hear you had a hot time up at old Ben's last night."

"Who told you?" Teddy demanded.

"I'd be willing to bet everybody in town knows by now. Sure was the talk of everyone at Petal's. Looks like you and your good buddy Rob got yourselves into a bit of trouble."

The snide tone in his voice rankled. "I'd say it was the little boys playing with matches that will be in trouble in the long run," Teddy spat at him. "Now if gossip was all that was on your mind I have things to do."

"Aw, Teddy, come on now. I was just teasing. I'm a little jealous you know, you do spend an awful lot of time with Rob Greene."

He had started out pleading and ended up accusing.

"Pete, who I spend my time with is absolutely none of your business, and I don't much like your intimating it is." Teddy glanced at the clock on the nightstand. It was a quarter to eight. She had slept in but it was still too early for anyone to be calling. "My eggs are burning," she lied, "bye." Teddy hung up the phone and lay back on the pillow fuming. "Damn that man makes me feel uncomfortable," she said to the ceiling.

Dressed, and the coffeepot doing its thing, she transferred the wet laundry to the dryer and contemplated the day. The drapes when she'd pulled them disclosed a gray, drizzly, morning. The man on the radio confirmed light showers, clearing to some sun in the afternoon. Teddy poured a bowl of cereal and sliced a banana on top.
The phone rang.
"Hello," Teddy said, holding the phone to her ear with her left hand while she extracted the milk from the refrigerator with her right.
"Well at least you don't still sound mad," Pete said. "Look I'm sorry if I upset you. Would you let me apologize by taking you to dinner tonight?"
"Pete drop it. I am not interested in going to dinner with you. Not now, and the way you're going at it, not ever. Good-bye." She clicked the talk button and disconnected the line.
It was only two steps to put the phone in its cradle. She didn't get that far before the instrument in her hand rang again nearly causing her to drop it in surprise.
"Hello," she said cautiously.

"Click!" went the line in her ear.

"Well good, maybe Pete decided not to apologize one more time," Teddy said, depositing the phone at last in its nest.

After breakfast she put on a heavy sweatshirt and took a second cup of coffee for an inspection tour of the garden. Weak sunshine was not quite dispelling the drizzle but had reduced it to a dampening mist. Everywhere she looked, the bright green of spring growth renewed the pending promise of the blooms and leafy pleasures to come. Everywhere, too, infant weeds gave assurance of future hours of work to be done. Teddy surveyed the probable path of her old-fashioned leach lines, terra-cotta tile laid end to end and most probably not even sealed but left for the liquids to seep out, dispersing them. She calculated the distances, not for the first time, and the number of tiles that would have to be lifted and perhaps replaced. If she called a professional it would not only be costly but they would of course have to get a permit for a septic repair, which would be subject to current regulation and inspection, and that could be very expensive indeed, in more ways than one. The kind of leach lines now demanded by building code, and the machinery it would require to install them, would decimate her garden. The only acceptable answer to her pocketbook, and for her beautiful garden, was to do it by hand, herself. Self-repair by the homeowner did not require a permit or an inspection, nor any change in the basics of an existing system as long as it could be returned to working order.

"You won't get done if you don't get started," Teddy reminded the wild fuchsia, which bobbed its first red buds in agreement. But it was also something she did not care to do with an audience. It would be better to wait until the curious got bored with the viewing of her purple-daisy-covered septic tank. "Don't need any crowd of shovel-leaners to watch me work and give advice." The fuchsia agreed again. Teddy sat her cup on a convenient stump and turned toward the beach, a long walk appealed to her, it always helped her think things through and she certainly had a lot to think about.

Chapter 18

The high tide had rearranged even the largest pieces of driftwood and left behind a wide clean band of beach, a sprinkle of stones, like freckles, at the mean tide line, but otherwise unmarked. Teddy always liked it when her footprint was the first of the day. It gave her a sense of privacy. She did not begrudge the seagulls and flitty little shore birds their sharp little tracks that spun fanciful designs across the sand. But the large dent of a pair of Nikes stamped into the sand by some two-hundred-pound jogger or even the barefoot trail of strolling teens left her with the sense that uninvited guests had just wandered through her living room.

Far south she spied the bright rainbow hues of a sand sailer, perhaps the one she and Rob had seen housed under one of the newer beachfront homes. It was moving at tremendous speed, swooping gracefully - tacking she thought they called it - back and forth across the beach, working its way farther south toward the river, then it would have to turn and come back.

They could have brought Ben's body up the beach from almost anywhere with one of those. Or in a car or pickup for that matter. "But then they would have had to carry it up through the garden," she explained to a seagull that sat still on the sand and listened attentively. "Ben was not a large man but a dead weight, up that hill would have been difficult and in the dark they would surely have left some kind of a sign, a broken bush, something, don't you think?" She had looked and found nothing.

The gull cocked his head and considered.

"No, I still think Ben came by the road, then he only had to be carried that short distance down the hill, you see."

The gull pulled his head upright, took two awkward steps by way of preparation, and with a bit of a hop slipped into the air, circling out over the cresting breakers and back over Teddy's head before he swooped north.

"Didn't mean to bore you," Teddy called after him and continued her walk south.

She watched the returning bright sail of the sand sailer begin to grow larger as the wind off the sea picked up and shifted slightly, whisking the light vehicle along at fantastic speed. The fat little tires, like the one on my wheelbarrow, Teddy thought, left a trail to mark their passage as the two passengers waved gaily and flashed on north. They had been so bundled up it was impossible to tell sex or ages.

At the river Teddy executed a wide U-turn, checking out the new angle the last storm had cut for the stream. The last time she'd walked this far the water had been running deep, and angled sharply north, cutting a long way up the beach before reaching the sea. Now the water was twelve to fifteen feet across, not so very deep, and wasting no effort in getting straight to its meeting with the Pacific, it doubled its width and spread in a wide fan where freshwater met salt.

The walk was doing her good, Teddy's spirits lifted. She picked out the fleur-de-lis trails of gulls criss-crossed on the sand and followed one with her eyes to where it edged around a small grass-topped dune. From behind the dune the end of a piece of driftwood, oddly bumped and very black, attracted her attention. Closer she concluded it was not driftwood at all but a boot.

Her heart beat faster, she stopped, then strode purposefully forward.

"Enough is enough. Damn it," Teddy lamented, feeling she had plenty of problems already. "I do not need another body."

With trepidation she rounded the hump of sand. The boot, she could now see, was sticking out of the side of the dune at an awkward angle. There might - or there might not - be a body attached. Teddy kicked at it gently.

It held firm.

She kicked again, harder, and the big rubber boot went flying, tumbling in the air, sending a swirl of sand pouring from its empty top, some of which managed to shower into Teddy's face.

"Pssttt." Teddy blew sand off her lips and began to laugh. "Paranoid, that's what you are Teddy Stanley." Then she remembered, with just a little bit of a quiver in her stomach, the newspaper article last year about the woman who had found a sneaker on a beach up north with a foot in it. Just to be sure, she retrieved the boot and felt it carefully to confirm it had only been filled with sand. The boot folded flat in her hand. Teddy smiled and sent wishes on the wind that whoever had lost it had not lost more. Seeing as it was not exactly biodegradable she tucked it under her arm to take back to the garbage can.

The rest of the way home she could not help but dwell on the fact that people, like things, were not always what they seemed. Ben certainly hadn't been. More than a good ole' boy and a sharp businessman, Ben was, at the very least, a petty thief if Rob's suspicions were right. Maybe he had been killed by one of his many investors? The Paileys, or Furst and Anna, or even Sonny?

Sonny would really hate being made a fool of, he might well have found violence an answer, might have heard about the septic tank having a vacancy, so to speak, and decided to take advantage of it. And Anna certainly was venomous enough to be a killer, though Teddy couldn't really see Furst in the role. But if Anna had somehow killed Ben, Furst would have helped her cover it up. More than fifty years of loving obedience would be a hard habit to break. Yes, and Marrianne Pailey had been heard railing at and about Ben more than once lately. What exactly was eating her and how far would she go to get even?

"And don't forget dear, money grubbing, daughter Trix." Teddy reminded herself. The puzzle was insidious, unable to shake its pull she put her mind to a plan of action.

"Like the damn drain tile, I just need to dig in and uncover all the dirty little secrets, one at a time," Teddy panted having climbed back up the soft side of the big dune that backed her garden.

The sun was stronger now. That and the exertion had Teddy feeling overheated. She stopped and eyed her garden critically. "Looking better every year," she concluded, satisfied with what she saw. "It is going to be beautiful this year when all the rhodies bloom." For weeks now she had done a daily inspection of the growing buds. Hard, tiny, green, upside-down tops since last fall, they had begun to grow and the pace was picking up. Soon they would swell to the point of bursting, their color barely concealed behind the pale-green wrapper that contained the flower until it could contain it no more and the individual blossoms that went to make up each fantastic bloom forced their way into the sunshine.

"Not long now." Teddy always awaited spring's glory with the anticipation of a small child at Christmas. She retrieved her empty coffee cup and checked out the garden plant by plant, bud by bud, as she climbed the hill to the house.

Her hand was on the door when the crunch of gravel alerted her to someone approaching on the road and she swung around.

"Morning, Teddy. I see your tourist business has slacked off," Furst called.

"'Bout time. I still can't see what was so all-fired interesting about my purple daisy seedlings," Teddy responded, coming down the steps to meet him.

"Well, life is a little slow around here, entertainment's hard to come by. And murder, particularly the murder of someone you know, is pretty fascinatin'." Furst leaned heavily on the sturdy cane that he'd been using the last couple of years to steady himself on his walks and waved his free hand toward the septic tank. "You got to admit the killer had some imagination. If you hadn't a got yourself a new lid it could have been years before old Ben was found. They'd a had to declare him dead eventually, of course, but it sure would have tied up his estate and business stuff for awhile."

Ben had pretty much precluded that himself with the trust, Teddy knew, but that was Rob's business and if and when he wanted to tell the world was up to him.

"Don't expect it makes much difference one way or another to his investment projects. You and Anna have a part in one don't you?" she asked prying more than she normally might have.

"More than one, more's the pity," Furst spat out, his voice filled with contempt. "We kind of liked the idea of investing in our own community, where you could see what was going on and maybe make a positive difference in the local economy. That was the sales spiel anyway. But I gotta tell you, Anna and I aren't the only ones hereabouts was beginning to get more than a little unhappy about those projects of Ben's. Cash flow never has been what he promised. Shoddy job of construction. And he just kept using the same local numbskulls to do the repairs. Couple of those projects paid out more in upkeep and repairs last year than income. Some of them repairs was just plain robbery. Complete new roof on a four-year-old building! Anna was so mad when she read the report I think she'd have killed him herself if she'd got the chance. I know she sure don't harbor no bad feelings about whoever did it. Bet she's not the only one would like to pin a medal on the fellow."

Furst was smiling, making light of it all but Teddy couldn't help but wonder again just how much of their assets were tied up in Ben's projects. Maybe Anna had gotten the chance!

They exchanged pleasantries about the weather and the prospect of spring and Furst continued on his daily journey.

Teddy decided she'd made enough excuses, there really wasn't any crowd of gawkers today. She got the tools and carefully uncovered three of the terra-cotta drain tiles before she stopped for lunch. It was clear what the problem was. They were buried less than eighteen inches below the surface and if there had ever been any gravel it had been assimilated, the tiles were nearly completely clogged with roots. Over lunch, a cup of leftover soup and some crackers and cheese, she figured her options. Dig them up, clean them out and put them back just as they were. They had after all managed to last a long time before becoming a problem. Or, she could deepen the trench and add some gravel to improve their chances of staying trouble free. Or, Teddy heaved a sigh knowing what she should do and dreading the drain - bad pun - she giggled, on her modest savings account.

I need to deepen the trench, line it with gravel and get some of that perforated plastic pipe and do it right.

A lot of work and expense but the more she thought about it the more she was sure it was warranted. After lunch her pick nicked the edge of the fourth tile and it split lengthwise.

"Well that decides that," she said aloud. "No sense spending money on those old-fashioned tiles when the plastic pipe will do a better job."

Teddy stared resentfully into the short section of ditch. The plan had been to dig up the tiles, clean them out, and put them back. Time and effort but no dollars involved. Even so she had not been looking forward to the endeavor. Now she would have to uncover the tiles, order the gravel, buy the pipe, and then remove the old tiles, deepen the trench and move the gravel with the wheelbarrow before laying the pipe and covering it. It was going to take a long time. It was going to take a lot of work. It seemed an unreasonable assault on her hard won security and pointed out how very near and threatening the possibility of financial disaster would always be. Butterflies took flight in her stomach and she felt overheated. Teddy picked up the shovel to remove the loose dirt from the hole but leaned instead upon the handle, head bent, eyes closed. The old familiar feeling of life snipping at her heels, wearing down her confidence and resolve, whelmed up to engulf her.

"Praying or napping?"

Her head came up with a snap. Pete was standing on the patio next to the picnic table grinning down at her. Angry at the intrusion, feeling vulnerable and invaded she opened her mouth to give him hell, "Pete..."

"Now Teddy, give me a minute. I just came by to apologize. You've been having it rough and I've been pushing too hard at all the wrong times. I'm sorry. I just want to be your friend. Anyhow I'm not going to ask you out anymore. Not for a while, not `til your ready. Okay?"

"Pete I doubt I'm ever going to be ready." Teddy shook her head tiredly. "Just go away and leave me alone. Please."

"Now Teddy, you don't mean that, you know you don't." Pete took a step toward the garden path and then catching the look on her face seemed to think better of it. "I'll see you at Petal's," he waved a hand in a sideways motion as if searching for an idea in the air. "See ya," he said lamely, turned, and left.

Teddy closed her eyes and hugged the shovel handle for support.

By four she had uncovered the main leach line and two arms that spread off it like tines on a pitchfork. One "tine" speared her bed of Shasta daisies and disappeared beneath one of her favorite rhododendrons. The central "tine" more or less stayed in the path that cut diagonally across the yard below the patio. The downhill course of drain tile was the least plugged, mostly because two tiles had been crushed just after it angled off, heaven only knew how long ago, and that arm of the drain system had been emptying out right there under the giant white hydrangea. Teddy wondered if the hydrangea was going to suffer a dieback when the new drainpipes were in place. She had a lot more digging to do to remove the tiles but for now she could see where they were and measure to determine the amount of materials she would need for replacement. It had been a lot of work getting even this far and Teddy was tired.

The whole time she had been digging her mind had been turning over her conversation with Furst. Motive certainly existed and she had thought of a dozen ways it could have come about, nearly all of them ending with Anna and Furst delivering Ben to her septic tank in their red wheelbarrow and then Anna following Furst as he drove Ben's car back to his house. It bothered her some that Anna, as far as she knew, had never driven a car. But in an emergency surely she could have managed an automatic shift on empty roads. The thing to do now would be to find out what they had been doing that fateful Wednesday night.

Her course of action clear, Teddy carried the pick and shovel back to the basement. Tomorrow she would watch for Furst and ask him to help her measure. Then she would grill him for an alibi. Feeling like she had accomplished something, Teddy decided she had earned a beer break.

It was the last one, "time to go to the store." Teddy sipped at the cold beer, shedding clothes on her way to the bathroom. A hot shower, clean clothes, a touch of makeup, then she finished the beer while staring down at the new scar running across her yard, the pink of the tile showing sharply against the mulchy dirt. She put her dirty clothes in the washer and inventoried the refrigerator and cupboard for dinner. Nothing particularly appealed. It was almost five, just enough time to get to the bank for cash and order a new bankcard. Then if she got beer but didn't buy anything perishable she could stop at the Sandy Inn for chicken. Suddenly the thought of broasted chicken, crunchy, greasy, delicious, deviled at her - served with jojo's - her stomach rumbled in anticipation, she could smell it, taste it almost.

"Time for some good grease," she decided reaching for her jacket. The jacket still had a smoky smell, having escaped the washing machine but it smelled no worse than it would after a trip to the Sandy Inn she decided, pulling it on.

CHAPTER 19

The parking lot was full. On weekdays they ran a perpetual special of half a broasted chicken. One dollar off the regular price if you ordered between five and six o'clock. In a rednecked, thin-pursed community like this that meant a flood of vehicles starting promptly at 4:59. The Sandy Inn was a beer-and-wine tavern, no hard liquor. They served breakfast (and beer) starting at 7, lunch from 11 to 5 and dinner from five until eight when the cook went home. The bar stayed open until 1:00 am to accommodate the devotees of the three pool tables (not to mention the video poker machines). The atmosphere was dark and smoky. Teddy knew for a certainty in a good light the place would have killed appetites. Still, once a month or so, the urge for crispy, crunchy, crusty chicken, washed down with an icy beer - sometimes even one of those designer ones from the micro breweries - drew her like a siren calling to the ancient Greeks in their tiny boats and she steered her car into the lemming line with the rest of the community for her grease fix.

Once her eyes had adjusted to the gloom Teddy located an empty table in the corner under the clock, one of the postage-stamp variety that was just right for dinner for one or drinks for six. Her favorite table, the one under an enormous elk's head, was occupied. When you ate there you somehow did not feel you were dining alone. Teddy lifted an eyebrow in hello to the elk as she passed. The glass eyes seemed to follow her.

It wasn't until after she was seated, her purse tucked under her chair, that she heard a familiar voice coming from the large group of gray hairs at the long table behind her.

"...doesn't hurt my feelings any I can tell you. Ben was a crook. Pure and simple. In Philadelphia we'd have put him out of business years ago." Marrianne Pailey was on a roll, must have gotten here early and been drinking wine while they waited to order, Teddy decided.

Frankie Ann, the waitress slid a frosty glass of draft beer onto the table.

"Chicken?" she asked, knowing the answer. "I saw you come in, put your order in already." Frankie Ann's red hair came straight out of a bottle, and it looked like it had been cut by a kindergartner with safety scissors. Her almost five-foot frame was wiry and shapeless at the same time. Black tights clad knobby legs and a deep-purple sweatshirt emblazoned with "Chicken out at the Sandy Inn" in neon orange hung from her shoulders to just above her knees, the long sleeves pushed up above her elbows. White sneakers completed the ensemble.

"Thanks," Teddy answered. "You got that Raspberry beer still?"

"All gone. Want to see the list?"

"Never mind. I'll stick with this."

Frankie Ann whirled away and Teddy sat back to peer through the gloom and see who else was here, wanting to check out Marrianne and her table-mates, but not wanting to be obvious.

At the bar a mismatched row of male bodies in Levi's, flannel shirts and dirty John Deere caps seemed intent on emptying the world's supply of long neck beer bottles. At the far end, a lone woman in Levi's, flannel shirt, and jewel-encrusted sandals flipped her brassy blond hair, much in need of a wash and a trim, and raised her hand, one finger pointed skyward then dipped down at her empty glass, in that universal signal for another one of whatever it was she was drinking. The heads were drawn together in groups of two and three. Eruptions of laughter and the occasional snort of derision added its dimension to the country-and-western music that was the perpetual background, almost a white sound among the beeps of the electronic poker machines, the thwack of balls on the pool tables and the undulating drone of human voices.

The tables nearest the bar always seemed to collect the good ole' boys and/or the good ole' boys-to-be. This time of day they were gathering for a postmortem on the day before going home to the little woman. If the little woman were lucky they would only have two or three beers before they remembered that she had said not to be late.

The middle of the room seemed relegated to the couples in twos and fours of a medium age range, late twenties to approaching gray hairs. Around the back edges sat the geriatric odd lot, the senior contingency. Ancient mariners who sat alone, scraggled from long years in the sun. Large tables of couples and broken couples - widows, and widowers - grouped together for safety, companionship and gossip, the women outnumbering the men two to one. Teddy was one of the few women who ever sat alone. Normally she preferred her own company to

161

the inane gossip. The gray hairs used to invite her to join them. She just never really liked any of them, or the things they talked about, all that much. Tonight she would have jumped at the chance. As it was, after nodding to sundry acquaintances, she sipped slowly at her beer and sat back in her chair trying to unravel the strands of conversation at the table behind her from the cacophony of babble, mechanical sounds, and music.

"...would have done better with the money under my mattress."

"...how could you not know what was happening in your own yard. I say she was in on it."

"I heard them arguing at Petal's, Rob Greene wanted control of everything and now he's got it, hasn't he."

"That daughter of his is really a cold one, not a tear at the funeral, and after, well I'd say she was celebrating not grieving."

"... was a dinosaur, couldn't do anything anyway but how he had always done it. That last batch of houses looked like they had been built in the fifties only they did a better job of it then."

"...owned a part of nearly everything in town, better than winning a lottery for Princess Trix."

Frankie Ann slid the plate in front of her and Teddy, noting she had sipped away her beer, smiled at her and pointed at the glass. Frankie Ann nodded and scurried away to clean a table (and pick up her tip) on her circuit back to the bar.

Out of habit Teddy picked up the wing and pulled it into three parts to cool. She also broke several of the potato wedges to let out the steam. The satisfaction in that first crunchy bite very nearly took her mind from her eavesdropping. The wing was reduced to just so many little bones and she was working on the thigh, before Marrianne Pailey's voice refocused her attention.

"...was a blessing as far as Trix is concerned. She had no desire to live in that barn of Ben's. Now she'll get a goodly lump from the insurance, she told me she owned almost half outright, not tied up in the trust. Wouldn't surprise me to find out she set that fire. She doesn't know how lucky she is, she'll never have to think about money again, not all of us have a nice fat trust fund." Marrianne sniffed at the unfairness of it all.

"But she'd have gotten the money when the house sold," a voice of reason opined.

"Who knows how long that would have been. I bet she'll have the insurance check by the end of the week." Marrianne lowered her voice conspiratorially and Teddy had to strain to catch her words. "From what she let fall at the house after the funeral, she needs the money. That boyfriend of hers..."

Frankie Ann arrived with her beer exchanging the frosty glass for the empty one without slowing.

"...odd couple if you ask me. Um what?" A male voice interrupted, from the sound of it, by an elbow. "Oh, well," he lowered his voice to a stage whisper that carried even better, "she is damn near old enough to be his mother, well-preserved mind you, but he could do better."

Teddy smiled and took a bite of potato dripping in dressing, no guessing who they were talking about now.

"I always think it's very odd, about her inheriting that house I mean," Marrianne Pailey was whispering too, but the high whine in her voice came in clearly. "Some very odd things are going on around here. I suppose now we'll never get a decent return from those apartments." The unspoken implication that it was all a plot against her personally and the rest of them peripherally was punctuated with two loud sniffs.

"Well at least Ben won't be taking advantage of anyone else, selling them on his schemes." It was a male voice Teddy couldn't place.

"No, and he won't be selling any more new houses that have to be completely rebuilt to be livable either." A breathy voice, as if the effort to speak was almost more than they could manage.

Howard Pailey? Teddy wondered, or a small, blue-haired lady at the far end of the table who had recently lost her husband to lung cancer and was still a heavy smoker herself.

Teddy ate slowly, more than savoring her treat, she wanted to get a look at exactly who had been at the table behind her. The gossip about her and Rob was old stuff but the anger directed at Ben and the speculation that Rob could be the murderer was important. Could be someone was casting shadows on Rob in an effort to direct suspicion away from themselves.

The group talked through their chicken dinners saying pretty much the same things over and over. Teddy thought she was going to have to order a third beer and eat the breast, which she normally took home for the next day's lunch. She had scraped the last of the ranch dressing out of the little paper cup with the last bite of jojo when Frankie Ann scuttered by with a handful of little plastic doggie bags and a sheaf of bills, they would of course each have wanted their own. The waitress in Teddy grimaced.

"I brought yours, too," Frankie Ann said, depositing the bill and the white plastic bag on the table. "You want another beer?"

"No, thanks, I always think I'm hungry enough to eat it all but I never quite make it," Teddy answered. *And if I had another beer I'd have to use the bathroom here before going home,* she thought, an experience to be avoided. The restroom here seemed to have a perpetual smell of urine, barf, and lysol that hit you in nauseous waves while you sat helpless with your pants around your knees.

"Two's my limit."

Frankie smiled, nodding in understanding, then in response to a hand signal, caught it would seem by the eyes in the back of her head, whirled away to get another pitcher for the foursome over by the pool tables.

Teddy made a slow job of reading her bill and counting the exact amount plus the 20 percent (but never less than a dollar) tip she always left for all but the worst of service. She knew how much work waiting table was and exactly how tired Frankie Ann's feet, legs, and back would be when she went home, never mind how hard it was to keep the smile on one's face. The group behind her dispersed in trickles as they accomplished the tasks of sacking up tomorrow's lunch and agonizing over the need for a tip at all. Teddy noted them carefully as they left. Only one couple, the wife in a wheelchair, was completely unknown to her. Howard Pailey thumped by with his walker, his sound-alike twin, the lady in the blue hair used the kind of cane that has four little feet for better stability. Most of them, Teddy knew, had either bought their home from Ben (or from one of Ben's salespeople) and/or had invested in one or more of his projects. Maybe it had been a true group effort. The thought caused her to chuckle.

Just imagine the whole group of them trouping down the hill with their canes and walkers, Ben on the lap of the lady in the wheelchair, to deposit him in the septic tank.

CHAPTER 20

The phone was ringing when she came in the door.

"Hello," she tucked the phone against her head holding it with a raised shoulder and crossed to the refrigerator to put the chicken away.

"Where have you been?" Rob demanded laughing. "I was about to call Sonny and mount a search party."

"I went to chicken if it's any of your business. What's up?"

"I'm turning over both sets of books, all the records, to my son-in-law, for a real audit first thing in the morning. Teddy, I spent the whole day comparing those books I found in Ben's office with my computerized records and I still couldn't get them to make sense. Maybe I just didn't want to believe what I was seeing, I don't know. But if what I think I was seeing is right it's not a pretty picture. There's almost no one in town who wouldn't have had a damn good reason to kill Ben, including me. Makes me sick to my stomach to think about it." He sighed deeply. "I need to talk, but not right this minute, I'm too tired. Want to meet me at Petal's for breakfast in the morning?"

"I'm not sure talking at Petal's is a good idea. Why don't you come here and I'll fix you something?" Teddy offered, thinking of how easy it had been for her to listen in on the table behind her this evening. Who knows who would be listening at Petal's, who might have been listening in the past and been inspired to murder. "How about French toast?"

"I'll see you at 7:30, that too early?" Rob asked.

"Come at seven if you like. You know I'm always up early." She thought about telling him some of what she had overheard and then decided that could wait for breakfast. "Your head feeling okay?"

"Achy, and I look like hell. I'm going to take a couple of those heavy-duty painkillers the doc gave me and get some sleep. See you in the morning."

"Bye," Teddy said and heard the click of the receiver on the other end. All that he had said - and implied - and all that she had heard through dinner swirled in her mind. She fixed herself a large glass of ice water and punched the button on the answering machine to replay the messages and see if anyone besides Rob had been looking for her.

One "Hi, what ya doing," from her daughter, two "Hi it's Rob, talk to you laters, and two hang ups.

"Why do people do that?" Teddy wondered. "They must know how aggravating it is."

The answering machine did not reply. She took her glass of water and went up to watch TV.

It was an uneasy night. Teddy dreamed of an army of angry golden-agers bludgeoning first Ben, and then Rob, and then herself, and dumping the bodies one after another into a gigantic septic tank. Then the pounding of the surf as the tide changed thudded through her subconscious and washed her into wakefulness. For more than an hour the events of the past week replayed themselves across the dark ceiling until at last she slept only to dream again of being trapped in a burning, endless maze, this time made up of towering piles of ledgers, boxes, and filing cabinets. She woke at six, sweaty and nearly consumed by a sense of panic.

"Hot flash," she decided getting out of bed. Did I forget to take my Premarin, she wondered on the way to the bathroom. The yellow pill she put out each night to ensure she took it each morning waited as usual in the little antique nut dish put there for just that purpose. Teddy did not like to take pills of any kind, certainly did not like the expense entailed in the cost of hormone treatment. But she didn't like night sweats, mood swings, or the panic attacks that swept in on her when she didn't take the pill either, not to mention the probable, unnecessary, aging of her body that would result. She popped the pill into her mouth and swallowed, pushing the fading memories of the night's dreams to the back of her mind where, with any luck, they would like most dreams, good and bad, dissolve completely.

Rob was late, Teddy felt a flush of concern as she poured herself a cup of coffee. The French toast was golden brown and stacked on a plate in the oven. The sausage patties were just about ready to be taken from the pan, the juice was poured, the table set. It was 7:35. He had said he was going to take some pain-killers, had he over-drugged himself and slept in? Her imagination began to work overtime. Had someone taken advantage of his drugged state and done him harm? The sound of a vehicle stopping on

169

the gravel road swung her around from the stove to peer out the window. Her heart was pounding.

Teddy pulled the door open and let out a sigh of relief. "I had you dead and buried," she called out with a grin.

"I'm not that late," Rob said, striding down the hill toward the porch.

"No, for you, you're almost early. I just had a troubling night. Guess the murders, the fire, and everything are getting to me."

"Me too," Rob said gathering her to him for a big hug. "Good morning," he said releasing her. "I hope you made lots of coffee, I have a ton of suspicions to unload."

"Lots, and I can make more. I have a few suspicions of my own."

Not until his plate was empty and he had almost emptied his second cup of coffee did Rob speak of his concerns.

"Teddy, Ben was ripping off his investors, there is no other explanation for the difference between the two sets of books." He waved a hand in the air as if searching for a tangible answer. "It wasn't just bad luck - storms damaging roofs - or even shoddy work and bad materials, though I'm sure there was some of that, too. Ben was inflating the cost of repairs, probably inflated the cost of construction, and keeping the difference for himself." He emptied his cup and stared for a minute into the bottom as if he might find some comforting message there.

"You mean Marrianne Pailey's tirades had some basis in fact?" Teddy asked, rising to get the pot and refill his cup.

"Looks like," Rob grimaced.

"Anna and Furst have been suspicious, too," Teddy said, and explained her conversation with Furst.

"Any of the investors who bothered to read that report were probably suspicious or should have been. I don't know how he expected to get away with it." Rob shook his head sadly.

"Well, he sure didn't," Teddy said returning the pot to the warmer having refilled both their cups. "Didn't it ever seem suspicious to you?" she asked gently, watching his face.

"I should have seen it. I mean, I knew something was wrong, but I guess I was too willing to blame it all on Dave or Keith and Jamie. I wanted to believe they were taking advantage of Ben's friendship. You know, getting him to give them the jobs and then doing slipshod work or using cut-rate materials. I still think some of that went on. But the truth is, Ben falsified those books. The numbers he gave me were pure fantasy. What really hurts is he used me to help him cheat the investors. He lied to me and caused me to mislead people. How could I have been so dumb?"

Teddy reached out a hand to cover his lying on the table. "You were grateful for all the good things he'd done for you. You loved him. You wanted to believe, that's all."

"I helped him rob people. If I had paid attention, not let all that good ole' boy talk get in the way..."

"Rob, you did nothing wrong, you are a victim like all the rest."

"Yeah, well I sure don't look forward to trying to convince the investors of that," Rob gave her a sad little smile, "but thank you for the thought."

"You wouldn't happen to have a list of those investors handy would you?" she asked him.

"I could name them off for you. You think one of them killed Ben?"

"Seems probable, doesn't it?" Teddy told him what she had overheard at the Sandy Inn the night before.

"My! My! But not liking Ben or feeling put out about the return on an investment, even fraud, shouldn't be enough to kill over. It has to be more." Rob was shaking his head, looking more than a little perplexed.

"You wait until you're seventy or eighty and someone takes advantage of you, threatens your financial security - your independence - and makes you feel like a fool. Then tell me you couldn't get angry enough to kill. Particularly in the heat of an argument maybe."

"Possible," he said slowly, his head turned to one side as he considered, "and several of those investors could have known about your septic tank being freshly pumped."

"Like who?" Teddy asked eagerly.

"Like Kevin's dad. Or Leroy's uncle, Sonny has a piece of every one of them. Sid Chapman and

172

his brother, both are investors, either one could have heard about the septic tank at Petal's and so could dozens of others. The list is endless." Rob emptied his cup and got up to get the coffeepot.

"I guess when you get right down to it I could be a suspect. I mean it sure makes me mad to think about what Ben has been doing all this time." Rob filled both cups and returned the pot to the warmer. "I sure wish we could have talked to Rene."

"Yeah, me too. I'm more certain than ever that's why she was run off the road. So she couldn't remember and maybe tell someone enough to zero in on the killer. But how do we prove it?" Teddy stirred a spoon of non-fat sweetened condensed milk into her coffee. "Not to change the subject but what do you think of the possibility of Trix having started the fire - to get some instant cash."

"Trix is that greedy but I'm not sure she would know the first thing about starting that kind of fire. Now that boyfriend of hers... maybe. But I don't see why either of them would have done it when it was obvious we were there. I mean my pickup was right out front," Rob shrugged his shoulders.

"Maybe they thought with you dead she would get control of the trust?" Teddy ventured.

"The lawyer made it pretty clear when we talked that if something happened to me, he and the bank take over, he must have told her that, too."

"Did he tell you or did you ask?" Teddy questioned.

"I think I asked," Rob answered, looking thoughtful. "And you're right, Trix probably never asked. I just don't think she's that clever. Deceitful and greedy, yes. But thinking through the idea of burning the house for the insurance money or plotting to get rid of me would be just too much work for either of them. I'd say by the time they left after the funeral they had realized she wasn't going to get her hands on it all straight off and were perfectly content with the idea of a nice big monthly check and letting me worry about all the details.

"Then why did anyone want you..., us, dead?" Teddy asked.

"Good question. Could be they thought there was something in the house that would have exposed them as the killer and they were afraid we had already found it. Or..." Rob took a drink of his coffee and then shook his head. "We've said all this before, we're beginning to go round in circles."

"I think we should see if we can find out just what some of our suspects were doing Wednesday night when Ben was put in the tank. And, I think we should find out if Sonny knows where Ben was killed. If it wasn't at his house someone had to return whichever set of wheels he was driving."

"The pickup," Rob said flatly.

"How do you know?" Teddy asked.

"The seat was back when I got in, way back, Ben could never have driven it that way. And Ben would have been driving it if he were going fishing. He always did," Rob said.

"So maybe he stopped to see someone on his way out of town?" Teddy offered, eyebrows raised.

"Maybe. It is odd Sonny didn't check out those vehicles better," Rob mused.

"Maybe he did, could be that's how the seat got back?" Teddy said, thinking aloud. "Maybe we should just ask him?"

"Maybe, but I could have been wrong before, being so sure Sonny isn't the killer, or isn't at least protecting whoever is. The good ole' boys are pretty tight you know."

Teddy sat her cup down and stared at it knowing that what Rob was saying was right. The good ole' boys she had known in her lifetime, not just here, had real blurry vision and worse memories when it came to one of their own and the law. The more serious the offense, the blinder they were. Drunk driving, hit-and-run, wife-beating, all just got shrugged, made a bad joke of, if you were one of the insiders. It was a good probability that Ben's fraud was no news to them, and if Sonny or one of the others and Ben had fallen out over it, well the good ole' boys would figure that was nobody's business but their own. Sonny and the rest of the gang could well have too many shared secrets for them not to back each other up.

"So what do we do first?" she asked.

"The dishes. Then you watch for Furst to take his walk and get him to help you measure like you said, and see if you can pin him down about that whole space of time between when I saw Ben last and he turned up here. I'm going to drive the books to the valley and get Ken started on the audit. Then I'll find an excuse to drop in on the Pailey's. Maybe I'll ask her to help me pick out some paint to redo the office, she's always complained it was badly coordinated. If necessary we'll visit with the entire

175

list of investors. Hell, there are only 1,500 people in town, how long can it take us to find out what every one of them was doing on a Wednesday night?" Rob was smiling. The shaven spot just above and behind his right ear with its red welted stitches, and the purpley bruise spreading across that side of his forehead and cheek contrasted violently with the rest of his pale, determined face. "Right this minute you and I are the only two people I know for sure didn't do it."

CHAPTER 21

Furst was only too happy to be of use. Teddy felt a little guilty asking him to negotiate the steep path since she could have managed the measuring perfectly well on her own. She felt even more guilty after she found out where Furst and Anna had been most of that Wednesday afternoon, evening, and far into Thursday morning.

"It's her emphysema, she gets to choking and sometimes the oxygen just isn't enough. So, I drove her up to the emergency room and they called her doctor and got her all fixed up." Furst shook his head, "We seem to spend one or two nights a month there, going to give her her own bed soon. They want her to stop smoking," he confided, "but Anna says it's her only pleasure, says it helps her nerves."

Well, that's two more who didn't kill Ben, Teddy thought, standing on her steps waving goodbye to Furst. And two possible witnesses who weren't at home to see anything of whoever did do it.

A white utility wagon roared up the road barely slowing to allow Frust time to move to the side and whizzed past her sending up a spray of gravel as its driver hit the brakes and turned sharply into the rental's parking spot.

"New neighbors again," Teddy observed.

Somewhere off in the wooded lot across the way a woodpecker, after its breakfast perhaps, made its familiar knocking sound as it dug into a tree for a tasty morsel.

"My, you are an early bird, I didn't expect you for another month or so," she called out softly so as not to frighten the often shy bird away.

The piliated woodpecker had been visiting in the neighborhood regularly each spring for several years now. Normally, according to Teddy's bird book, they preferred deep woods and seclusion from man. But this pair seemed inclined to vacation at the shore. Looking and sounding like Woody Woodpecker from the cartoon, they were easy to identify and, if one stood very still, fascinating to watch but the slightest movement would send them into hiding. Teddy waited, still and quiet, searching the dense foliage, but though she could hear them she could not spot their red plumage. At the rental house, major unloading was taking place, accomplished with much door slamming. The woodpeckers fell silent and Teddy went in the house.

"What ya doing?"

Teddy looked up from her digging to find herself the subject of earnest inspection. A small boy, seven or eight she thought, and a smaller girl, both with red-blond hair and a generous amount of freckles stood on the edge of the patio peering down at her.

"I'm digging treasure. You staying next door?"

"Yes'em. We're having a vacation. My name's Orin, she's Hanna. What's yours?"

"I'm Teddy. Mom and Dad know you're out?"

"Mmmhuh. Mom said we could walk to the end of the street, the corner and back," Orin answered.

"But we can't go to the beach until Dad comes too," Hanna added.

"I see," Teddy said, stopping to lean on her shovel. "I suspect walking to the corner did not include going into people's yards. Your mom might get worried if she looks and can't see you, don't you think?"

"Yeeees," Orin said slowly making it into a three-syllable word. "Don't you like visitors?"

"Sometimes, but I've had a lot of them lately and I have a job to get done here." Teddy waved her hand at the long hole with its lining of root-filled pink tiles.

"I guess you don't have any children for us to play with?" Hanna sounded hopeful.

"Sorry," Teddy answered with a smile. "All my children have grown up and gone away."

"Well, okay, we better go then," Orin said, and taking Hanna's hand turned and started up the path. After a few steps he turned back and said, "those are real pretty flowers on your porch."

"What?" Teddy asked not sure what he was referring to.

"On your porch, the white flowers, they don't have any smell but they're real pretty," Orin explained.

"Thank you," Teddy said, still confused. She dumped the shovel full of dirt she had just removed from the hole and lay down the shovel. Curious, she followed the children up the hill.

179

Sure enough, there on the top step was a terra-cotta pot containing an orchid, three spikes of creamy white blooms. They were beautiful. They were also alarming. Teddy checked the watch in her pocket, it was after four, she had come out after lunch, sometime before one she thought, and hadn't been back to the front of the house since. If the children had been able to find her in the garden surely whoever delivered the flowers could have. She looked for a card and found none.

"Hummh?" same source as the roses probably she thought. But who? Why?

"Orin! Hanna!" an anxious female voice called.

"That's mom," Orin explained, "We got to go now. Bye."

"Bye," Teddy said absently her mind busy trying to remember if she had so much as heard a car. "Damn, there is enough mysterious stuff going on without this. Where the hell am I supposed to put it?" The pot was heavy and Teddy decided it could stay right where it was for now.

Might as well get a drink of water while I'm here, she decided. Once in the house she checked the answering machine. Three messages, all of them hang-ups. Aggravated more than worried, Teddy reached for the telephone book to ferret out the directions for getting the number of the last call received. Picking up the receiver to dial, the phone rang in her hand causing her to jump.

"Hello?" she said, her heart thumping.

"What were you doing, hatching that thing?" Rob asked her.

"You didn't happen to call earlier and not leave a message did you?"

Teddy answered his question with a question.

"You know I wouldn't do that. I know how much it irks you."

"And you didn't send me orchids?"

"Orchids? WOW! Not me. I take it someone has sent you orchids?"

"Sometime in the last three, three-and-a-half hours, while I was down in the yard. They were delivered, or materialized, or... or I don't know what, but they're here. I don't think I like this, Rob. There was no card. Nothing."

"It is puzzling, but Teddy, not exactly threatening."

"I suppose," she agreed. "So what did your son-in-law say?"

"That he would get me a report by Friday. He also suggested that he get a second report from a friend of his since we're related, just to be sure. Then I took Marlo to lunch and played with the baby for a while. She seemed to think grandpa looked funny."

Rob's voice sounded relaxed. The visit had done him good, Teddy thought.

"I had a message from Sonny waiting when I got back. He said he had a report on the fire. I asked him to meet me out at your place at five. That all right with you? I thought you'd want to hear what he's got to say."

"Sure, sure, I'd like that very much. Thanks. You going to ask him about where Ben was killed and the cars?"

"I thought we could. And maybe even what he was doing that Wednesday night."

"How we going to manage that?"

"I haven't the foggiest idea. But we have almost half an hour to come up with something. See you at five."

Teddy hung up the phone and made a dash for the shower.

CHAPTER 22

"Teddy, I wish you'd quit digging up your yard. Until we get Ben's murder all sorted out anyway. It looks like you're getting ready for a mass homicide out there."

"Good evening to you, too, Sonny," Teddy said, standing back so Sonny could enter. "I take it you've inspected the yard. Find anything interesting besides my drain field?"

"Good looking white flowers there on the step. They wasn't there before," he said by way of answer.

"No, they weren't. That arrived this afternoon and I wouldn't mind knowing from where or from whom."

Sonny raised an eyebrow but said nothing.

"Rob just called to say he was on his way. He got hung up at the Paileys'," Teddy informed him.

"What was he doing there?" Sonny demanded.

"Well, I don't know exactly. But the Paileys are investors in several of the projects Ben put together, maybe it had to do with business."

"He didn't say anything to me about those projects and I own a fair piece of more than one myself," Sonny said indignantly. "And I ain't been real happy about the return neither."

Sonny looked as if he had more to say on the subject but the crunch of tires coming to a stop on the gravel road drew their attention.

Teddy opened the door and she and Sonny watched as Rob ambled down the slope.

"You look just like Frankenstein. You know, all stitches and bruises," Sonny said cheerfully.

"Yeah, well I can tell you that if his head felt anything like mine it's no wonder he went around terrorizing the neighborhood. You got any more of that Advil?" Rob asked Teddy.

"I'll get it," she turned toward the bathroom.

"So, how'd the fire start?" Rob asked, sitting down at the table.

"With a match," Sonny began.

"Duh!" Teddy commented, returning to hand Rob two orange tablets.

"Like I said," Sonny continued, "it was lit with a match, only took one in the laundry room, one in the kitchen. The chief said the arsonist had wadded up paper soaked in bacon grease, piles of it in the laundry room and more in the kitchen. Used a hell of a lot of drippings, must have been saving up for months."

"It was all there," Teddy said quietly, remembering the cans of drippings and the bags of paper when she had cleaned out the laundry room cupboards. "In the cupboards, the grease was in the cupboards, the paper was in the closet. I thought it was odd..."

"Not so odd," Rob interrupted. "Ben's wife use to save up the grease to mix with seeds and make up feeders for the birds in the winter. Everyone has paper stacked up somewhere."

"Ben's wife's been dead for years," Sonny said incredulously.

"I suspect Ben just kept filling the cans and sticking them in the laundry room cupboard out of habit. He may have even meant to make up the bird feeders himself but as far as I know he never did."

Rob popped the pills in his mouth.

"Don't you want some water for that?" Teddy asked. "Or a beer, or coffee - juice?"

"I don't know about Rob but I'll take a beer if you have one," Sonny said.

"I'll have the juice, thanks," Rob said. "I have enough of a headache already."

Teddy poured Rob's juice and got out two beers. "I wonder if they knew the grease was there or just lucked out?" she said, sitting down. You know there was some lighter fluid, too."

"And lots of oil and rags in the garage," Rob added.

"The Chief said they knew just what they were doing. Started a fire in the laundry room, another in the kitchen, and I think were getting set to start one in the garage when you opened that door and got yourself konked." Sonny paused to take a mighty swig of his beer. "Said there were signs, rags, oily ones most likely, piled near the door into the storage area. Pretty plain they thought you were both in there and they didn't mean for either of you to get out."

Sonny took another drink of his beer and set the bottle on the table with a thump.

A cold chill shuddered down Teddy's spine. She had already been sure that whoever had started the fire had meant for them to die in it but she'd wanted to be wrong.

"I'll bet you surprised the hell out of them when you opened that garage door. And they sure didn't expect Teddy would be able to get out. I know for a fact Ben nailed them doors onto the patio shut, years ago. Bought a stove off a him once and he had to use a pry bar to pull them nails so's we could get it out, and he nailed it right back up after. Reckon our killer just didn't count on you being so determined," Sonny grinned at Teddy.

"You try facing down a raging fire and see how determined you get," Teddy snapped.

"I take it you agree we did not set that fire to trap ourselves then?" Rob asked.

"For now," Sonny said, "Course I only got your word for it that it happened like you said. Nothing the Chief found said it didn't. But nothing much left to say it did either. All them windows busted and burned, Teddy might have been outside the whole time, so might you."

Teddy was stiff with indignation. "Right, and then I hit Rob over the head and nearly killed him just to make it all look plausible."

"Could have," Sonny said flatly.

"Sonny," Teddy began menacingly.

"He doesn't believe that Teddy," Rob put a hand on her shoulder and patted it gently, "or he wouldn't be here talking about it, he'd be arresting us. Right Sonny?"

"Right for now," Sonny agreed. "I just ain't seen any good reason why you would. Stands to reason if there were something in that house incriminating, Rob, you could simply have searched for however long it took to find it. You were in the catbird seat time-wise, nothing to rush you. No, it's more likely someone else had a hair up their behind over something they was afraid you would find and that's why the house was burned. I think getting you with it was just a bonus sort of."

"One that didn't work out," Rob said.

"Yeah, I hope they weren't too disappointed," Teddy said.

"I hope they won't try again," Sonny said, downing the last of his beer.

"'Nother beer?" Teddy asked him, rising to get it before he could respond. "Man, I don't envy you trying to get so many people to remember what they were doing the night Ben must have been killed. I mean nobody makes notes about what they do, when, after a day or two it just sort of all blends together. Bet you'd have a hard time being sure of your own whereabouts." It sounded lame to her, but she'd said it and now waited for Sonny to reply, fingers crossed.

""You'd be right if it wasn't Wednesday we were talking about. That's poker night, we don't play for money of course," Sonny cleared his throat nervously, "but we was playing at Keith's, eight until after one. We were talking some about Ben but we wasn't out killing him," Sonny said wrenching the top off the bottle.

"We who?" Rob asked.

"Keith, Dave, Harry, Jamie, and me. Same old gang as always, 'cept Ben." Sonny stared at the bottle in his hand, his face reflective. "That Wednesday's turning out to have been a real social evening for a lot of folks. Seems like almost everyone was visiting, or meeting, or something with someone else. I've damn near filled up a notebook making

187

notes on who was with who, where." He took a swig from the bottle. "Spent a whole lot of the week cross-checking and scraping paint off of green pickups."

Rob looked at Teddy and she raised an eyebrow in answer. She had asked the question about where, the ball was in his court now. "Speaking of pickups, "Rob said, "When I got in Ben's old clunker, you know, to get out of the garage the other night, I didn't have to put the seat back."

Sonny looked at him obviously unsure of the point.

"Sonny, Ben was a good six to eight inches shorter than I am, somebody, other than Ben, had been driving that rig. Unless of course your guys moved it back when they went over things out there?"

"I...," Sonny seemed surprised and at a loss for words. "I ain't real sure who checked the vehicles," he cleared his throat, "but I imagine that explains it."

"So, you think he was killed at the house then?" Teddy asked.

"At his house? Nothing to indicate that, or I'd a had that place locked up. Made Trix stay in town. What made you think that?"

"Well, if both vehicles were there..." Teddy started to explain.

"Don't you think I thought of that?" Sonny's face was getting red. "Teddy, I know what I'm doing. Ben could have been picked up and driven off to someplace we ain't found yet to be killed. Weren't no signs of a struggle or blood or anything anywhere in that house. That don't mean he wasn't abducted from it, killed out in the woods maybe. And there weren't no fingerprints on those rigs but who you'd expect. Ben's and Rob's," Sonny leveled his eyes sharply at Rob for an instant, "and Keith's, Jamie's, and the kid from the gas station, too. All people who'd had reason to be in those vehicles recently. Now is this interrogation over or you two got any more questions you'd like answered?"

"Sonny, he was my friend," Rob began.

"And it was my septic tank he ended up in," Teddy chimed in. "We are naturally interested in finding out what happened."

"I'm more than interested, it's my job. You two just sit back and let the professionals do what needs to be done," Sonny scolded. There was a hard edge to his voice that strengthened the warning in his words.

"I don't suppose they found my tote, or what was left of it in the ashes. I was kind of hoping not to have to get my driver's license replaced." Teddy changed the subject slightly.

"Teddy that house pretty well burnt down to nothing, like a pile of yard trash. There ain't nothing much left but the cement foundation full of water and a bunch of twisted, melted metal. Them filing cabinets of Ben's, the metal ones, supposed to be fireproof, well they wasn't. Filled with ashes, the ones that didn't come all apart. There was some mighty fine scotch stored in one of those cabinets. Real shame," he shook his head in remorse and downed the last of the second beer in a long draught. "No playing at detective now, you hear? You was lucky to get out of that house alive. Might not be so

189

lucky next time." Sonny stood as he was talking and finished his admonition, hand on the door, "Take care now. Night."

"Guess we've been told," Rob said as they heard Sonny's car spit gravel and move off south.

"He was lying, twice. Or at least not sure he was telling the truth," Teddy said.

"About what, how do you know?" Rob asked.

"About playing poker for money to start with, everyone knows they play for money. Didn't you hear him clearing his throat? And then again when you asked him about the pickup. He wasn't sure, he was covering. Sonny always coughs or clears his throat when he's unsure or stretching the truth."

"Humm." Rob said considering what she said. Then he smiled at her. "I'll take your word for it, I mean, I never dated the man."

"I was going to ask you if you'd like some dinner but I'm not sure you're worth the effort. Want some more juice?"

"Yes please, and dinner too, if it's not too much trouble. I'll tell you all about my lovely little chat with Marrianne and Howard," he offered by way of a bribe.

"So tell me," Teddy said, going to the refrigerator for the juice.

CHAPTER 23

"They were at church."

"Aw come on now. On a Wednesday night?" Teddy was skeptical.

"Potluck and bingo. Half the town, or at least half of those over fifty were there for dinner and most of them stayed for Bingo. Honest." Rob held up his right hand, grinning at her.

"Okay what did they do after Bingo? It's generally over by 10, 10:30."

"Marrianne, Howard, the Hesters - she's the one in the wheelchair, Carol Pepper - she's..."

"The one with the cane, I know," Teddy interrupted.

"John and Retta Carson, and Joanna Bennet all went to the Highway House, for coffee and pie. Howard said they left there as Riley was locking up, that makes it twelve o'clock or so," Rob finished up.

"Rob, you know as well as I do that Riley locks up whenever he feels like it, he'll stay open all night if he's got a big spender or shut up early if he wants to get rid of a bunch of poor-tipping, dessert-splitting seniors. It could have been anywhere from 10:30 to 2:00am." She shook her head, "Guess they could have sat there hatching the plan and then, high on caffeine, gone out and killed Ben." She giggled remembering her image from the night before, "the bunch of them together could just about have managed to carry Ben down the hill, but the truth is I just don't see it. Maybe Sonny's right, maybe we should stop trying to figure this out."

"And let Sonny do it?" Rob made a face, "I'd be more comfortable with that if there didn't seem to be somebody trying to kill us. I don't know about you but I don't like the idea of someone waiting and watching for opportunities to shove us off the road like Rene or serve us up flambeau."

"You're right, I know you're right. I just feel kind of foolish. I mean, I thought Anna and Furst or the Paileys seemed so logical and now that seems so silly." Teddy's hands had been busy while they were talking, a large pot of water put on to boil, two mild and one spicy Italian sausage links put in a nonstick pan with a little water to begin to cook. On the counter a green bell pepper, a can of tomatoes, the kind cut up in their own juice, ready to use, a package of bow pasta and a container of fresh shredded Romano cheese awaited her attention. Teddy added a dash of salt and a splash of olive oil from the squat little bottle that sat on the counter to the heating water.

"I just can't think of anyone it doesn't now seem silly to suspect."

"I know what you mean." Rob leaned back in his chair, his head against the wall, his eyes shut. "I think whoever is doing all this must be getting pretty desperate. I mean, when they put Ben in your septic tank they didn't expect he'd be found for a good long time. They must have pretty much relaxed and felt safe. When you found Ben they got scared, started trying to cover their trail." He sat up and opened his eyes. "They weren't worried about Ben's being missing. I mean they didn't seem to be concerned about who heard what or evidence or anything until after the body was found."

"You're right," Teddy had been cutting the green pepper into bite-sized squares and paused, knife in hand. "After Ben was found, when everyone started talking motive and opportunity, they got real panicky, started worrying about who might have heard what, and what Ben might have stuck away that would point to them. Probably thought they had all the time in the world to go through Ben's stuff as long as he was only missing. But whatever they didn't want us to find, it would have implicated them eventually wouldn't it?" The water was about all boiled away in the sausage pan and Teddy poked at the casings with the tip of her knife to release the juices and keep them from splitting.

"You'd think so. Maybe they just didn't think that far ahead. Or," he lifted his chin as a thought apparently came together in his mind, "maybe they had been looking already. I mean we know we weren't the first to go poking through Ben's things. He, they, could have been doing it systematically before Ben got himself found pushing up your purple daisies. Then, when that happened, they had to step up the search or destroy the evidence altogether. The other afternoon, when we were out there looking was just their first chance maybe."

"Uh huh," Teddy agreed as she opened the can of tomatoes. "They'd have been afraid to go out to the house right after the body was found, I mean first the sheriff was all over the place and then you had it cleaned up and Trix was there. They could'a burned it with Trix in it and done us all a favor," she said with a small smirk playing across her lips.

"Sonny would really be after my hide then," Rob reminded her.

"Oops, sorry, you're right." Teddy poked at the sausages with the point of the knife again, testing them for the firmness that would indicate they were cooked through. Dissatisfied, she allowed them to continue to cook and began to set the table. She paused beside the table, silverware in hand, to stare at Rob's face. "You look awful," she said with concern.

"Thanks, I feel awful. And I am not going to feel a whole lot better until this mess is cleared up and I know just what it was Ben was playing at with the investors, and the contractors and with me, too, for that matter." He chuckled in a self-deprecating manner. "I may have had a better motive for killing Ben than I thought. Could be the killer was just a little faster than the rest of us in figuring out what Ben was doing." His face settled into a sad frown.

"Hey, whatever Ben was doing, he really did care about you. People sometimes do bad things for what they think are good reasons. I'm not excusing him, I just don't believe his motives were all bad where you're concerned, no matter how it turned out." Teddy said it like she meant it, praying silently she was right.

"Thanks. I'm glad you're my friend."

"Yeah, well I like you, too." Teddy gave him a big grin and then turned back to the stove. The water was on the verge of boiling and the sausage, in their now dry pan, seemed done. She removed the meat

194

to a cutting board and poured a teaspoon or so of olive oil in the hot pan, adding the green peppers. "I think we should just wait and see what your son-in-law and his friend have to say, then maybe we'll have a better chance of figuring it all out." She sliced the sausage into generous bite-sized ovals, returned the meat to the pan, and poured the can of tomatoes over the top. The water in the big pot was boiling furiously and Teddy emptied the bag of pasta into it and set her timer.

In a matter of minutes she had made garlic toast, poured two glasses of wine, and then when the timer dinged drained the pasta and tossed it quickly with the sauce and a generous amount of the cheese. Teddy ladled heaping servings into the wide pottery bowls, more like smallish pie plates, that she used for pasta and stews, and sprinkled more cheese on top.

"Mmmm. This smells wonderful," Rob said appreciatively when she sat his in front of him.

"Sorry, no salad, the lettuce was more than a little past its prime," Teddy explained.

"Don't need it and don't apologize. This is great."

They concentrated on the food for a bit and then the conversation drifted to Teddy's drain-field plans. Teddy told Rob about her adventure with the empty boot on the beach, embroidering it just a little to make him laugh.

"I tell you I've begun to see bodies and plots everywhere. By the time I got back to the house I was convinced it was really possible Anna and Furst had put Ben in there." Teddy laughed at her disillusionment. "I guess something like this brings out the amateur detective in all of us. Can't you just see me doing the Jessica Fletcher bit?"

"Does that make me the honest but not quite bright sheriff?"

"No, you're the kindly but overweight doctor."

"Gee thanks," Rob speared the last bite of sausage from his plate.

"Want some more?" Teddy offered.

"No thanks, I think two servings is sufficient. It was really good, as usual." Rob looked at his watch. "I should be getting home, in case my son-in-law calls. The sooner I face the truth of what Ben was doing and deal with it the better."

"I thought he said it would be Friday before he knew?"

"Emmhuh, but just in case." Rob laid his napkin down and stood up.

"Well, call me as soon as you know anything. Maybe when we know exactly what Ben was doing we'll know who he was doing it to, and who was mad enough about it to kill." A thought struck her. "You know, no matter what Ben might have been playing at, with the double set of books and all, he might have been killed for another reason altogether."

Rob gave her a grim little smile. "Possibly. But it's the only thing we have to go on. Now, I'm going to go home, take another one of the Doc's heavy-duty little tablets, and get a good night's sleep." He opened the door. "You want me to bring that in first?" Rob asked, indicating the orchid.

"Don't know where I'm going to put it," Teddy said, "but bring it on in."

"Your secret admirer has good taste, this thing is beautiful."

"Yeah, he seems to be well-heeled, too, but it's making me just a little nervous."

They put the orchid on the old cedar chest that Teddy used as a bedside table and then Teddy stood on the steps and waved Rob off. His taillights had just disappeared to the south, she could still hear the pickup rounding the corner toward the highway, when her ears caught the sound of a motor being started behind her.

Teddy swung around to stare into the dark in the direction of the Bensons. There were no lights and the cloud cover did not allow for any from stars or moon but she could hear a vehicle backing out of the Benson's drive. It was too dark under the trees to tell whether it was a car or a pickup. It backed into the street, the brake lights glowing red as it halted and then drove off slowly north.

A cold shudder ran down Teddy's spine. "Probably the same neckers as the other night back for a little more of the same." She wasn't convinced. Neither was she hot to go off in a rush to check it out even if they were apparently gone now. "I'll go over in the morning," she announced firmly. Back inside, she checked carefully to be sure her door was locked.

Perhaps it was the wine with dinner, or having got the chance to talk things out some with Rob, or even that the surf was well-behaved and constant through the night but even the unsettling reoccurrence of an unknown visitor in the Benson driveway did not trouble her sleep. Teddy woke a few minutes after six, refreshed and unable to remember whether she had dreamed or not. If she had, she decided it must have been pleasant, the uncomfortable ones always seemed to linger in her mind.

The day had promise of being a nice one. The sun, from its position low in the east, was shining across medium-sized breakers, bleaching the foaming crests and the resulting wash a gleaming white particular to early mornings. Only a few grayish clouds huddled far on the horizon, the blue sky reflected in the sea sparkled back a deeper, crisper blue than it had been in some time.

When Teddy took her second cup of coffee out to inspect her garden and plan today's attack on the drain field the brisk little breeze off the sea, while not quite warm, was more welcoming than it had been since last fall. She breathed in a lung full of the clean air and felt very good about life in general and her small corner of the world in particular.

Teddy tuned the radio to the station that played the eternal music of the thirties, forties, and fifties and turned up the bell on the phone full blast, in case Rob called. Then she shouldered her weapon of choice, her pickax, and got to work, determined to get the job finished and covered back up before the septic tank was again full enough to flow into the leach lines.

By noon the last of the root-choked sections of tile were removed and the trenches deepened. Teddy was tired but feeling good about her accomplishment.

Over a sandwich and a tall glass of iced tea she figured the amount of gravel that would be needed and made the call to the quarry. Then she called the local building supply and ordered a half-dozen ten-foot sections of drainpipe, the accompanying fittings, and a can of mastic to stick the pieces together. When she put the phone down, Teddy allowed herself to be tired, physically. She had undoubtedly overdone and was going to suffer for it.

"A good time to check out the Bensons and turn up the hot tub."

Yes, indeed, she thought, a good soak in the hot tub before bed tonight would be just the thing to short circuit the aches and pains that were otherwise going to be her reward for her morning's effort. Teddy took the Benson's key from its place in the drawer and headed out the door and up the slope to the road. There was a path across the vacant lot that got well worn each summer but she had not cleaned it out yet this spring. That was generally something she and Minna Benson did together, would do, she was sure, when they were down next. Right now it would just be too much hassle to try and get through.

First she checked out the house, walking around as she had the other night to check the windows from the outside and then using her key to give a quick inspection to the interior. All was as she had last seen it. Even the drive looked as if there hadn't been a car there since they'd left. "It's the pine needles." she decided aloud. There had been a car there last night and at least once before as well.

Teddy circled back down the side of the house to the big deck that spread across the west side and wrapped around both the north and south ends of the house. On the south end, tucked discreetly next to the shingled tool shed with its red metal roof and mullioned windows that made it look like an upscale child's playhouse, was the hot tub. Lon and Minna had installed it the year after they'd gotten one for their home in Eugene.

"Nothing like it," Lon would say, relaxing with a glass of his favorite wine, up to his neck in the hot bubbling water, "after a day of weed-pulling or tree-cutting." Free use of the hot tub was Teddy's in exchange for keeping an eye out in general and checking on the chemical balance of the tub now and again when Minna and Lon were away for extended periods.

Teddy checked the chemicals and decided she would wait and put some more chlorine in after she got out, then raised the temperature dial two notches. She didn't like it too hot, you couldn't stay in as long if it were too hot.

It was the burgeoning buds on the dark lavender rhodie beside the shed that caught her eye. Just behind it to the left was the terminus of the path, choked normally this time of year with over-eager salal and berry. Someone had obviously been using the path recently.

"Damn!" Teddy said aloud, feeling a lump rising in her throat.

Well, so, it hasn't been neckers, nor anyone casing the Benson house for other unsavory reason. Whoever it was had been parking in the Benson's drive and then using the path to...

The thought froze as Teddy stepped off the deck and crossed quickly to where the trail entered the morass of salal, blackberry, wild rhododendrons and seedling trees jammed together like teens at a rock concert under the canopy of giant spruce, hemlock, and pines.

Teddy paused to admire from a new angle the spectacle of the broken pine hung sideways in the air and then slowly, carefully pushed her way along the overgrown path watching for the signs of recent passage. It wasn't a matter of just broken and torn branches, there were signs of clipping. They had brought their cutters and snipped as they went, in the dark yet! Teddy found it a startling idea. About three-quarters of the way back to her house the path veered out of its normal route and around the top end of a large pine that had been a fatality of the last storm. Obviously rougher going, but the trail maker had pressed on. The newly broken trail ended abruptly only yards short of her woodshed. There a large stump offered a place to sit and rest, and a perfect view of her front door! Teddy felt slightly sick to her stomach. Who, she wondered, and why? She also wondered if they drove a green pickup and started fires.

CHAPTER 24

Teddy began carefully retracing her steps to the Benson's yard, wanting to show the newly broken trail to Rob just as she had found it. The panic in her chest vied with her determination to be calm and think her discovery through.

"They were watching."

Watching her house while Rob was there. They had left when Rob left. Did they follow him home? The panic asserted itself again and she quickened her pace, breaking into a run as she reached the street. She flew down the slope to her door trying desperately to remember where she had left the phone before spotting it on the table. Teddy punched in Rob's home number and then disconnected. "He'll be at the office, dummy," she scolded herself and entered the office number.

It took four rings for Becky, the secretary/receptionist to answer.

"Good afternoon, Raymond Realty." Becky's slightly whiny voice droned into Teddy's ear.

"Becky this is Teddy, is Rob in?" Please, please say yes, she prayed.

"I'm sorry, Teddy," there was the sound of another phone ringing in the background, "darn, hang on just a bit will you? I'm here alone."

Becky didn't wait for Teddy to answer but clicked her onto hold and left her standing with her heart in her throat imagining a million things at once, none of them encouraging. In what seemed like an eternity Teddy heard the line click again.

"Like I was saying, Rob is out showing a house. He said for you to try his cell phone if you called."

Relief flooded Teddy's chest followed by a modicum of embarrassment at having jumped to conclusions. "Thanks Becky but just leave a message on his desk will you. I always hate disturbing him when he's with a client."

"He said I was to tell you not to worry about bothering him. He was real firm about it," Becky's voice lowered conspiratorially despite the fact she had said she was alone. "I think he's real worried, about the murderer you know. I think he's worried about you, too, after the fire and everything. And he looks just awful."

Becky had worked for Ben and Rob for more than five years now, ever since her husband had gone out for another six-pack and called three weeks later to say he wouldn't be back, would she forward his last paycheck. Forty-five, with three children in their early twenties, she had never lived anywhere else, never worked except during the summers as extra housekeeping help at one of the local tourist motels. Rob had hired her, trained her, and put up patiently with her rather flat learning curve. Whatever Rob said or did was all right with her, including his relationship with Teddy. Occasionally, she was rather too protective. Rob said it was empty-nest syndrome. The real estate office in general and Rob in particular had become her chick.

"Anyhow, I think he really wanted you to call the cell phone," Becky finished.

"Okay, but leave him a note, too, in case he's somewhere up a canyon where that thing doesn't pick up." Teddy ceded.

"Sure thing," Becky answered. "Someone's coming in the door, got to go." The line went dead.

Teddy disconnected and then dialed Rob's cell phone.

On the fourth ring the answering machine picked up and Teddy's heart sank. She wanted to hear his voice, now, just to be sure he was okay. She needed Rob to help restore her perspective. Surely there was a logical explanation for the path cut by the watcher.

Yeah, like the killer is waiting for just the right opportunity to kill you because...?

"Hello." Rob's voice interrupted the answering machine message and her less than cheerful speculating.

"I'm sorry to bother you but I really needed to talk to you," Teddy began to explain.

"No bother, they liked the house and are going to go home and think about it. I'm on my way back to the office now. What's up?"

"This may sound silly but..." Teddy told him about the lights she had seen after he left the night before and about the freshly clipped trail. "I panicked a little I guess. I thought he might have followed you home."

"Well if he did he found another nice stump and just watched the house, I didn't hear or see a thing. After one of those pills the doctor gave me I sleep pretty soundly. I think you better call Sonny,"

"You don't suppose it was Sonny?" Teddy asked hopefully. "You know, just being nosey about if you were going to stay, maybe spend the night."

"I think Sonny's plate is too full right now to have time to worry about whether you and I are sleeping together and he sure wouldn't have bothered to snip out a path. Sonny'd just have parked up the road and watched from the comfort of his patrol car."

"You're right I know, just wishful thinking. I don't much care for any of the other possible explanations I can come up with."

"Me neither." Static broke up the line. "I'll be there as soon as I can. I have to stop at the office on my way through town."

"I'm not sure what good you can do - I mean it's just a path across a vacant lot. I'm probably being silly to find it so threatening." Teddy did feel just a little silly. What after all had happened? Someone had clipped out an existing path and sat on a stump. Was there a law against it?

"Too damn much is going on for this not to be connected somehow. I don't like it. I'll see you as quick as I can. We can decide then if we want to call Sonny. Okay?" It was more of a statement than a question and brooked no denial.

"Okay," Teddy replied, feeling much relieved that she had not been able to talk him out of coming.

Almost before she had gotten the receiver back in its cradle the phone rang.

"Hello," Teddy said catching it before the second ring.

"Teddy?" an all too familiar voice asked.

"Pete, I'm kind of busy just now," Teddy said, perturbed.

"I guess I must have been thinking of you when I dialed. I meant to call Harry, some of us investors are getting together to compare notes and maybe sue your good buddy over those projects of Ben's." He chuckled nastily, "I wouldn't want to be in his shoes just now. You may be putting your bets on the wrong horse."

"What?" Teddy asked.

"It's just possible your friend is a murderer as well as a thief. Wouldn't be the first time thieves fell out," he said with relish.

"Pete, I imagine Harry is waiting for your call," Teddy said coldly and hung up.

She had gotten two steps from the phone when it rang again. Not feeling like any more vexing conversations Teddy waited for the answering machine to screen the call. The machine picked up on the third ring and the caller promptly hung up.

"Damn! That is just plain rude."

She was three steps from the phone when it rang this time. Teddy grabbed it up before the second ring.

"Listen you pervert, I don't know what your game is, but I don't want to play. If you don't have the good manners to leave a message you're no one I want to talk to."

"Whoa! I don't know who's been lighting a fire under your pot but don't go boiling over all over me," Sonny's voice echoed a slight amusement.

"Sorry Sonny. I've been getting a lot of weird calls lately and I guess they're getting to me. That and everything else that keeps happening."

"There something going on you should tell me about?" he asked.

"I..." Teddy wavered. It seemed like every other half-hour for days now she had been ready to cast Sonny as the bad guy. On the other hand if he were the bad guy he would already know what she was going to tell him and if she didn't he might get suspicious that she was suspicious.

"It's probably nothing, I think somebody's been watching my house, or following Rob or..."

"Maybe you should tell me all about it," Sonny's voice evidenced immediate curiosity.

"Can you come over now?" Teddy asked, making a decision. "Rob is on his way and then I'll only have to go through the whole thing once."

"Be there in twenty minutes, have to make one call first." As if to illustrate his interest in getting there quickly, the line clicked dead.

Teddy replaced the receiver and then stared at it warily, daring it to ring. The receiver lay innocent and quiet in its cradle. But she knew better. It was a coiled snake just waiting for her to relax her guard. She made a pot of coffee and set out the last of the cookies hoping all the while that Rob would arrive first and she could tell him what she had decided and why.

Ten minutes later, with great relief, she opened the door as Rob came striding down the slope.

"Now show me this path," he demanded.

"Sonny is coming I'll show you both at the same time." Teddy explained about the phone calls and how she had come to ask Sonny to come out. "I don't lie very well and then it came to me that if I did lie he would know it was because I was suspicious, if he's guilty that is. And if he isn't, then we need to tell him, right?" she concluded.

"Right," Rob agreed. "I think it's time to tell him everything, except of course that we're still not certain he isn't the killer. Then we'll see what happens."

"What do we do if...?" Teddy began.

"Hell if I know," Rob said, "We'll just have to play it by ear."

CHAPTER 25

It did not help that when Sonny arrived he had his service revolver strapped around his waist. He didn't usually wear it Teddy knew because his ample heft made it just plain uncomfortable when he sat down, the gun in its holster digging into his side. She looked at Rob, the look of concern that passed over his face making it clear he, too, had noted the weapon. The next minute Rob's face was all smiles and welcome.

"Glad you're here, Sonny. Teddy wanted to wait and show us both her discovery at the same time." Rob smiled reassuringly at Teddy and taking her hand started up the slope to the road.

"So you're saying someone parked here at least twice watching your house?" Sonny asked, standing in the Benson's drive.

"Last night and last Friday, too. Could have been more often, could have been two different people I suppose."

"Let's see this path," Sonny interrupted.

Somehow with Sonny and Rob trailing along behind it all seemed a great deal less sinister than it had earlier.

"The Bensons are in Hawaii and I sure didn't do this," Teddy said, pointing at the salal and berry clippings littering the path.

"Silly thing to do unless you're planning to use a path frequently," Sonny observed, leading the way into the vacant lot.

"You mean he plans on coming back often?" Teddy asked in alarm.

"Seems that way," Sonny answered.

Teddy turned questioning eyes on Rob behind her.

Rob nodded silent agreement, a grim set to his jaw.

As they neared the stump at the end of the path Sonny held up his hand for them to stop. "I think it would be better not to go tromping around in here too much."

"You think there might be clues or footprints?" Rob asked.

"I think if it looks like a herd of elephants has passed this way our watcher might get scared and not come back." Sonny shooed them with his hands in the direction of the Benson's. "Let's us go get some of Teddy's good coffee and talk about this and I want to hear about the phone calls, too."

Rob looked startled and opened his mouth to speak and then shut it.

Seated, as it seemed they had often been lately, at the little table, coffee cups in hand, Teddy lifted hers to her mouth and then set it down without drinking. She explained about the frequent hang-ups.

"At first I thought it was just Pete. But I'm beginning to think it's part of the murders, someone checking to see if I'm home or trying to scare me. And if scaring is what they had in mind they're doing a good job of it."

Sonny made a couple of notes in his crumpled little book and then flipped back through several pages. "Well I got me an idea, but we better see how it plays out first," Sonny said.

210

Teddy couldn't decide whether Sonny was showing real concern about this odd turn of events or was doing a very good job of pretending, too.

Rob cleared his throat, met Teddy's eyes momentarily, and then squared his shoulders as if getting set to do a particularly distasteful job. "There's more still."

Sonny looked from one to the other of them as if he could read what they had to say off their faces.

"Well?

"It's all just suspicion, I won't know for sure until tomorrow, but I found something unsettling in Ben's financial records. It could be the reason he was killed. I don't know."

Sonny opened his mouth to speak but Rob rushed on.

"I know you said to tell you if I found anything out of the ordinary. That's why I'm telling you now. I'm just not sure what, if anything, it is. It could still turn out to be nothing."

"But you don't really think so, right?" Sonny asked.

"No, whatever it turns out to be, I think it's probably pretty serious. Serious enough to be a motive for murder. I felt like I owed it to Ben to have it checked out, an audit of the records before I said anything. But so much has happened, obviously the murderer thinks we know something, Teddy and I. Anyway, I took the books to the valley to get checked out by two good CPA firms."

"Those books are evidence in a murder case." Sonny's voice was rising and he was flushed slightly.

"We don't know that for sure, Sonny," Rob interrupted.

"What we know for sure is that you withheld information in a murder investigation. Rob, it wasn't your call." Sonny's face was now more than slightly flushed and his voice dead serious. "I been rushing my butt all over town checking out alibis and looking for motives and you were busy crossing me up."

"Sonny, it's not like that at all. I couldn't tell you what Ben's books mean and I'm familiar with his business and have been studying them for a week now. I think at the very least Ben was fudging on his taxes big time." Rob sighed, "And he was scraping extra out of the projects, and working some kind of financial mumbo-jumbo with Keith and the boys. But nothing to point to any one suspect anymore than anything you already knew. Honest."

"It may surprise you some, but the police have access to CPAs and other experts, too. How do I know you aren't having those books doctored up for your own purposes?"

Rob and Teddy both opened their mouths to protest but Sonny rushed on.

"I don't think you killed Ben, but my opinion don't matter. It's what can be proved with the evidence, and I have to provide the state with all the evidence, including that you didn't turn over those books the very first minute you noticed they was odd." Sonny drained his cup and sat it on the table. "Could I trouble you for a refill?" he asked Teddy.

"Sonny, so help me, you got it all wrong," Teddy protested, rising to get the coffeepot. "Rob didn't know the books had anything to do with the murder to start with and when he did..."

"You two thought I might be a suspect, too, on account of me being one of Ben's investors?" Sonny finished her sentence with a smirk.

"I wanted to be sure. It could have been just a different way of keeping records. That's what we were doing up at Ben's, besides getting the rummage ready. And we did find his records only, well, the fire..."

"Did you ever consider that if you had spoke up sooner I might of got those records out of there before they tried to barbecue you?" Sonny shook his head. "I could still make a case for you two having set that fire."

"Blaming it on us would be one way of covering up; for yourself, or maybe one of the good ole' boys. Make you look good in the elections, too. But we didn't do it Sonny. We didn't kill Ben and put him in the septic tank, and we didn't run Rene's car off the road, or set fire to Ben's house. And we didn't clip that path out there. And I think in the long run we could prove it," Rob paused as Sonny rose from his chair.

Teddy felt a chill run through her and a need to shout out something, anything, to stop what was happening.

Sonny's hand went to his gun. "In the long run our murderer don't have much choice. He's going to have to kill you. The murderer is afraid if you two don't stop mucking about you're going to stumble onto the truth," Sonny grasped the gun, holster and all, and itched it up and down a couple of times vigorously, resettling it. "I think that's why he's been watching, probably working out how to do it." Sonny sat back down and reached for a cookie.

Teddy let out a breath she'd discovered she'd been holding and took a large drink of her coffee. Rob's face had paled, making the bruising stand out, his hands were flat on the table pushing against it as if he had been getting ready to stand, he relaxed as she watched, a small smile twitching at the corners of his lips as he eased back in his chair.

"So, what do we do now?" Rob asked.

"We, don't do nothing," Sonny said firmly. "I make arrangements to pick up those books and the reports from your auditors in the morning and get them double-checked by my own people. And I stage a little snipe hunt for our pal who likes to sit on stumps. The only thing I need from you two is for Teddy to sign this little paper I had faxed me this afternoon before I come out that says it's okay to tape her calls so's I don't have to get a court order." He fished around in his shirt pocket and pulled out a much-folded piece of paper, which he spread on the table in front of Teddy.

"Rob?" Teddy said looking at the paper as if it were covered with Chinese characters.

Rob took the paper and read it quickly. "It's just what he said."

Teddy read it quickly herself and then took the pen Sonny offered and signed.

Sonny folded it and put it in his pocket with a smile. "Now, we'll just see who we catch." He turned a serious face to Rob. "I ain't going to lose all my

214

money in those projects of Ben's, am I? If I thought that, you'd a been right in suspecting me."

"No, the projects are sound and run correctly, which I promise you they will be, the income is going to improve starting the very next quarter," Rob answered with a confident smile.

"Good," Sonny said. "You probably better be ready to explain that to a lot of folks. I hear there's talk of a lawsuit."

Rob looked surprised and Teddy remembered Pete's call.

"There's a meeting somewhere tonight, Pete said he was going. I almost forgot," Teddy said.

Rob shut his eyes and shook his head slowly. "This gets much worse, if Ben weren't dead already, I'd kill him."

Sonny laughed then looked thoughtful. "There is one more thing you two could do if you would. It might be helpful if you was to have breakfast at Petal's tomorrow and kind of let it be heard that the two of you are having dinner here tomorrow night. Let on that maybe that you have things to talk about, but don't let on what."

"Doesn't that kind of make us sitting ducks?" Teddy asked.

"Yep," Sonny answered. "But no more than you already are. And don't go talking to no one, even each other, where others might hear, not about the phone calls, or the line being tapped, or nothing else to do with all this, hear?"

"Swell," Teddy said, "I've got a shirt with little red-and-blue bullseyes all over it, I'll just wear that."

"You ain't never been safer than you're going to be for the next few days so don't worry none," Sonny reassured. "I'm going to have people watching both of you twenty-four hours a day."

"Are you sure that's a good idea?" Rob asked. "I mean everybody knows everybody's business around here. That kind of effort would be known by everyone in town an hour after you gave out the schedules, and several of your officers are related one way or another to your most probable suspects. How you going to know who to trust?"

"You're right, could be setting the fox to guard the hen house, but I don't see what else we can do," Sonny said scratching at his gun belt in the folds of his belly.

"We can keep it just between us and maybe Heitzer, he's new and not related to anyone hereabouts," Rob suggested. "He seems capable enough to be watching Teddy. I'll come to dinner and then leave and if the fellow in the car doesn't follow me then I'll come back to help. I can park at the State Park and walk up the beach."

Sonny looked skeptical.

"You could use the Benson's" Teddy offered. "I have the key, and I know they won't mind. You could see the path and my front door, sort of."

"All right, all right. Just you two, and me, and Robo Cop."

Phil Heitzer had graduated top of his class at the state police academy. Nobody knew quite why he had applied for the opening on Sonny's staff. The rest of Sonny's people were more Mayberry RFD than NYPD Blue. Heitzer had shown up his first day

216

pressed and polished to a fine sheen. He said yes sir, and no sir, when addressed by Sonny and took his job dead serious and by the book, hence the nickname. Nobody knew quite who had coined it, but it had been all over town by dinnertime. Heitzer took it as a compliment and had been doing his best ever since to live up to it.

"What about tonight? I don't want Teddy here alone," Rob said, standing and turning to stare out the window at the gathering gloom of early evening.

"Well, if you'll stick around until after supper I'll get Heitzer on the job tonight. If we're lucky maybe you won't even have to bait the trap in the morning." Sonny seemed pleased at the possibility.

Teddy didn't feel so lucky, but it was at least doing something to draw the killer out and make him expose himself. That was a whole lot better than going around imagining impossible scenarios and jumping at shadows. She got up and went to the drawer for the Benson's key. A sharp jab in the small of her back when she rose reminded her of why she had gone to the Benson's earlier in the first place.

"Any reason I shouldn't take a quick soak in the hot tub before I fix dinner?" she asked.

"Not as long as you take Rob with you," Sonny said, with a bit of a grin and a wink at Rob.

"Sonny," Teddy began menacingly.

"I only meant he looks like a good soak would do him a world of good," Sonny defended, hands raised palm out. "Honest."

"You just be sure to tell Heitzer to leave the kitchen door open, I'll come up through the Benson's garden and we can spell each other," Rob said grimly. "That fresh-clipped path out there gives me a real bad feeling."

"Doesn't thrill me much, either," Teddy said. "But what if our path-clipper follows Rob, how's Heitzer going to get to his car in time to follow them?"

"That's my part," Sonny said, "I'll park out on the highway where I can see both corners and, Rob, you leave here going south so you go back by me and I can see you good, anybody comes out of either street after that is our man. No one comes out I'll go in to back up Heitzer. We could have him all corralled by the time you get back. Presuming he shows up." Sonny looked at his watch. "If I get back to the office now I should get a good chance to talk to Heitzer without any other ears getting involved. You two enjoy that hot tub now." He wiggled his pale eyebrows and grinned, then he stood, itching furiously at the place where his holster rubbed and put a hand on the doorknob. "Remember this ain't no TV adventure, this here is a real killer we're baiting, no heroics, and Rob you be real sure you're not seen when you come back. You ain't going to know if he's here or where he's at if he is. Got me?"

Rob nodded without answering.

Sonny went out into a heavy mist that was almost rain and lumbered up the slope to his car. They watched him swivel his head in the direction of the Benson's drive before he got in the car and crunched off.

"So, what's for dinner?" Rob asked. "I never quite got lunch today."

"You've munched out enough on the cookies," Teddy pointed to the empty plate, "you ought to be able to last another hour or so. I'm dead serious about needing a soak in the hot tub. I did a whole lot of digging this morning and if I don't soak it out now I'll be in bad shape in the morning. If nothing else, I want to be sure I'm up to running if our great scheme doesn't work out." Teddy managed a small grim smile. "I'm going to put my suit on. Lon keeps a baggy old pair of swim pants on a peg in the shed if you want to join me. Otherwise you can get yourself a beer and watch the news."

"You are not going over there by yourself. I guess I could play voyeur and just come watch." He wiggled his eyebrows in an imitation of Sonny.

In the long run Rob had donned the putrid-green baggies Lon kept in the shed and joined Teddy in the hot tub. The steam from the tub merging with the mist cloaked them in an alien space where only the whisper of the ocean could be heard and the trees were contorted into gray-green living walls, unmoving in the heavy stillness of the deepening dark.

"Emmmm," Teddy moaned softly for about the fifth time.

"It does feel good," Rob agreed in hush tones that seemed to go with the hush around them. "You come over here often - by yourself?"

"I don't generally have the pleasure of a good-looking fellow for company. Sometimes Minna and I enjoy a soak and a glass of wine. We had peach schnapps once. That was nice. Mostly it's just little ole' me and whatever little creatures care to look on.

219

You see bats some nights in the summer. When it's clear I just lay back and watch the sunset or count stars. This mist is kind of like sitting in a cloud."

"I think I'm going to have to have one of these at my place. Sonny was right, I can feel the soreness melting away." Rob slid down so the water covered his shoulders and lapped gently at his chin. They sat quiet for a long while, each lost in their own thoughts.

"What are you doing?" Rob asked, as Teddy leaned out over the side of the hot tub.

The surface of the water erupted into bubbles as the underwater jets spurted into action offering massage from every direction at once.

"It's on a timer, this is your ten-minute warning. When it goes off we get out, okay?"

"Couldn't we just set it for another ten minutes, this is great."

"Maybe," Teddy agreed. "But the idea of meeting our 'watcher' as he turns in the Benson's drive, me standing there in my wet bathing suit and a towel, is a little unsettling."

"Good point, but we don't even know for sure he's coming," Rob pointed out. "I mean you only saw him twice, several days apart."

"He could have been here every night and I just didn't notice him."

"He cut that path last night, those clippings are fresh," Rob reminded her. "This feels sooo good."

When the timer cut the jets Teddy leaned out to reset it for another ten minutes. "We meet the killer on the way home, I plan on running like hell."

"I'll be right behind you," Rob assured her. "What's for dinner, you never did say."

"What is this preoccupation with food," Teddy asked, changing position so a jet of bubbling water was pounding into her left shoulder, a primary ache spot.

"I told you I was hungry."

"Well, I've got pork chops in the freezer, if I bake them in a hot oven we could eat in about half an hour. Pork chops, mashed potatoes, and little peas?"

"Sounds good to me. Got any more of that red wine?"

"About a glass apiece. Remember, you're supposed to be alert this evening. I don't want you sleeping through my murder."

Rob reached out and pulled her into his arms. "Nothing, I repeat, nothing, is going to happen to you. I promise." He held her close.

Teddy was finding it very reassuring, enjoyable even. The timer dinged and the jets went quiet.

"Time to get out I guess," Rob said softly in her ear.

"'Fraid so," Teddy answered rising, "I think I'm hungry, too."

Somewhere out on the road there was a sound that could have been a footstep on the gravel, or a raccoon, or even a pine rat. Teddy and Rob froze, and then with a finger to his lips, making an effort to cause as little noise as possible, Rob stood and stepped over the side to the deck. He paused and they listened, straining their ears. The muffled scrunch of gravel reached them again. Rob looked toward the shed, obviously wishing for his clothes and then when the sound came again, closer, started barefoot across the deck to the stairs up to the drive. Teddy sat on the edge of the hot tub, swung her legs out and slipped her feet quickly into her rubber thongs.

Rob had gotten as far as the bottom step and Teddy was half way across the deck toward him when they both heard a polite sort of cough. Then Phil Heitzer's face appeared slowly around the corner of the house.

"I thought it was most likely you," he said quietly. "The sheriff said you'd probably be in the hot tub when I got here. Aren't you cold?" he asked, eyeing first Rob and then Teddy as they stood dripping in the mist.

CHAPTER 26

The aroma of the pork chops baking in their bed of sage-seasoned celery and onions was beginning to fill the small house and a prick with a fork confirmed that the potatoes were just about ready to be mashed. Teddy tore the lid back on the frozen pea's cardboard box and administered a shake of salt and a miniscule bit of butter. She put the box in the microwave on a paper towel and set it for three minutes on high.

"Tomorrow night I'll bring you a pizza," Rob said. He was seated at the table watching Teddy move efficiently around the tiny kitchen.

She looked worried.

"You know, Teddy, he may not even show up tonight. That's why we need to bait him tomorrow, and he might not come then."

"I don't know whether to hope he does or hope he doesn't," Teddy said, draining the potatoes at the sink using the pot lid, held so the water could escape but the potatoes couldn't. "I'm sure not looking forward to the idea of the confrontation but it would be good to have it done and over with. You know what I mean?"

"Exactly. It's one of those occasions when your choice would be none of the above, only we don't get a choice. There is someone out there who has been watching us, quite probably the murderer, and we have to find out who it is. Should I pour the wine?"

"Please. I know you're right." Teddy dropped another bitty bit of butter into the pot with the potatoes, followed by two shakes of salt and four of pepper and then whipped them with the electric hand mixer she had ready on the counter. Finished, she put the lid on the pot to keep the potatoes warm and opened the oven to check on the pork chops.

"Done?" Rob asked hopefully.

"Done," Teddy confirmed, removing them from the oven.

Once, while they were eating they had heard a car on the road. Listening, frozen in their seats, they heard slamming of doors and laughter coming from the rental house. Conversation had been limited to how good the food tasted, how much Rob's grandchild had grown, and the probable costs involved in putting a hot tub like the Benson's on Rob's deck. Only when they were clearing the table did they return to the murders.

"I don't know about you but I almost peed my pants when Sonny started reaching for his gun. I thought we were dead for sure," Teddy chuckled.

"Me too," Rob agreed, grinning. "When he started itching and twisting I almost couldn't keep from laughing. Would have served us right if he'd been the killer. We were kind of dumb about the whole thing, sitting right there asking for it." Rob handed her the last of the dirty dishes as she loaded the dishwasher.

"What time tomorrow, breakfast I mean?" Teddy asked, shutting the dishwasher door.

"Meet you there at 7:30. That ought to be about prime listener time. We want to be sure as many of the regulars as possible have a chance to hear us talking. You know there's one thing to think about, everyone's gotten so used to the two of us I'm not sure we're worth gossiping about anymore."

"So, we could talk about using the hot tub again, that ought to get us talked about," Teddy suggested with a giggle.

"And scare our path builder off, maybe. But I guess we could just sort of hint that last night was fun, let's do it again tonight and let them draw their own conclusions as to what," Rob offered.

"That'll work. That ought to burn up the phone lines for sure. You sure you're ready to do that kind of damage to your reputation?"

"Like I keep telling you, it seldom hurts a man's reputation. Marrianne and Anna and the rest of the pious crowd will smirk and blame you for being the hussy they always suspected you were." He looked at his watch. "I'd better get going, I think I left here about this same time last night, not much later anyway."

Teddy stood in the door to watch Rob climb the slope to his pickup. "See you in the morning," she called after him. It took great effort not to look in the direction of the Benson's.

"7:30, I'll be there. Night." Rob waved, ducked into the pickup's cab, and started his engine.

Teddy had the urge to call out and stop him. What if the murderer was out there, ready to follow him? What if Sonny wasn't able to keep the unthinkable from happening? What if Rob was run off the road, like Rene, before Sonny could stop it? The panic rising, Teddy lifted her hand and forced herself to smile and wave.

This is all really silly if no one besides Heitzer is watching.

Teddy returned indoors and turned on the dishwasher. Then, determined to keep to her normal routine as much as possible, she went up to watch TV and read.

Two hours later, having read the same page at least a dozen times and still not sure what it said, she turned off the lights before allowing herself the luxury of a peek out the north window toward the dark and silent shadow of the little brick house. Teddy took her book and went down to bed to try and watch an old movie and read that elusive page again.

She slept fitfully. Dreams of dark halls that became towering, maze-like tunnels of salal and berry-lined paths going on without end, interspersed with the pleasanter images of Rob and herself holding each other close in the hot tub. Then the hot tub would turn into a vast roiling sea of bubbling water and Rob was nowhere to be found. Once during the night Teddy had come awake with a start and been unable to identify just what had awakened her. Finally, a little before six, floundering alone in the sea again and aware she was dreaming, she had swum up out of the sea into full wakefulness.

Teddy was early. It was only 7:20 when she entered Petal's front door. Even so, Rob was waiting, sitting in the booth opposite the cash register. Chosen, Teddy was sure, for its prime visibility. Now we see what kind of actors we are, she thought, still harboring a hope in the far corner of her mind that perhaps Rob would tell her Heitzer had caught the intended quarry, even before he had gotten back up the beach to help, and it was all over.

"Morning Teddy," Rob said, only a little louder than usual, as she slid into the booth. The booths either side of them were empty but Keith and Jamie sat in their usual booth near the window and there were a full complement of regulars at the counter. Sitting facing the back of the room Teddy could see Kevin and his dad Harry in a booth beyond some obvious tourist types - they were dressed by Eddie Bauer not J.C. Penny. The place was only half full but Teddy knew it should fill up over the next half-hour.

Her attention on "counting the house" she did not notice Alice approach with the coffeepot until her shadow fell across the table. Teddy looked up and then felt suddenly ill. She had expected it to be Rene, the sense of loss very nearly brought tears to her eyes.

"You need a menu?" Alice asked. "Billy said to tell you we got biscuits coming out of the oven in another ten."

"Then I'll have two biscuits when they're ready, a side order of bacon, extra crisp, oh, and honey for the biscuits." Teddy smiled up at Alice and hoped her voice sounded okay. They were supposed to make people think she and Rob were up to something, make the killer curious. Weeping all over the table wasn't in the script.

Rob had apparently already ordered, Alice topped up his cup and scooted off.

He reached a hand across the table and held hers. "Missing Rene?" he asked softly and squeezed gently.

Teddy gave him a smile of thanks and squeezed back.

"I can't tell you how much I enjoyed dinner last night," he said much louder. "I thought I'd pick us up a pizza when I come out tonight. What do you like on yours?"

Well, that must mean they had had no luck last night. "Black olives and mushrooms and pepperoni if you like. Actually I like almost anything but anchovies." Teddy answered, trying to make it sound as casual and clearly audible as possible. "What's your favorite pizza topping?"

"You're going to think I'm crazy. I like pepperoni, black olives, and pineapple. It's really good, honest."

"If you say so. I'll tell you what, get them to do a half and half, you know with the mushrooms and the pineapple and I'll give it a try."

"Alice, get me my pancakes, I'm in a hurry," a loud impatient voice bellowed from behind her. Rob looked up.

Dave must have joined Keith and Jamie, Teddy didn't have to turn, she recognized the voice and the demanding attitude.

"Hey, Rob, leave your girlfriend there for a minute, I got to talk to you," Dave shouted across the two empty booths that separated them.

"Can't, here comes Alice with my breakfast. Catch up to you later. What time you getting to work? I'll stop by." Rob was relatively sure Dave hadn't done a minute's worth of work on either of the current jobs since Ben's body was found.

"That's what I want to talk about," then Dave lowered his voice a hair, still loud enough to be heard everywhere in the restaurant, "outside."

"I'll see you at the Harbor Court site, at 9:30. I need to see how things are going." Rob moved his cup aside so Alice could set down the big oval plate containing a cheese and onion omelet, ham, hash-browns, and toast.

"Didn't I feed you enough last night?" Teddy asked, awed.

"That was last night." Rob replied digging into the hot food.

Kevin and Harry Bates paused on their way out at the cash register to pay their bill.

"Morning Kevin, Harry," Teddy said, "How's it going?"

"Just fine if I can ever convince my dad I can afford to buy my own breakfast," Kevin said, with a big smile that took any complaint out of his words.

Harry Bates turned from the register, his change in hand. "Taking the kid to breakfast is the only way I can get eggs and bacon anymore. The wife has me on a low cholesterol diet. Doctor says she can't have eggs and bacon, so I don't get any either. Go figure. Don't suppose it would hurt to take off a few pounds, though." He patted his belt line and winked at them. "Listen Rob if you're going out to Harbor Court later, would you mind stopping by for a chat before you head back this way. I got a couple of questions about some of those projects, you know the ones Ben put together."

"Sure Harry, see you as soon as I finish with Dave. Probably about 10:30. Okay?"

"Just fine boy," Harry said, putting a fatherly hand on Rob's shoulder, "No problem, just want to ask a couple of questions."

"Come on dad, I got to get to work," Kevin urged.

Harry laughed, a deep rumbling kind of laugh. "Used to be I was always waiting for him. Now he's the one with places to go and things to do." Harry was still laughing at the changes life brings as they went out the door.

Alice brought Teddy's biscuits, bacon, and honey and refilled Rob's half-empty cup without so much as a smile. The place was filling up. All around them the hum of voices increased, Teddy tried to separate out the different conversations. The tourist family was trying to decide whether to go to the aquarium before or after lunch. The semi-regulars (summer people who owned a place just north of town) were deciding on breakfast, they would have the pancakes, they always did. It was sure a lot easier to keep hold of the thread of the various conversations if you were moving back and forth with a pot of coffee and could see who was saying what. Someone seemed to be doing a lot of shushing behind her and she caught an angry tone that sounded like it might have been Dave once.

"We finished that bottle of red wine last night, I'll pick up another bottle or two. Same kind?" Rob asked.

Teddy knew she was not holding up her end of the deal. She smiled gratefully at Rob and said,

"Yes, since we both seem to like it. It ought to go well with tonight's pizza."

Marrianne Pailey harrumped at Teddy's elbow and followed her husband's lead by sliding into the booth just behind them. Teddy giggled.

Rob nudged her foot under the table and with a lift of his chin toward the counter, called her attention to the fact that Pete was waving at her from where he had just taken a seat.

Teddy waved obediently.

"Don't forget, I might be a little late tonight. I have to show the Willis place at four," Rob remarked.

"Well just try not to be too late, you know how hungry you get."

By the time they had finished their breakfast (and their little charade) Teddy was sure there wasn't anyone in three states who wouldn't know by lunch that they were having dinner together, again, tonight. Even Alice, who'd always seemed blessed with the ability to blank out all conversation that wasn't a request for service, was looking at them questioningly.

Rob crowned the performance by picking up both tabs when he rose to go and then leaning down and planting a kiss on Teddy's cheek. "Remember, we have lots to talk over."

"See you tonight," Teddy smiled up at him. She intended to linger, as she usually did, over her coffee. Rob paid the bill and then stopped at the table, where, despite his earlier hurry, Dave was still sitting with Keith and Jamie. Teddy heard Rob ask Keith about the progress on a repair to one of Ben's rentals and then suggest that they should all have a meeting the next morning at 10, in Ben's old office and get their schedule figured out. The grumble level in the tone of conversation from that end went up considerably after Rob left.

Alice came to top up her coffee cup but suddenly the coffee just didn't taste as good as it usually had.

"Thanks Alice, I think I've had enough," Teddy said, and after fixing her lipstick slid out of the booth.

"Teddy," Pete called, "going home? Thought I'd stop by later and see if you needed any help with those leach lines."

"Got it handled Pete, thanks anyway." Teddy started toward the door, nodding and smiling to those she knew.

"Morning Teddy," Keith said, eyeing her speculatively.

"Morning Keith, Jamie, Dave." Teddy gave them a smile and a nod and passed on out the door, mildly surprised that they had not offered so much as one off-color remark about her and Rob, nor even mentioned the fire.

"Most unusual," Teddy told the double-trailered lumber truck that held her hostage on the curb while it managed to slow to a mere ten miles over the speed limit through town. Before she crossed the street to her car she turned and looked back through Petal's window to see Dave with Jamie and Keith turned in their seats, staring back at her.

CHAPTER 27

Teddy stopped at the post office to clean her box of several days worth of junk mail and almost threw away the water bill that had gotten stuck between the pages of a catalog from a company Teddy had ordered from once, more than six years before. It struck her that by now any profit they had made off her purchase had been used up in printing and postage. The Paileys came in as she was leaving.

"Morning, Marrianne, Howard," Teddy nodded.

"Morning, Teddy," Howard replied with that odd little movement of the head he used that made him look like he was withdrawing even while he was moving forward.

"Mmmmhuh," Marrianne mumbled, tugging Howard after her through the door.

Teddy went to the grocery store for lettuce and ended up with three bags, two of which actually contained food products. The tall woman behind the meat counter had paused midst whacking up baby back ribs and waved her cleaver in greeting.

"What you like the looks of today? We got those nice hams on sale, I'll slice one up for you."

A pound of pepper bacon, a pound of super-lean ground beef, and a sliced ham later she leaned over the counter to hand the paper-wrapped packages to Teddy and winked at her knowingly. "I hear you're cooking for more than one nowadays."

Teddy couldn't believe the word had gotten around so fast, then she spotted one of the regulars who had been at Petal's for breakfast in the checkout

233

line ahead of her and knew the source. After that she stopped at the bakery to pick up some dark rye to go with the ham. A man Teddy recognized as part of the gray-haired group that had been with the Paileys at the Sandy Inn was sitting at one of the little tables along the bakery's window wall having coffee and raisin rolls with a heavy blond woman Teddy'd never seen before. He stared at her frankly on her way out and as Teddy passed by the window she could see him talking animatedly and gesturing with his pastry.

Boy, I wish my life were half as interesting as everyone else seems to think, Teddy thought, unlocking the car. Then it struck her.

It is.

At least right now it was. In fact a little less interesting wouldn't be such a bad thing.

"Never happy are you."

Teddy spent the rest of the morning awaiting the delivery of the gravel. She was going to have them dump it on the level patch where she normally parked the car, then any leftovers could just be raked out. Someday, she promised herself again, she would build a garage there. Until then a nice graveled parking spot wasn't all that bad.

Puttering around the wild iris patches that scalloped down both sides of the front slope from the road, Teddy eyed both the slope and the two possible paths down into the garden she could use to deliver the gravel to the leach line trenches and concluded that either way it was going to be one nasty, time-consuming job.

"Maybe I should let Pete come help me after all. That would certainly serve him right and dampen his ardor."

No, she decided, no matter how hard the job, what Pete would expect by way of a thank you made that an unacceptable idea.

The gravel arrived at 10:30, just as they said it would, and ten minutes later the driver had his check and was rumbling north on his way back to the highway. Teddy stood staring at the pyramid of rock trying to figure out why it looked like too much to get moved and not enough to fill the need.

A subjective inspection of the three long trenches convinced Teddy they should be cleaned out just a little better before she started moving rock. It was well past time for lunch before she stopped, with a third of one and all of another yet to go.

"Enough for one day," Teddy declared to a gull who sat watching from the roof. She was muddy and sweaty and wishing the job were done and over with.

Her muddy shoes came off on the porch. One step inside the door she shed the rest of her clothes then went to pile them in the washer and take a shower. Hungry, head wrapped in a towel, body wrapped in a short terry robe, she fixed half a sandwich and a glass of milk.

It wasn't until she'd finished eating and put the dishes in the sink that she noticed the lights on the answering machine flashing. The first message was from her younger daughter wanting to know if she would come a day early for Dee's birthday party in two weeks so Teddy could watch the children and she and her boyfriend could have a night out. "Maybe," Teddy said to the machine. The next message was a beep as were the three after that. "Well Mr. Smarty Pants, if Sonny did his job, we should know who you are by now." The thought was cheering. Maybe the pizza and wine tonight would be a celebration, they might be done with all the mystery at last. Hugging that thought to her Teddy got dressed and spent the remainder of the afternoon reading.

Going on four o'clock the phone rang.

"Hello," Teddy answered and then held her breath.

"Teddy, this is Sonny. Just wanted you to know they have you all hooked up now."

"Now! I thought you were going to get it done this morning. There were four beeps on the answering machine by lunch. I've been waiting for you to call and tell me you knew who was doing it and why. Maybe even that you had the murderer."

"You didn't want much, did you? It's not as easy as you think, even with a signature. Especially since I had to time it just right so's everybody in town didn't find out. Had to get the phone company manager alone and threaten him with arrest for impeding justice if he told even his wife."

"Especially his wife," Teddy commented, "she's the worst gossip in town and has the next five contenders for the title on speed dial."

"Exactly, anyhow it's done now. He'll call again, he ain't got what he wants yet." Sonny sounded very sure.

"What about the audit? Did you pick it up? What did it say?" Teddy asked.

"I picked it up first thing this morning and hand-delivered it to the state unit that specializes in just such things."

"But what did the reports Rob was supposed to get say? You got those didn't you?"

"Teddy, I got them, but they are evidence now and none of your business."

"None of my business! Sonny I have had a body stored in my septic tank, had my yard become a draw for the local busy bodies, lost a good friend, been almost burned to death, harassed by telephone and watched by... well, by whoever did the watching. It most certainly is my business."

"Like I told Rob," Sonny insisted paternally, "it's my business to take care of these things. You two just stick to the plan this evening and it will all work out just fine. I got everything under control. Hear?"

"Sonny I hear, but I don't like."

Sonny didn't let her complete her protest. "Got to go, there's things got to be arranged. You two did good at Petal's this morning. I've heard several versions of it myself, including two suggestions that you knew who the murderer was or at least knew something you had your heads together over." Sonny laughed, "I even heard you was shacked up together, had been some time now. Had it hinted that maybe you and Rob had killed Ben 'cause he found out. You and Rob just enjoy your pizza and hope our fish has taken the bait. Heitzer and I will handle the rest." The line went dead.

"Why that pompous ass," Teddy steamed with no one to listen, she slammed her phone back into its cradle. "I wouldn't trust him to handle anything more complicated than a school crossing. And we're just supposed to sit here and leave our lives in his hands."

She looked at the clock. She was going to have awhile to wait before she could talk out her uneasiness over Sonny's plans with Rob. He wouldn't arrive for at least an hour and a half, maybe longer. Teddy reached for her jacket, maybe a walk on the beach would help.

Teddy walked north - past the Benson's, past the new houses on their cement pillars, past the polyglot assortment of fifties-and-sixties-style motels interspersed with pods of tiny little beach cabins clinging low and close together to the top of their dunes. The tide was out and she walked on the firm sand as it ran parallel with the highway, ignoring the occasional mechanical grumble of the big rigs as they rattled and roared, picking up speed on their way out of town. When she arrived at the entrance to the bay she could hardly remember what she had seen, her mind had been so busy reliving the past couple of weeks, building scenarios only to tear them down and start off on a new tangent. So many of the possibles seemed so improbable. But then Ben's and Rene's murders would have seemed pretty damned improbable if someone had suggested them three weeks ago.

Teddy looked to her right toward the compact community nestled another half mile up the bay side with the big graceful bridge that spanned the wide river dwarfing it. Still firmly established in its own time warp, the town seemed never to have, either physically or emotionally, gotten out of the sixties. A Northwest coast, red-necked, sixties to be sure, but the sixties none the less.

The last time she had walked this far it had been morning, she had gone on into town. Rob had bought her lunch and given her a ride home. Teddy knew Rob was not at his office now, no hope of a ride unless she wanted to try and catch him at the pizzeria. She did a one-hundred-and-eighty and headed back south focusing on the crashing surf, letting its unceasing rhythm massage her mind into an acceptance of all things she could do nothing about.

By the time she crested the dunes into her own garden the churning that had gripped her mind and body for days had at least subsided. It would be tough but she could handle finishing the drain-field's repairs. She would play her part, eat the pizza, and let Sonny catch murderers.

Which isn't to say I won't keep alert it's just that it isn't really all my responsibility.

A trio of crows perched on the sea end of her roof cawed their greeting as she climbed the hill reminding her that she had stale bread and some cereal that had been open too long to put out on the big stump she used as a bird feeder.

"You three wait right there," she called up to the crows. "I have goodies for you."

CHAPTER 28

It was getting dark. Teddy had the table set and she'd changed her clothes feeling the need to dress up some in honor of the occasion. It was not, after all, everyday that one played bait for a murderer. By local standards she was dressed up indeed - khaki knit pants and tunic and her favorite gold hoops, the ones Stan had bought her just before he died. Now Teddy worried at the backs of the earrings and watched out the window for Rob.

It was March, barely, the sun still setting early in the evening. It had been a glorious sunset, boding well for tomorrow's weather, but the afterglow was fading fast and in the west, the pale turquoise sky was turning sapphire behind the black skeletons of the trees. Looking east, Teddy could barely make out the outline of the woods across the way, black against a black sky. It was clearing, it would be cold tonight and later there might be stars.

Headlights slid their white glow up the street followed by the outline of a vehicle, a van, Teddy could tell when it passed. She watched its taillights veer right and stop at the rental house. Disappointed she turned to the stove and then remembered she wasn't cooking dinner, there was nothing that needed to be turned down or stirred. Nothing to do but wait. But not long maybe, the crunch of tires from the road pulling her attention back to the window. It was a pickup and it stopped. She heard the door slam and seconds later her motion lights came on and illuminated Rob striding down the slope, pizza box in one hand and a grocery bag in the other.

"Sorry I'm running late," he apologized, putting his burdens on the counter. "It's the first time I was ever unhappy to have somebody want to make an offer, but they really liked the house and they're leaving for Wisconsin in the morning, so it was now or maybe never."

"No problem. I don't suppose you noticed if there was anyone parked in the Benson's drive on your way past?"

"Not a soul, place looks deserted," Rob noticed Teddy's look of concern, "just as it's supposed to. I had a long talk with Heitzer last night. He brought his sleeping bag and provisions, wasn't going to leave the place today, just stick around and keep an eye on you." Rob got the corkscrew from the drawer and took a bottle of wine from the bag. "They were on sale so I got four bottles, stick the extras away, we'll drink them eventually."

Teddy opened the pizza box and inhaled the spicy aroma of pepperoni mixed with the musty mushroom scent. "No pineapple? I was looking forward to trying it."

"Next time. But I did get them to give us extra black olives." Rob poured the wine. "I'll take two pieces to start. Oh, here, you might want to look at this." He handed her several sheets of paper, the fine print across the top of the upmost identifying it as a fax.

"What's this?" Teddy asked but she could see that it was from Rob's son-in-law and she read greedily.

Rob sipped at his wine and had consumed both of his pieces of pizza and gotten a third before she quit reading.

"Wow!" Teddy commented, taking a drink from her glass. "But doesn't that just leave us back suspecting everyone?" The gist of the short report seemed to be that Ben Raymond had been cheating everyone. The IRS, his investors, his contractors, Rob, everyone - big time.

"Mostly," Rob nodded in agreement his face grim. "He didn't care who he was stealing from."

"But what did he do with the money?" Teddy asked. "He wasn't exactly a conspicuous consumer." She noticed that she had managed to consume an entire piece of pizza without remembering a bite of it. "Want some more?" she asked, rising to get herself another piece.

"Please," Rob held out his plate. "Ben's trust lists several pieces of property elsewhere in the state and some in Montana. I know he's had some of them for years but I suspect now that either I am going to find major improvements or additional properties. What a mess." Rob refilled his glass and topped off Teddy's. "I'd be willing to bet that one of those filing cabinets that burned contained the answer to your question."

"Why? I mean I know he liked buying property and holding it long term. I remember hearing him give that spiel more than once when he brought clients in to breakfast, about land being the true inflation hedge and rising in value even when the economy was soft or at least holding its value. But what was he going to do with it all eventually?"

"I don't think he every thought that far ahead. He got so wound up in acquiring - I'd guess it was greed and his way of keeping score. You know, some men collect big-boy toys - cars, boats, trophy wives. You have to have heard it, probably from one of the good ole' boys, 'he who dies with the most toys wins'. With Ben it was land. But I'm sure going to have to have a nice long talk with the attorney. I think the trust needs to pay back some of it, all of it, if we can figure how much and to whom. It seems so convoluted. I'll know more when Sonny and the state people get through with the books and give them back, then I can sit down with the lawyer and my son-in-law, Ken, and trace it all backward. If there's property out there I don't know about, it'll find me at tax time." Rob stared into his glass for a minute as if the answers might swim to the surface in the crimson wine.

"Not to change the subject but just how are you planning on moving all that gravel down into the back?"

"By wheelbarrow, and I'm not looking forward to it."

"I may have a better answer for you. Jamie's been using it at the Harbor Court site, I'd thought it was in the garage up at Ben's and been burned."

"What?" Teddy asked, more than interested in anything that would ease the job of moving all that rock.

"It's a mini dirt-mover, sort of an overgrown Tonka Toy, Ben got it to do pathways with up on his place when his wife was alive. It's got all the standard tools, scoop, bucket, blade, but the whole thing will go down a three-foot-wide path. Dave had a tarp over it when I got there this morning. I think he was kind of hoping I wouldn't notice. I'll haul it over and we can move that gravel in no time without doing too much damage to the garden or your back."

"How did your talk with Dave go? He going to cooperate with you?"

"Well, there's another puzzle for you. He laid into me the minute I got there about how he hadn't been paid for a month and he wasn't going to do anything more until we sat down and renegotiated not just that, but all the jobs. I tried to explain that I'd have to get the bank records before I could tell where we stood - because of the fire, and because I was having the books audited. He just kept saying he didn't care what my problems were, he wasn't doing another lick of work until I paid up. He was really hostile. Then when I spied the dirt mover, butter wouldn't melt in his mouth," Rob chuckled, "went on about how good it was that it had been on the site and not in the garage. He even volunteered to come move the gravel for you."

"Doesn't sound like I can afford him. Do you think he was trying to keep the dirt mover without your knowing?"

"Seems that way. I got the good ole' boys coming in in the morning for a little setting up of ground rules. From here on in all jobs go out for competitive bid - starting with the existing projects if they don't agree to finish up with them my way. And I guess now is as good a time as any to explain about Ben's bookkeeping."

"That will certainly give everyone something to talk about besides our private lives." Teddy told him about her experiences at the grocery and the bakery and what Sonny had said he heard.

"Sounds like my ears should have been burning all day," Rob laughed.

Teddy eyed the clock nervously.

Rob followed her glance and then stood up, "I think it's show time."

"I don't have a good feeling about this. Please be careful," Teddy implored.

"Come on, I'll help you put the dishes in the dishwasher, then we'll go out and say good night, just like the other night. And Teddy, no matter what, you keep your door shut and locked until Sonny or I tell you it's safe to open up. Okay?"

"You know, we're going to feel real silly if the only audience we have is Heitzer. In fact, I feel silly already, knowing you and Heitzer were over there baby-sitting me all night."

"MMmmmh," Rob agreed, with a smile, "and we will keep on baby-sitting until this thing is cleared up and we catch the creep."

It took only seconds to put the plates and silver in the dishwasher. Teddy walked out on the porch with Rob. "Call me after your meeting tomorrow," she said raising her voice slightly.

"I will."

Rob had gone down one step, far enough to trigger the motion lights, he turned and then with a wink took her in his arms and kissed her soundly, lingering over it ever so slightly. "Sleep tight," he said, smiling, and strode up to his pickup, waving to her before he got in.

Teddy gulped down her surprise and waved back.

Well, of course, it was just for show. Play acting.

But it had been very nice. *Very nice!*

Teddy watched Rob drive off and then looked expectantly toward the Benson's. There was no sight nor sound of a car. She went back inside, locking the door carefully behind her. Teddy turned off the kitchen lights and went upstairs turning the TV on but muting the sound. She wanted things to look normal but she didn't want to miss hearing whatever activity might occur from the direction of the Benson's driveway or the stump in the vacant lot. It took every bit of self-discipline she could muster to keep from looking out her north window. A half-hour later she was beginning to think they should give it all up as a foolish idea when the shots rang out.

The first shot had been preceded by a shout. "Halt?" was that what she'd heard, she wasn't sure. Then almost immediately there had been two more shots followed by hollering and much thrashing and snapping of underbrush and one or two yelps plus a very understandable "Shit!" and an equally loud and discernible, "Damn!" ending in an unmistakable, "Fuck it! Fuck it! Fuck it!"

Teddy had stiffened with the first shot and been galvanized into action with the second two. By the time the yelling had begun she had gotten down the stairs and, forgetting Rob's admonition to stay inside, wrenched the door open just in time to see a large male figure, in dark pants and jacket with a ski mask over his head, bust out of the undergrowth near the shed. He headed up the slope toward the road followed closely by Heitzer who grabbed for the man just as he crossed the edge of the motion light's sensors. The lights flashed on momentarily stunning both men and the masked man changed directions abruptly, lunging downhill toward the garden and the beach. Heitzer sprawled full length his hands holding fast to what purchase he had, the escaping man's jacket came away with a rip.

That shirt, I know that shirt, Teddy thought trying to remember just where she had seen it before. The running figure disappeared around the side of the house.

Teddy heard a siren approaching and the squeal of a car making a fast turn at the corner beyond the Hanby's house.

Rob crashed out of the underbrush from the vacant lot and rocketed down the hill after the fleeing man. With a final unwinding moan of his siren, lights flashing, Sonny's patrol car skidded to a noisy stop. Heitzer, regaining his feet followed after Rob, followed by Teddy, followed by Sonny waving his service revolver in the air in one hand and a flashlight in the other, all the time yelling, "halt, damn it, halt," at the top of his voice.

The leader of this odd parade had crossed the patio and reached the dark of the garden below with no sign of heeding Sonny's demands when Rob, using the steep path for a launching ramp flung himself through the air toward the running figure.

There was the sound of not one but three crashing bodies as Heitzer dashed across the patio and also flung himself into the blackness.

For the next several minutes the air was blue with remarks of the kind Teddy had not heard since she had tried to explain to Hal why she wanted a divorce. None of them very explanatory, and most of them anatomically impossible.

Teddy halted at the top of the path, peering down into the darkness erupting with howls and lamentations.

"I've broken my fucking leg!"

That did seem to indicate at least one injury.

"Get your knee out of my face you..."

Sonny huffed to a halt beside Teddy and shined his light toward the cacophony, disclosing a many-armed-and-legged monster grappling about on the ground. With his gun aimed high toward the dune Sonny fired off a single shot.

The monster fell still.

Sonny played his light back and forth across the scene. At first Teddy thought the man in the ski cap had escaped. Only Heitzer and Rob, climbing to their feet with much groaning, were immediately visible. A deep moan off to the left indicated their fish had not gotten off the line. Sonny clomped down the path and shined his light on the man lying face down, wedged at the bottom of the narrow trench Teddy had cleaned out that morning, one leg twisted awkwardly beneath him. The gray-plaid shirt was unmistakable.

"Pete! Why?" Teddy cried out.

"Teddy you got any lights out here?" Sonny demanded loudly.

"I... yes. I... I'll go turn them on. Rob you okay?" Teddy called before going.

"I think so. I'll let you know as soon as I take inventory."

By the time Teddy had turned on the row of low-voltage lights that rimmed the patio and, for good measure, every light in the house with the drapes pulled open wide, Sonny had used his cell phone to call for an ambulance. Rob and Heitzer had managed to pull Pete from the trench. They'd left him lying on the garden path, his head pillowed on a pile of dirt, and climbed back to the patio level.

"Now will you two tell me just what in the hell went on here?" Sonny bellowed.

"He arrived about an hour-and-half ago. Came up the street, no lights, and parked in the drive over there," Heitzer said indicating the general direction of the Benson's. "That's when I called you, just like we'd arranged. You told me..."

"I know what I told you, Heitzer, to watch him and keep me advised. I'm sitting out there expecting you to tell me he's following Rob, or that he didn't, so's I could come in and help with the arrest. I seen Rob turn onto the highway and no one followed, then I seen him pass back by me on his way to the State Park. You said our watcher there, was just sitting, not doing much of anything. I was on my way here, next thing I know all hell's busted loose."

"That's what I'm trying to say, Sir. He didn't follow Rob right off but before you could get here he comes back out of the little path - headed toward his car I think - anyhow I thought I'd better stop him. Only he didn't halt, he ran back into the vacant lot. So I fired a warning shot and I ran after him. He kept running, crashing around all over the place."

"How'd you get in the middle of this?" Sonny asked, turning to Rob.

"I was coming back up through the Benson's garden when I heard the first shot. By the time I got up to the deck Heitzer had fired again and I could hear them both out there in the dark."

"So you just waded in after them?" Sonny asked, shaking his head.

"Well, yes," Rob answered a little sheepish.

"Heitzer, if it was anyone else,... but I expected more of you." Sonny was still shaking his head.

Teddy suspected if there had been more light they would have been able to see Heitzer blushing. As it was his shoulders drooped and he was biting his lip.

Pete, all but forgotten on his dirt bed, moaned loudly. "Doesn't anybody care that my leg is broken."

CHAPTER 29

The ambulance was the last to arrive. Furst and Anna had hobbled down the street. A round dozen partiers, wine glasses in hand, poured out of the rental, even Sid had arrived and was taking pictures with great glee. Sonny called for backup - for crowd control. The entire night shift, one car, two men, had arrived, siren going full blast just ahead of the neon-lime-and-blue emergency vehicle.

The two sheriff's deputies pulled their guns and rushed down the slope scattering wide-eyed vacationers in every direction.

"Put those guns away!" Sonny ordered. "The suspect ain't going nowhere. Just move this crowd back up to the road and give us a little space down here." Teddy's little patio wasn't really filled, but Anna, Furst, and the pushier of the rental people were standing at the edges peering curiously down into the dark at Pete. Sid had managed to edge his way down the far path and was busy documenting Pete's predicament from every angle, the flashes as his camera clicked away giving the scene even more of a party atmosphere.

"Damn it Sid, get that thing out of my prisoner's face," Sonny yelled. "Pete you don't go talking to him, hear me. You do your talking to me right after Heitzer here reads you your rights."

Sid knew his rights, as far as he was concerned, as a member of the press, his right to get his story exceeded any other right set forth in the constitution. He sidled closer to Pete.

"Why'd you do it, Pete?" Sid asked.

Teddy had brought a blanket to cover Pete against the onset of shock from the broken leg. Now he grasped the edges and pulled it up over his face. Sid took another picture.

"Why did he do it?" Teddy asked softly, having another of her conversations with Rob's shirt pocket as she stood close against him for warmth as well as comfort. She had brought out the blanket for Pete but not gotten her jacket. The sky was clear, starlight supplementing the lights that blazed from the house and the patio, but it was getting cold.

"He's an investor but," Rob sounded as befuddled by the turn of events as Teddy felt. They stood back next to the house out of the east wind that whistled coldly down from the road.

Sonny and Heitzer stood at the top of the path, their backs to the wind and the crowd, deep in quiet conversation. Sonny would lift his head occasionally to shout at Sid or a member of the crowd that was edging too close. Heitzer would nod ever now and then. Finally he climbed the hill to the patrol car.

By the time the medics had Pete ready to transport, Anna and Furst, the rental people, everyone but Sid, had been shooed up to the road. The party atmosphere remained; someone from the rental had gone back for the wine and brought back extra glasses.

The medics fastened Pete into the basket-like stretcher and were bringing him across the patio when he turned his head and spied Teddy and Rob clinging together.

"You shouldn't have let him kiss you, not right in front of me like that. It wasn't right. You have to tell him he doesn't have to come see you anymore. I'll take care of you." He may have said more but the attendants had kept walking and Pete's voice was lost as they climbed the hill to the waiting ambulance.

Sid snapped a picture of the back of the medic's head and then swung and blinded Rob and Teddy with a close-up shot.

"Damn it Sid get off my property," Teddy raged, feeling the stress of the evening, of everything that had happened since she had accepted the offer of the used cover for her septic tank, shredding her composure.

"Now!" Rob added as Sid had adjusted his camera to take one more shot.

"Sid, the lady has asked you to leave. Do it now or I arrest you for trespass, I mean it," Sonny said with menace.

"Just going. Just going," Sid smiled still gleeful. This was, after all, not just great local news, he could see his pictures in papers all over the state maybe even in the nationals.

"Rob, you go get some coffee into her, get her warmed up. I gotta go question my prisoner," Sonny directed, moving up the hill.

"You haven't really arrested him yet, have you?" Teddy asked as she and Rob followed. "I mean you didn't read him his rights or anything yet." Teddy was sure she hadn't missed hearing that.

"I'll take care of that when I know I'm doing it just right. He ain't going nowhere on that leg. By the time they get him in a cast I'll have had me a nice chat with the DA and won't be no mistakes made."

They had reached the porch.

"Sonny, no matter how late, you come back here and tell us why..., what..., you know what I mean," Rob said. "Please."

Sonny just nodded in the affirmative and kept on to his car. The crowd sensing the party was over split in two. The rental people, still all talking at once and laughing, headed back to the right. Anna and Furst stood looking lost and very small and old in the bright cold night. Sonny barked an order in the direction of his back-up officers getting ready to leave, and as Rob closed the door Teddy saw Anna and Furst being offered a ride home.

It was suddenly extraordinarily quiet and Teddy was exhausted. She collapsed into the nearest chair, pulled the jacket that had been hanging on it around her and watched without saying a word as Rob made coffee.

When the pot began to make its comforting sounds Rob turned and Teddy saw for the first time that he had ripped one of the stitches on his head, a trickle of blood flowed down the front of his ear and was drying there.

"You need cleaned up. Sit," she ordered, vacating the chair and going to the bathroom for a wet cloth and the hydrogen peroxide.

"What's with you and that stuff. It stings," Rob lamented.

"It kills the germs," Teddy said, firmly dabbing the blood away.

"Ouch!"

254

"Sit still, I'll be done in just a bit."

By the time Teddy had cleaned and disinfected Rob's head and the new scrapes on his arms and hands, the coffee was ready.

"I'm hungry, got anymore cookies?" Rob asked, delivering the cups to the table.

"Just a package of Oreo's, in the cupboard over the refrigerator. You and Sonny cleaned out all the homemade."

"Oreo's are just fine." Rob got the cookies and then opened the refrigerator door. "I forgot, you like white stuff in your coffee."

"Thanks. It feels good just to hold on to the warm cup. I know it wasn't that cold out there but..." but she was chilled through.

Maybe that was why it all still didn't make sense to her. It was like doing a jigsaw puzzle. Looking the whole time for a particular yellow piece with a red knob to fit a red and yellow space and then discovering when you got down to the very last piece that what you wanted all along was a brown piece with a green knob. Or that the piece was missing altogether. Pete was either a brown piece with a green knob or, he wasn't the killer at all and there was another explanation for everything. But that was silly. He hadn't even bothered to deny it, just babbled some foolish thing about Rob having kissed her.

"You okay?" Rob asked concerned. He was sitting at the table his cup in his hand, staring at her.

"Tired, confused, cold, still." Teddy glanced up at the clock, not even eleven. It felt like it should

255

be nearly morning. "You think Sonny will be back soon?"

"I think I should have told Sonny to see us first thing in the morning, you need some rest. Why don't you go ahead and get to bed and I'll call Sonny."

"No, please, I don't want to be alone now and I do want to know what's going on. I want to know what Pete says when Sonny talks to him. What could he possibly say?"

"Hey, I'm not going anywhere if you don't want me to, why don't we go upstairs, it's warmer up there and we can play cribbage or watch an old movie if there's one on."

"Cribbage. Cribbage is good." Teddy jumped up and got the cards and the cribbage board out of the drawer and headed up the stairs. "You bring the cookies."

It was 1:45am, they had finished two pots of coffee and the bag of Oreos. Teddy was two games up on Rob when Sonny finally called to say he was on his way. They had not talked about Pete and his possible motives. Teddy felt as if she had speculated so much in recent days on the who and why of it that now all she wanted was the facts of the thing. Rob shook his head once as he lay a crib out to count and commented, "It just doesn't add up." The crib added up fine, twelve points. Teddy knew he was referring to Pete and the murders.

Teddy made another pot of coffee, ready for Sonny's arrival then decided that what she really wanted was food. "Anymore coffee and I'll never get to sleep."

"The caffeine bother you?" Rob asked.

"Some, but I was thinking more that I'd have to spend the rest of the night peeing." She took eggs and ham from the refrigerator. "Over medium or scrambled?"

Sonny arrived, without the siren and lights this time. Rob opened the door.

"Got any beer?" Sonny asked without preliminaries, "I am full to the top with coffee. But I wouldn't mind some ham and a couple of those eggs," he added, catching sight of Teddy's activity in the kitchen.

"You talk, I'll cook," Teddy offered, "Rob get the man a beer."

Rob got them all one.

Sonny lowered himself into a chair with a sigh. "I ain't never had such a night, not in a long, long time anyhow. That Pete is crazy as a loon or doing a damn good job of pretending to be. He claims all he was doing, skulking out there in the dark on that stump, was protecting Teddy here from you."

"From me?" Rob looked from one to the other of them in confusion.

"Yep, he told me you'd been paying her unwanted attentions and getting her all mixed up and he was just making sure you behaved yourself 'til such time as she came to her senses."

"Came to my senses and what? And what does that have to do with Ben and Rene's murders?" Teddy put a plate heaped with fried ham, scrambled eggs, and rye toast in front of each of them and went back for her own.

"I kept asking him about Ben and Rene, he kept talking about you and Rob. Like I said, the man is damn crazy or damn clever."

"Let me get this straight. Pete said he didn't kill Ben or run Rene off the road?" Teddy asked.

"He's not saying anything, not about the murders no how," Sonny explained.

"Is it possible he didn't do it?" Rob asked.

"Oh, he did it all right," Sonny answered. "It's the only thing that makes any sense of this mess."

"But why? I mean, why Pete any more than anyone else. Rob, you said he wasn't even a very big investor?" Teddy struggled to understand and couldn't.

"He's not by comparison," Rob said. "But it may be a larger part of his total assets, or maybe he's just been losing it ever since his wife died and no one really noticed. Maybe the possibility of a financial loss was the straw that broke the camel's back. That, and you not giving him a tumble. He hasn't made his interest in you any secret."

"No, but..."

"Ain't no but about it, Teddy. Now it ain't your fault I know, and it ain't your problem no more. Pete's in jail and the rest is up to the DA. You got any more of that ham over there? Another beer wouldn't hurt my feelings none either."

A half hour later, having rehashed the evening and its improbable outcome several times, Sonny and Rob both left. Teddy turned out her lights and collapsed into bed to dream of an army of ski-capped

258

men crashing about in the vacant lot and marching in neat lines to lay like dominoes in trenches. Then Rene was pouring her coffee, strong coffee. She kept promising to tell her a secret, she would go off and pour coffee for Ben and Pete and Rob all seated alone in separate booths and return to promise all over again. There was a crack, loud like the sound of gunfire, and Teddy came awake with a start, not sure if the sound had been part of the dream or real.

What was real was the smell of coffee, strong and burnt!

"DAMN, DAMN, DAMN," Teddy shouted rushing to the kitchen.

She had forgotten about the coffee. It had taken all night for the full pot to cook down to nothing, then it had shattered. Teddy sat down at the table and stared at the bits of glass on the counter.

"DAMN, DAMN, DAMN."

CHAPTER 30

First she had a good cry. Then Teddy took a shower and got dressed. She would go to town for breakfast, well lunch almost, she decided. The crowd at Petal's would be thinned considerably by the time she got there. No time like the present to face whoever was there and see what the gossips were making of things.

She opened her front door carefully, fully expecting to see a yard full of gawkers, Mom and Dad back with the camera for a shot of the empty leach line. Nobody! There wasn't a soul in sight, well, that was better. Teddy relaxed a little and began to feel that life might return to normal after all.

A female voice on the car radio had just finished complaining "Did I Shave My Legs For That?" when Teddy turned onto the highway. Next was the local news.

"Peter Mettler, a suspect in the murder of local Realtor and landlord Ben Raymond, was arrested last night at the home of Teddy Stanley, on Arlington Drive. Ben Raymond's body, for those of you who didn't know, was found in Ms. Stanley's septic tank a couple of weeks back. Sheriff Sonny Hubbard says a second charge of murder - that of a local waitress run off the road under suspicious circumstances - may be filed this afternoon. A two-car accident resulted in two injuries and a long wait for those in the northbound lane of the bridge this morning."

Teddy switched stations. "Rene, she had a name, Rene Pullman, she shouldn't be treated like a footnote."

"Sheriff Hubbard says Teddy Stanley was not arrested at this time. The sheriff indicated there was no evidence to show Ms. Stanley was involved in the slayings. Well, I don't know about you folks but I'd say hiding a body in your septic tank was involvement. Call in and let's hear what you think."

Teddy turned the radio off. "That Crandall Belker has a big, stupid mouth and an empty head, twisting the truth that way." She could feel the anger rising in her. Then she smiled. Rene had always said that man would say, or do, anything to keep his ratings up, said someday someone would shoot him. Maybe she should call in and offer him the next vacancy in her septic tank.

Billy raised his spatula in salute when she entered Petal's. There were two regulars at the counter, neither one looked up from their coffee, but then neither of them could see or hear well enough to read a paper or listen to the radio. Retired the two of them always came in late, ate breakfast and drank coffee for close to three hours most every morning in veritable silence, walking the four blocks to the Elks in time for the card room to open where they spent the afternoon, still in silence, playing rummy. Alice, in the middle of delivering three plates piled with pancakes, sausage, and eggs to a table of tourist types, nodded at Teddy with questions all over her round face. Well, the morning talk had been hot if they'd got Alice's interest. Teddy slipped into a booth three-quarters of the way to the back wall, facing the front. There wasn't anyway of evading the questions that would be asked but at least she would be able to see them coming at her.

But Alice was the only one who said a word and that only to speculate that Teddy was probably glad it was over and an arrest made. It was the lull between the regulars who ate early and the tourists who tended to sleep in so that breakfast became brunch. Teddy indulged herself with sausage and French toast and cleaned her plate, surprised that she could be hungry after her late night meal.

Deciding not to push her luck, Teddy skipped the post office and returned home. The answering machine was blinking. Her heart thudded for a moment. "Dummy, it's probably Rob, or Sonny, or one of the girls." Teddy's scolding stopped cold as the machine beeped and rewound. There was no message! "Easy, it's just someone who didn't leave a message, it doesn't have to be connected to the other calls," Teddy reminded the kitchen. But it left a little chill in the pit of her stomach.

She called her daughters and brought them up to date, giving them the light and laughable version of the prior evening's events, then she put on her grubbies and went back to work on the leach lines.

Toward afternoon traffic up on the road picked up. Mostly cars driving real slow. Where the body was found must be more exciting than where the killer was captured, Teddy decided. By four she was done, completely, with readying the trenches for the gravel. She went in and took a quick second shower, fixed herself half a cheese-and-pickle sandwich, opened a beer and made cookies.

Baking was soothing, productive, and self-indulgent all at the same time. Twice, in passing, Teddy had eyed the answering machine daring it to parent more upsetting calls. It had stared back mute, unblinking. The house took on the kind of smell that had lured Hansel and Gretel. There were oatmeal-cranberry-walnut cookies cooling on sheets of wax paper spread over newspaper on the table, lemony sugar cookies in the oven, and two pans of molasses bars waiting their turn. All the batter made, Teddy stood at the living room window watching the sun edge its way into the sea, waiting for that final second when it dropped like a coin through a slot. The air in the garden below her hung in a gold cloud and a gold satin welcome mat spread across the wet sand to the water's edge. Downstairs the timer ticked, standing sentry over the oven, ready to summon her at the appropriate time. It seemed the first truly peaceful time in days but in the back corner of her mind were a pile of unanswered questions. Slowly she began to pull them out and line them up, sure she wasn't going to like the conclusion they would insist on.

A greasy-spoon waitress, lost off the side of the road might just be part of the background in the murder of one of the community's good ole' boys but it mattered to Teddy. And for the life of her she couldn't imagine what Rene could have heard that would have made Pete so afraid that he needed to kill her. If Rene had heard something, then who had Pete been talking to? Where did they fit in this crazy picture? It was true that Pete had the requisite green pickup. Did the paint match? Even if you accepted that Pete had gotten so upset over the lack of performance of the projects and killed Ben, maybe accidentally - the coroner did say he fell as opposed to being hit - why hide him in her septic tank? Just to escape discovery? Could be, however, there were so many other simpler ways to have handled it. Big as Pete was, it had to have been a horrific job, digging up the daisies, hefting Ben down the hill and putting the daisies back, and that motion light would have been going on and off. Had Sonny ever talked to the renters that were next door that night? Who had moved the seat in Ben's truck? Why, oh why, would Pete have wanted to burn Ben's house with her in it?

The truth was she could fix answers of a sort to every question if she tried, but most of the answers took a real stretch to accept.

Teddy baked cookies, mindlessly filling the sheets and putting batch after batch in the oven, batch after batch out to cool. By the time the two pans of bar cookies were baking, the oatmeal cookies were tucked away safe in the cookie jar. The timer had almost twenty minutes to go and it was full dark outside. Teddy was no more convinced in her mind that Pete was the killer than she had been when she started. But if he weren't, why the odd behavior?

The phone rang and caused her to jump. She went and stood beside it while it rang a second and third times. Her knuckles were white on the back of the chair she was gripping by the fourth ring. The machine picked up and she listened to her own voice asking for the caller to leave a name and number.

"Teddy! Where are you?" Rob's anxious voice demanded.

"Right here," Teddy said, having grabbed up the receiver. "I had another of those calls, at least it was another hang up. It might not be connected. Rob I don't feel like it's all over. Does that sound crazy?"

"It's all been pretty weird, it's going to take a while to digest it all and have it make any kind of sense. The big one I can't answer is why, if Pete is so crazy over you, he tried to burn us both out at Ben's. Listen, I just called to see if you were all right, and ask a little favor. After I got the boys all sat down and laid out the rules this morning I told them I'd want to be using the little dirt mover one day next week. They hemmed and hawed and then Jamie reminded me that the trailer it rides on has a weird hitch Ben had made up. The only way to use it is with Ben's old pickup. Would you mind going out there with me Monday morning to pick it up?"

"To get that rock moved, anything. But tell me how did your little showdown go. Didn't they put up any kind of a fight?"

"It was sort of a dull thud. They looked grim when they came in, and I thought Dave was going to get into his rut about not having been paid again. I was all prepared to promise him I would see to it that he got everything Ben owed him but he didn't even open his mouth except to try and talk me out of using the dirt mover. Keith kept saying 'of course, of course,' when I explained about the audit and that there would be some adjustment of the accounts payable. Jamie mumbled and shook his head in the affirmative every time Keith said it, and Dave just sat there with clenched fists. It was eerie. I was all prepared for this big battle. I mean Ben was ripping them off, too." Rob laughed nervously, "you know Teddy, they didn't even ask me about last night. Listen I've got a slew of things I've got to get done in the office, I probably won't see you until Monday morning. I'll pick you about eight, okay?"

"Come at 7:30 and I'll fix you breakfast," she offered.

"It's a deal. Hey, don't let all the nonsense on the radio get to you."

"No problem. I'm saving my real irritation for the paper when it comes out. Sid seems to go in for bad pictures and tabloid-type headlines."

Teddy went to bed early and slept badly. In the morning she skipped the shower, mindful that the two yesterday had put a lot of water into the septic tank, pumped or not. If it was going to be Tuesday, maybe Wednesday, before she had the leach field reconnected and recovered she had better start conserving.

CHAPTER 31

Sunday morning turned out postcard perfect. Teddy inspected her garden and the leach-line trenches, coffee cup in hand. They would deliver the pipe and fittings tomorrow sometime. She plotted the needed moves; gravel in the bottom of the trenches, pipe joined and in place, gravel over the pipe, a run of tar paper over the gravel and dirt back on top. Broken down into steps it was, bit by bit, all something she could handle, particularly if Rob brought the dirt mover to help with the gravel. She could, of course, do it with the wheelbarrow but it would take so much longer, not to mention ache so much!

Her walk around the yard showed her that while she had been occupied with murder mysteries the weeds had not been idle, pushing up in flowerbed and path alike. At the bottom of the hill the daffodil bed's population of little green spikes had quadrupled, many of them six-to-eight-inches high, now with tight yellow buds waiting for just the right warm day to burst forth. Wild grasses and dandelion made the beds look messy and Teddy decided the daffodils would be the priority today. Plans made, she climbed the hill to the house for a second cup of coffee and some breakfast.

While she was eating she saw the people from the rental walk past slowly, talking and pointing. "So glad we could provide a little excitement for you to tell the folks back home about," Teddy observed, though of course they couldn't hear. When she cleared the table she picked up two petals that had fallen from the now fully opened roses. A closer looked convinced Teddy it was time to dump them. An icy chill ran down her spine. Pete sent the roses, she'd bet anything. Pete put the roses on her steps and the orchid. Pete sat on the stump watching her door. That added up, Pete who couldn't be convinced that she wasn't interested in him. Pete the pest, the persistent wooer, impossible to discourage. It had been annoying. When, how, had it turned murderous? That still didn't add up. If Pete was going to start killing people shouldn't it have been her or Rob? The dark thoughts were interrupted by the arrival of a car. An oddly familiar couple got out. "Mom and Dad!" Teddy exclaimed recognizing them. Dad had his camera slung around his neck and was busily snapping pictures of the front of the house. Teddy stepped back out of the line of sight and crossed her fingers. "Don't knock on my door," she whispered. "Take your pictures and go away." She stood still waiting, not daring to peek out the window.

There was the sound of feet on the steps and then three loud raps on the door.

"Hey, Teddy, you in there?" Dad called out.

"She's probably down in the garden. Come on I want to see where they got him," Mom said.

Teddy seethed. She was being held hostage in her own home by a couple of nosy, rude, self-important senior citizens. Trespassers! That's what they were. For a second she considered calling Sonny but it seemed a bit extreme. However, she could have a little backbone and tell them to get out, she decided, reaching for the doorknob.

When she got down to the patio and could see them below her in the garden she was flabbergasted. Mom was down in the trench, stretched out where Pete had lain with Dad standing at the other end prepared to take her picture. How could they have known? The local paper wasn't due out until Tuesday. Dad stepped closer to the edge to improve his shot and collapsed the edge of the trench.

"Get out of there and get out of my yard. Do you know how much work it was getting those trenches dug? You're trespassing. If you don't leave at once I'm going to call the sheriff!"

Dad looked up in surprise and slid into the ditch the rest of the way, sitting down with a plop, which jarred his hand and set the camera off with a flash. Mom sat up, indignation all over her face.

"Now you've ruined his shot, you shouldn't sneak up on people like that. Do it over Hon," Mom whined.

Dad attempted to rise but found himself stuck, his ample girth securely wedged in the trench, his struggle to rise loosening more dirt from the edges to slide in around him fixing him even more firmly in place.

"Oh my God, he's being buried alive. Do something. Do something!" Mom screamed, panicked. She scrambled to her feet and attempted, without success, to climb out of the trench. The more she tried the more dirt slid down from the edges. The woman began to scream in short grunt-like gasps that were punctuated with a high-pitched plea for "Help!" from Dad.

Teddy frankly felt more like laughing than helping, try as hard as she could, she could not stop the giggles of outright glee.

Mom's screams escalated and a bevy of renters returning from their walk rushed around the house to the patio to see what was going on.

It took several minutes for two of the men to tug Dad to his feet and the three of them almost landed back in the ditch before they got him completely out. The young man who had given Mom a hand was rewarded by Mom clinging to him desperately, sobbing her thanks.

Teddy went to get her shovel from the basement, laughing and angry all at the same time.

It was lunchtime before she'd restored the trench. When she went in to clean up, the lights were blinking on the answering machine. Heart in her throat she pushed the button.

"Hi Mom, some wild picture of you and Rob in the morning paper, glad they caught the guy. What was he doing in the hole? Call me," Teddy's youngest daughter chirped.

A second call was from the Portland paper wanting an interview. The third was her eldest child demanding to be called ASAP.

Teddy called her daughters and learned that the daily papers had printed several of Ben's pictures, predominately the one of Pete in the trench but at least one had used a shot of Teddy clinging to Rob. It did explain Mom and Dad's visit.

After lunch Teddy kept her head down over the daffodils and ignored the assorted rubber-neckers that drove by slowly up on the road. Few bothered to get out of their cars and that suited her just fine. Twice the phone rang, she heard it faint behind the "beach music" coming from the radio. She ignored that, too.

About four-thirty she heard Furst's familiar voice calling to her from the patio.

"Hey, Teddy, give those weeds a rest."

"Hi, Furst," Teddy called back, feeling an achy twinge in her back as she straightened up. Her short-handled weeder still clutched in her hand she climbed up to visit. "All the traffic bothering you?"

"We do seem to be getting more cars down the street than normal. One, this morning, circled three times while Anna and I were eating our breakfast. Guess all that will die off now that Sonny's made an arrest. Sure didn't imagine it to be Pete though."

"I'm still having a hard time believing it," Teddy motioned Furst to a seat at the picnic table and sat down herself. "I certainly didn't understand how twisted his feelings for me were. I thought it was, you know, just a lot of flirting and teasing. He kept asking me out and I kept turning him down."

"Well, I guess Anna and I owe you an apology there. We been seeing Pete coming and going quite a bit lately, several weeks anyhow, starting back before you found Ben Raymond in the septic tank even. We kind of assumed you and him was getting serious. Seemed logical." Furst did not point out that Pete was more her age than Rob and that Anna had felt him eminently more suitable for Teddy to be seeing, though Anna hadn't thought Teddy was good enough for Pete either. "I'll bet you're glad to get things all wrapped up."

"Sure," Teddy answered, sure as she said it that it wasn't really over. Not until all the pieces fit a whole lot better than they did at the moment. "Furst you saw Pete the other night, you feel sure he's the one killed Ben?"

Furst considered solemnly before answering. "I guess if I had to say absolutely, like on a jury, I'd have me a few questions. I expect Sonny and the District Attorney must have got the answers to their questions satisfied and we'll hear it all in time. They don't tell the public everything - save it for the trial - that kind of thing. Thing is, I do wonder why'd he put Ben in your tank. I mean, feeling like he does about you, you'd think he'd a kept the body and all this mess as far from you as possible. What I read about that fire up to Ben's place don't make much sense either. I'd have wanted all those records to be found if I were him, to be able to prove Ben was stealing from his investors, maybe get my money back. What good did it do to burn up all the evidence of Ben's dirty dealings? And, 'cept maybe being jealous over you," Furst winked at her softening the implication, "I can't think what he was doing trying to burn you and Rob up with the house."

"Exactly," Teddy nodded her agreement. "The problem is, I can't come up with any other answer, either. If Pete didn't kill Ben, who did? Say Pete was obsessed about me, stalking me. That would explain a lot of what he's done. The things we know about. Watching the house, even the flowers that have been showing up on my steps. That's all weird, but I can see all that. It's when I try to connect Pete to Ben and Rene's deaths that it seems too much to swallow."

"From what's being said I'd still say more than a few around here had reason to wish Ben dead, including me and Anna. Could be we ain't ever going to know for sure why Pete done it. Could be he's just gone round the bend and it don't make no sense because he don't make sense any more," Furst speculated.

"Emmhuh. I guess," Teddy nodded in agreement, wanting to accept the notion. Accepting that Pete was out of his mind and therefore acting irrationally made it easier to accept the inconsistencies in the events of the last several weeks. But it did not lie comfortably on her mind.

When Teddy went in to clean up, she was relieved to find that both callers had left messages. Not that she was going to call either TV station back, but it was nice to know for sure just who it was you were ignoring. The ache in her back screamed for a soak in the hot tub but Teddy could not bring herself to venture out into the encroaching dusk alone. She settled for a quick hot shower. Snugged into her old chenille robe, first she mixed a double batch of German pancake batter for the morning then she warmed some soup and made cheese toast and took a tray up to the living room to see what was on in the way of old movies. Surfing the channels, she rejected the made-for-television murder, lust, and mayhem, and narrowed it to a ridiculously young and skinny Elvis Presley in "Love Me Tender" (murder, lust, and mayhem of the western variety) versus an equally young, but unarguably better fit, Sean Connery in "Goldfinger" (murder, lust, and mayhem made for the big screen). The Bond film was just starting and the TV guide promised a second early Bond film to follow. Sean Connery's suave smile won out. Somewhere in the middle of the second film Teddy roused herself from a dream where Mom lay nude and golden in the leach trench while Sean Connery stood casually at the other end in his Saville Row suit, sipping a martini, Dad's camera around his neck. Teddy turned off the television and headed for bed, stopping at the top of the stairs to gaze out her north window in the direction of the vacant lot. A gust of wind rattled through the treetops, and a low mist spun among the dark branches with a diamond glimmer of stars visible in snatches. She sighed deeply, uneasy still, and continued down.

The pounding of the changing tide woke her in the early hours from a disturbing chase through long halls whose doors opened onto burning rooms or impenetrable walls of scrub pine, berry vine, and salal. Pieces of paper covered in columns of figures and money, bills of every denomination, floated teasingly in front of her leading her on. Teddy had reached out to grasp a long, number-filled sheet that hovered just out of reach when the walls around her began to come crashing down. Slowly she reached up through her sleep and the halls, the swirling cash, and financial records faded, the familiar sound of the heavy surf asserting its claim on the shore worked its magic and having first woke her from her nightmare, proceeded to lull her back into peaceful sleep.

CHAPTER 32

Monday Teddy was up early. By the time Rob arrived for breakfast she had made the bed, vacuumed the house, cleaned the bathroom, dusted, and dug out a jar of the huckleberry syrup she'd made last summer. The bacon was crisp, the coffee was hot and the stack of thin, eggy pancakes growing steadily when he scrunched to a stop on the road.

"Good morning," Teddy called up to him. "My you look," well there was no other way to say it, "you look sort of green." The bruising on his cheek and forehead had passed through the purple-blue phase and entered the puce-yellowy-green.

"Good morning, you look nice yourself. What smells so good?"

"Huckleberry syrup, I'm heating it. How was your weekend?"

"Lost. I spent the last two days trying to get reorganized. Every time I thought I had things all lined out so I could handle it in an orderly fashion some little bomb exploded."

"Oh," Teddy said, and waited, sure an explanation would be forthcoming.

Rob took the coffee cup she offered and sat down. "I signed a whole stack of checks, bills for materials from the lumber yard, hardware store, that kind of thing. Teddy, I made a point of identifying which job and so on for every screw of it. Then Keith stops by with a bill for materials he says he's already paid for, wanting reimbursed. Some of it the exact same things! And boy did he hem and haw when I asked him about it. Claimed he must have picked up the wrong invoice, grabbed it back out of my hand and took off. I mean, maybe he did just get it confused. Pretty soon here came Dave back on his, "I haven't been paid kick," claiming to have forked out in advance for the materials out at Harbor Court instead of charging them to the account. And I've been trying to chase down some pipe. The plumbing stuff supposedly already in the ground inside the foundation forms - they are supposed to pour cement Thursday - Harry wanted to know the other day why it looked like we were building twice as many units as we had permits for. Said he counted the plumbing pieces the afternoon they were delivered and it was at least twice as many as were needed for those sixteen units. Dave says he's crazy, it was just the right amount and it's all ready to go. Jamie called in this morning, says he still needs half of it to be delivered or he can't finish up in time. Tried to tell me it wasn't ordered, then when I told him I had the bill for all of it in my hand, said it must have been stolen from the site. Teddy, I can hardly wait for Sonny to get those records back to me. I spoke to Ken and he confirmed my numbers, the ones from the office computer were pure fabrication. I have to tie down all the loose ends and figure out exactly how Ben was doing it. If I'm going to avoid a nasty lawsuit against Ben's trust I'm going to have to get a handle on the problem and get the investors together and explain what happened and how it's going to be fixed."

"Wow! You have got a mess going. And it doesn't sound like any quick answers." Teddy set a plate in front of him. "It's going to take as long as it takes, you know. Don't let it get to you."

"MmMhuh," Rob answered, his mouth full.

"Rob, do you really believe Pete killed Ben and Rene?"

Rob swallowed and sighed. "Teddy, I honestly don't know? It seems so improbable. But then what is probable about murder. I mean I never would've thought of Pete as someone to go off the deep end over a woman either. Even you," he said with a bit of a smile and a raise of an eyebrow.

"Gee, thanks. But even if I can accept that he was irrationally fond of me, to the point of becoming a stalker, still, killing Ben - that's a whole different thing. And killing Rene! None of it makes sense."

"So you think there is still a killer out there then. That Pete's watching us from the vacant lot only had to do with his fascination for you?"

Teddy nodded, "I don't mean to sound vain, but I think so." She went on to explain about Furst and Anna having seen Pete's car often.

"But that could be because he had planned to put Ben in your septic tank all along," Rob reasoned between mouthfuls.

"Nobody, not even I, knew I was going to have that tank pumped. No, I think he was watching me - you and me together," she shuddered, "creepy feeling."

"You think the man is crazy enough to be a stalker, irrational in his feelings for you. But not irrational enough to be a killer?"

"Not a killer over what you tell me was a rather small investment."

"Ten thousand dollars. One of the three smallest investors," Rob supplied. "Frankly I want to believe Pete is the murderer and that this nastiness is about to begin to unravel itself. I have every intention of sorting out Ben's mess, reimbursing every dime he stole from whoever he stole it from, even if I have to liquidate his entire trust to do it. I called the lawyer at home Saturday, we're going to meet Wednesday morning and get to work on it. Now, no more speculation. Let's go for a nice ride in the country and forget our problems for a bit. Okay?" Rob took her hand and gave it a gentle squeeze.

"Okay." Teddy smiled back.

It was a beautiful day. The second week in March blowing in crisp and clear, sweeping the blustery gray of winter off to the horizon where it hung in the form of a thin dark line above a sapphire sea. To the east, over the tiers of ridges stepping up to the peaks of the coastal range, the sky was decorated with gauzy clouds in a big hurry to get somewhere. Rob was in no hurry at all, he drove at a leisurely pace through town, slowing even more to wave at Kevin and Harry going into Petal's and did not accelerate all that much once they'd passed beyond the city limits. Teddy was amazed at how much more budded out or even in bloom the trees and shrubs were along the sheltered corridor of the river since their last trip up to Ben's.

"If I couldn't live by the sea, the river would be nice. Look at that dogwood peeking out between the spruce." Teddy's own little dogwood tree was still clutching tight to its tiny buds.

In front of them, a monster of a motorhome swayed its way along the snaky road at a good ten-miles-per-hour below the speed limit. There were few places legal for passing, and several miles yet to the first turn out where a polite driver of a slower vehicle would pull off and let faster traffic past. (It was Teddy's experience that few motorhome drivers were that thoughtful. Many seemed to think if they weren't in a hurry you shouldn't be either and held the road by dent of their size.) Behind them another behemoth cruised close on their bumper, dwarfing Rob's green pickup.

Teddy noticed Rob was watching his rearview mirror nervously. Checking the mirror on her side she could see that there were really two motorhomes behind them and then an ancient red car, badly rusted and in places actually taped with what looked like duct tape. Behind that was a green pickup, older than Rob's, and apparently in a hurry. As they rounded a sharp curve she could see the driver pull it close up to the red car's bumper and left into the oncoming lane. There was a double yellow line, but he was obviously one of those that took it as a suggestion, not an absolute. Repeatedly the green pickup danced out into the oncoming lane, pulling back when it was found to be occupied. Teddy could not take her eyes from the mirror as the pickup apparently found the space it had been seeking and accelerated, passing the red car and disappearing behind the motorhomes as the road swung them back in the opposite direction.

"Ooohhh..." she whispered bracing herself as Rob pulled the car far right and laid on his horn. The pickup had pulled round both of the motorhomes and begun to slide into the space that Rob's pickup already occupied. In the oncoming lane a giant brown pickup/cab-over camper barreled downhill, hugging the right edge of his narrow lane. A steep bank rose high on his right leaving him nowhere to go, somehow he squeaked by the two green pickups. Rob was concentrating on staying on the road, one wheel in the ribbon of gravel that trimmed the pavement before the earth dropped away for a fern-and-berry-covered plunge to the river. Teddy leaned forward trying to see the driver of the other pickup but without ever hitting his brakes the pickup driver shot into the opening left by the passage of the camper and whooshed around the motorhome ahead of them.

"Man I hope his wife has him well insured!" Rob said, recentering his pickup in his lane.

"Are you kidding, that kind doesn't get killed. They just go about forcing others off the road and afterwards sit in the bar talking about what a great driver they are and how they just missed being involved in the accident they caused."

The motorhome ahead did pull right into the wide spot designed for that purpose and Rob waved his appreciation as they passed. Several minutes later they came to the place, no longer marked except in Teddy's memory, where Rene had gone into the river.

"Rob, do you think Rene's death could have been an accident after all? Maybe that same idiot even."

"Did you notice the red plastic cover on the tool box in the back of that pickup? I think the idiot was Dave. He's the only one I know with that red-topped box. His wife gave it to him last Christmas."

"Dave? Where do you suppose he's going in such a hurry? He doesn't live up this way."

Rob didn't answer right away, concentrating on making the left turn into the woods. Three cars and a water district truck passed, headed for town before the oncoming lane was clear. Rob swung the pickup across the lane and into the graveled road. Soon they were moving slowly under the canopy of trees, bright glints of blue teasing through, along with an errant sunbeam or two to dapple the road. In the short time since their last visit the deciduous trees dotted among the evergreens had begun to leaf out and bright flags of new green waved them on.

When they rounded into the clearing where before they could have seen the house, the empty space marked by a jumble of blackened rubble and the ruins of a garden brought back flashes of that frightening afternoon. Teddy raised a hand to her chest, sucking in a deep breath.

Rob turned sharply off the drive on to the track that led back to the little guesthouse in its private glade.

The faded denim blue pickup stood like a faithful horse right where it had been left.

"I had some people in the office a couple of weeks back looking for a place just like this to retire in. I think I'll give them a call. This bit could be split off easy enough, say three acres and access. It's a shame for it to go to pieces from lack of care," Rob said, eyeing the cozy log cottage with the golden mass of daffodils in full bloom beside the deck. "I brought some gas, that gauge has been broken forever."

The wild grasses in the open space were lush green, knee deep, and dotted with a small purple wildflower Teddy could not name. She climbed down from the pickup to examine them while Rob emptied a red container of gas into the elderly vehicle.

"Better follow me. Just in case. We'll go out to Harbor Court and get the dirt mover and take it back to your place. You mind having this parked at your place for a few days?"

"No problem, I've always thought it was a kind of nifty old darling of a truck. What you going to do with it?" Teddy asked.

"Don't know, think I might keep it. Buy it from the trust maybe."

"Mmmh. Just what everybody needs, two pickups."

"It's got some good memories for me, of Ben and the good times, the good things." Rob put the lid back on the gas container and put it back in the bed of the green pickup. "Ready?"

Teddy followed Rob, driving his green rig across the grassy track and back to the driveway trying not to let memories of the last time spoil the beauties of the place and day. Twice going down to the highway she readjusted the seat, having first not slid it up enough and then found herself too close so that her knees were hitting the dash. She managed at last to find the right spot just as Rob slowed in front of her in preparation for the turn onto the highway. Teddy had the clutch in, a foot on the brake, one hand on the wheel, and the other on the seat release when she came to a full stop in order to click the seat into position. Rob turned and, before she could change gears and follow, an enormous bronze motorhome towing a matching luxury sedan filled the space behind him. Cautiously Teddy followed after. She flipped on the radio and for several minutes drove, content to speculate at the lifestyle one lived traveling the country in a mobile upscale mansion-come gas guzzler and listened to Doris Day lament "I said my pajamas," followed by Perry Como vowing "I'm not sick I'm just in love." She noted the antenna dish on the motorhome's roof and the TV camera mounted above the wide back window. A bumper sticker proclaimed, "Smile you're on Candid Camera," Teddy smiled and offered a small wave.

Out of the corner of her eye she caught sight of a green pickup in her side mirror. Already in the oncoming lane, it barreled past her and the bronze vehicles in front of her giving her only seconds to identify the red-lidded tool kit in the back. The bronze sedan swung wildly on its moorings as the motorhome's driver hit his brakes. Teddy hit her brakes, too, managing not to rear end the rapidly slowing and swerving duo. Somewhere beyond the bronze motorhome, Teddy heard horns blasting, one seemed older, less electronic somehow, and she knew that was Rob. There was also a squealing and screeching sound. Teddy slowed more despite the fact that the motorhome had resumed its forward speed. She checked her rearview mirror, then, watching cautiously for oncoming traffic, slid out a few feet into the oncoming lane in an effort to see around the motorhome. The curviness of the road twice offered her flashes of green ahead and once of powdery blue. Teddy grasped the steering wheel firmly and concentrated her attention on what snatches she could get of the activity on the road ahead of the motorhome. Her heart leaped when she saw, through the trees across a hairpin turn, the blue pickup and the green one side by side hurtling downhill, and around the next bend a cloud of dust rising as Rob's right-hand-side tires churned up gravel at the edge of the pavement.

"It might have been the same idiot who killed Rene, but it sure wasn't any accident," Teddy decided aloud. Now her eyes swept not only the road ahead of the motorhome but the verge, afraid of what she might see. It was with relief, when on another switchback, she spotted both pickups still nearly parallel. The relief was quickly superseded by a scream when a large economy-sized U-Haul van, coming from town, squeezed the pickups both into one lane just as they rounded once more out of sight.

Two more sweeping curves passed and Teddy failed to catch sight of either pickup. Her heart pounding, her knuckles white from gripping the wheel, Teddy checked the rearview mirror giving serious consideration to a little illegal passing of her own. A near steady stream of oncoming cars forced her to reconsider.

Down at last, to the gentler, wider curves near town, almost level with the river as it widened, getting ready to meet the sea, Teddy spotted Ben's pickup directly ahead of the motorhome. The green one was no longer anywhere in sight.

CHAPTER 33

"If you loved me half as much as I love you," Rosemary Clooney's lush voice intoned as they turned into the cul-de-sac that would be Harbor Court Town Homes. Rob came to a dirt-spewing stop behind Dave's green pickup with its tell-tale, red-topped tool box. By the time Teddy halted the new green pickup behind the old blue one, Rob was standing in the middle of the maze of strings and stakes and trenches that marked out the placement of plumbing and foundation forms for the first of the buildings, hands on hips, his green pallor considerably reddened.

"Dave," he yelled, "where the hell are you? And just what in the hell were you up to?"

The "court" terraced down three levels from the top of the cul-de-sac, the lowest level at the bottom of the turn-around so that the townhomes would all enjoy a modest peek at the estuary far below and about a mile away. The property had been cleared back to within fifteen or twenty feet of its edges on all sides so that a fringe of small pines and spruce mixed with salal and berry acted as a visual fence. On the north side a half-dozen mature spruce stood majestic guard over the edge of a ravine that separated the development physically from a six-street grid of ranch-style homes built in the sixties. At the bottom of the ravine was a small creek with a wide flat spot on the near bank where Rob and Ben had hauled in an old picnic table. It had become the "office" for the project, sheltered as it was from wind and rain.

Keith's rig was parked in the middle of the space that would be the last building to go up, the whole site should have been swarming with activity but it was deserted. Almost hidden behind Keith's vehicle was the bright orange mini dirt-mover, a chuggy little hum indicating its engine was running.

Rob turned and started walking toward the break in the vegetation that marked the top of the path into the ravine. "Keith! Dave! Damn it, what's going on?" He broke into a run.

Teddy scrambled from the pickup and started after him.

"Rob, wait for me."

A cool blast of wind off the water caught the door and slammed it, catching the corner of her sweatshirt/jacket. By the time she had opened the door and freed herself, Rob's head and shoulders were just visible as he began to go down the decline.

Teddy took the direct route; over a small stack of gray conduit, across the string barrier, across corner of the yet-to-be-poured foundation, and across a shallow trench with its filler of black pipe. She leapt easily over two more trenches, tripped over a string strung taut between two stakes, pulling one out of the ground, and came to a dead halt at what was the final trench between her and the open ground.

It was like her dream - like Mom and Dad in the trench - like Pete! Only he wasn't painted gold, wasn't yelling, and it appeared to be his head not his leg that was broken. Dave lay at the bottom of the narrow, shallow, ditch, twisted on his side to fit, the entire right side of his head a crumpled bloody mess. Teddy screamed.

It was an amazingly loud scream it seemed to her. And it went on, like a siren. It didn't stop, she couldn't stop it. She stood frozen, screaming, listening to herself scream and trying to distance herself from the screaming so she could take hold and make some sense of what was happening.

"Teddy?" Rob called, "What is it?"

Somewhere at the very back of her mind she heard Rob calling, knew he was coming, but she was unable to pull her eyes from the trench. The body had been partially covered, dirt from the sides of the trenches, maybe. It reminded her of Pete and the blanket. She wondered if Dave would be able to pull his dirt blanket up to cover his face when Sid came to take his picture.

"Teddy what...?" But now Rob could see what and stood across the trench from her, the flush of anger drained out of him. "How? Why? I don't understand."

Rob took a long step across the trench and pulled Teddy to him turning her face to his chest. With a sob Teddy stopped screaming and leaned into him, willing the earth to stop spinning, her stomach to quit its seasick lurching.

"If Dave was driving his pickup just now, trying to shove you into the river, how could this have happened so fast? It doesn't make sense."

"Oh, it will make sense all right by the time I finish explaining to Sonny how Dave discovered it was Rob here all along doing the stealing." Keith stepped out from behind his truck, deer rifle in hand, a single clicking noise signaling that he now had the safety off. He raised the gun as he neared so that it was pointed at Teddy's chest. "I got it all worked out, and this time Teddy isn't going to go mess it up by digging up her damned purple daisies."

"Keith, be reasonable." Teddy still felt seasick, but the world had slowed and the ground felt firmer beneath her. "Rob did not kill Ben, I know he did not kill Ben."

"Sugar, I know he didn't kill Ben, too. Dave did. It was an accident, ole' Dave there had such a short fuse. Ben wanted to retire, wanted to stop the gravy train. Me and Dave and Jamie, we didn't see it that way. But Ben was determined, said this was the last project, the last time, that this time we weren't going to be able to talk him out of it. Then Rob would be running everything. No more double billing, no more little repair jobs for big pay, no more kickbacks. Maybe even no more work, Rob was always talking competitive bid." Keith had come to stand close beside them, he waved the gun toward Dave and then quickly brought it back to bear on Rob and Teddy. "Dave just couldn't control his temper. We was going to talk to Ben, that's all, when he came for poker. Ben brought the digger down that afternoon," the muzzle of the gun waved momentarily in the direction of the little dirt mover. "Dave, he starts in demanding. But Ben wasn't having none of it. Said he was tired, wanted to retire, that he'd made enough money and so had we or at least we'd just have to be satisfied." Keith laughed bitterly, "the old fool, just cause he was tired and had enough, he was going to end it for all of us. I, we, we all had got used to having the sure job, the extra money."

"So you three killed Ben?" Rob asked.

"No, I told you, Dave did, and it wasn't murder. It was an accident. Dave and Ben got to arguing, right here." The end of the gun waved again. "Crew was gone home. No one here but Dave and Ben and Jamie. Ben said no, it was final, this was the last project and he didn't feel like working it like normal, wanted to turn everything over to Rob right away. Rob was going to be in charge, we'd just have to do it his way or not at all. Dave pushed him. Jamie told me Dave just pushed him, you know how he does, with his finger on your chest when he's mad and trying to make his point." Keith's voice was tired, filled with confusion. "Jamie saw it all, Dave is making his point and Ben, he steps back to get away from the finger poking him sort of, and he slips a foot in a hole or something and goes down and hits the back of his head against the machine." The gun waved again toward the little dirt mover. "And he was dead. Just like that. But it was an accident. I believe that."

"Then why'd he end up in my septic tank? Why did..."

"Why didn't you report the accident to Sonny?" Rob interrupted, "And why are you pointing that gun at us now?"

"My wife is a very beautiful and a very expensive woman. She don't like it when she don't have money for her pretties. Dave and Jamie, they came by my place soon as it happened, scared. We came up with this plan. At first we was just going to

290

drive Ben way out, like up to where he goes fishing and set up his camp and just leave him. Make it look like some vagrant maybe came by and did him in. We was going to do it after poker, I mean it would have looked odd if we hadn't been there for poker and all."

"Where was Ben during all this planning?" Teddy forgot all about feeling sick, or even scared, now she was just curious.

"Dave and Jamie'd left him up here. Covered him with the tarp Ben brought to cover the digger. Left his rig here, too."

"The three of you left Ben lying here dead under a tarp and spent the evening with the sheriff playing poker?" Rob asked, incredulous.

"Yep. Kick in the head isn't it? Old Harry had him a fine run of luck that night. But he said something gave us a great idea. Leastways it would have been. I mean putting Ben up in the woods meant we would probably be able to finish out the project, maybe even bamboozle Rob into letting us start up on the Tree Tops condo project Ben had talked about. But when Harry mentioned his kid having pumped your tank - I don't even know how the subject came up. Something to do with the new codes on tanks and leach fields I think, Harry was going on how the old ways were sometimes better. Anyhow, he starts telling us how your old tank didn't really need pumping even after all these years, probably wouldn't need it again for another thirty or more. Well hell, I figured if Ben weren't dead, just disappeared, it'd be a good long time before Rob got full control and in the meantime we could sort of do business as usual and get a little aside."

"But the trust," Rob shook his head. "Ben had already signed it."

"Yeah, well we didn't know that then did we?"

Keith's face was purple. Blood pressure? Anger? Teddy wondered which or both.

"So you guys decided to put Ben in my septic tank."

"Yeah. After the game broke up we came out here, wrapped Ben up in the tarp, loaded him and some shovels in the back of his pickup and drove him out to your place. Didn't take no time to get him in the tank. Boy you should have seen Jamie jump when your motion light come on. Then we came back here, Dave followed me, and we took Ben's pickup back to his place. And it'd worked too, if Harry's boy hadn't gotten the lame-brained idea of getting you that lid. We might not have been able to keep Rob from messin' up the gravy train eventually but nobody'd ever known Ben was anything but missing. It was perfect."

"Not too perfect," Rob said. "You still seem to have some loose ends."

"Not much longer I don't."

The gun waved again and Teddy moved closer to Rob. Keep him talking she thought, keep him talking, maybe Rob will think of something or someone will come by or... The problem was the 'or' list was very short and improbable. "Why did you kill Rene? What threat was she to you?"

"The last time we'd had breakfast with Ben he'd talked some about his fishing trip but mostly about how he was retiring, going to be going fishing all the time. Talked about how Rob would run things different, and we'd argued some. Dave, he didn't always exercise good judgment about what he said, when. Him and me got to worrying about what Rene might have overheard - smart old bird, she might have put two and two together eventually - we was willing to chance it until Ben gets himself found. Then Dave there got to worrying again and waylaid her on her way into work Friday morning. Jamie and I didn't have nothing to do with it, honest."

"Like I suppose you and Jamie didn't have 'nothing' to do with trying to burn us alive up at Ben's?" Rob asked. His arm tight around Teddy, he edged them both back a half step for the second time.

"Records had to go. I'm too old to spend time in jail, and the kind of fraud we done ain't looked on too kindly much anymore. Used to be, you just paid off a building inspector or two, donated to a judge's campaign, got you a good tricky tax man and relied on the good ole' boys to take care of their own. But it don't work like it use to. Too many don't understand. Too many here now from someplace else. Even if they hadn't give us motive for murder them records of Ben's would have put us in jail, sure. We'd been up there a couple of times, weeding out stuff, would have looked odd if everything'd just gone missing, like Ben. Then we ran out of time so we messed up your computers good, busted them all to pieces, don't know how you got together what you took to the auditor. But Ben had ledgers, contracts, plans, receipts all over that house, weren't no other way to be sure we got it all. Getting rid of you was just a bonus, Teddy there, just a part of the package."

"Gee thanks," Teddy muttered.

Rob pulled them back another half step and Teddy felt her heel encounter space. She tried to remember the trenches she'd crossed. Was there a trench behind them? Maybe it was just a soft spot? "Don't you have an awful lot of bodies to explain now?"

"It's just one more mess of Dave's for me to clean up. I been cleaning up after that ole' boy since the day we met. Got tired of it. Fool, taking out after the two of you today was the last straw. We're sitting there eating breakfast and he looks up and sees you waving to Harry and Kevin and he jumps up and is out the door, don't talk it over, nothing. And then he don't do the job. Comes sliding back here whining about how we got to make a run for it, that you was sure to have recognized him and figured it all out. Ain't no place to run to, no money to run with. I'm too old. Jamie and me, we came out here to finish up with the digger 'counta you said you was coming for it. I was sitting there, motor idling, and Dave was ranting on. It just seemed like a good idea. I flicked the lever and bam, the bucket got him a solid one right on the side of his head. Thunked just like that shovel I hit you with in Ben's garage only it did a better job. Dave flew sideways and landed right where you see him, real neat like."

"Where's Jamie?" Teddy asked, curiosity still edging out fear. She could feel Rob's arm, tight and reassuring, around her waist and she had tested her heel over the "empty" space enough to be sure it was

294

the trench. Did Rob know it was there, did he have a plan? "Did you kill him, too?"

Keith grinned. "Teddy, sugar, you do have the damnedest imagination. Jamie's not much one for blood, gets real queasy. He's down to the creek being sick. He'll be along in a bit."

The motor on the idling piece of machinery sputtered and coughed.

"Damn, that thing was damn near empty, going to run out of gas before we finish what we have to get done. Didn't have time to shut it down when I saw you two steaming up the road. You'd been just a little bit longer, ole' Dave could have got all the blame and never been found, not till they tore down these town houses anyways. But now I'll just have to catch you in the act of killing my good friend and do what comes naturally. Ain't no doubt about you two conspiring lately on something. Got lots'a witnesses to that. Few years back they'd a even given me a medal or something. Things have changed some but I'd bet I don't spend a single night in jail." Keith raised the gun. "It's time I got this over."

Three things happened. Rob took one more half-step backward into the waiting ditch carrying Teddy with him, a rock the size of a big man's fist thudded solidly into the back of Keith's head, and the gun went off.

Rob had managed to twist as they fell, landing Teddy in the ditch with himself more or less on top, actually the ditch was neither that deep nor that wide. Harry, with an agility that belied his years, not to mention his girth, came running from the direction of the ravine, pelting additional rocks at a confused and bleeding Keith who dropped the gun and made for the cab of his truck.

Whether or not he had any intentions of making a run for it was academic as Sonny arrived, as usual, a wee bit late for the real action but just in time to bluster and clean up the mess. Risking life, limb, and the suspension of his brand-new car, Sonny bumped up over a small berm and across the recently graded ground to physically lock Keith in a triangle formed by the trenches of the building's unfinished foundation, the dirt mover, and the patrol car.

"Teddy, what is it with you and holes in the ground? Don't you two never wait for the proper authorities before taking action?" Sonny grumbled getting out of the patrol car.

"MMmmmmpht." Teddy replied spitting dirt.

CHAPTER 34

Rob had managed to break his left arm and had a bruised hip to match a blackened left eye.

Teddy had the kind of scrape on her knee she hadn't had since she was seven and learning to roller skate.

Harry, referred to forever after by family members as Harry the Hero, required of his wife, and got, all of his favorite foods for dinner.

Sonny retrieved the still retching Jamie from the creek bank, called for Heitzer to come get the murderers, took pages of new notes, and got his picture taken in time to make the regular edition of the weekly paper. LOCAL SHERIFF SOLVES MURDER/FRAUD CASE Sid promised the headline would read.

At the hospital, Teddy had been explaining the details of Dave Dexter's wild last ride to Sonny when Harry and Kevin arrived.

"The keys were on the floor so we thought we'd bring it on down and see how he was doing," Harry explained, handing over the keys to Ben's pickup. "We left Rob's rig right where she was, couldn't find the keys."

Teddy reached into her pocket, and withdrew the keys and a crumpled torn sheet from a ledger. The piece of paper she had stuffed in her pocket in Ben's basement when the lights went out. Three columns headed with initials, D.D.,K.T., J.M. And lots of numbers. Teddy had no idea what they might mean but it was undoubtedly evidence. Silently she handed it to Sonny.

Sonny accepted the gift, eyed it, smiled, and stuffed it into his notebook.

Rob was getting a cast put on. Teddy, Sonny, Harry, and Kevin retired to a table in the hospital cafeteria for coffee and donuts.

Teddy started again with the saga of the trip to-and-from Ben's. "It's how Dave killed Rene, it just didn't work the second time," she concluded. "What I want to know is how you both managed to show up right when you did. Honestly Harry you were the answer to my prayers."

"Well," Harry grinned, "you know I saw you two going through town this morning. Kevin and I no more get in the door and Dave takes out of there grumbling something about doing it right this time. Kev and I have breakfast and I don't give it another thought until later I'm out in the yard - you know our house backs onto the ravine next to the Harbor Court property. Anyhow I'm out there putting up the wife's new bird feeder and I catch sight of someone down at the picnic table. Well that ain't so unusual, but then after a while I hear this screaming and I decide to go investigate. First I find Jamie chucking up a year's worth of breakfast, blubbering about how the money wasn't worth it and the killing has to stop. The screaming had stopped but now I'm curious, so after I get Jamie cleaned up and calmed down some I decide to come on up to the work site and take a look."

"Don't nobody in this community have the sense they was born with. You should have called my office.   Everybody's got to play detective," Sonny moaned and reached for another donut.

Harry looked hurt.

"I was just curious, and Jamie weren't going nowhere. Anyhow I climbed up and I get to the top of the path and see Keith holding a gun on two people, I know it's Keith because I recognize the shirt from seeing him at breakfast. And I know it's Rob and you because I know his rig and who else'd he have with him. Anyway I creep up in the bushes close as I could get and not get right out in the open and I hear bits and pieces. Rob caught sight of me I think. Keith kept waving his gun and Rob seemed to be trying to back the both of you out of it. I couldn't figure out what I could do to help, then I started picking up rocks, used to be a fair pitch when I was a kid, won all the prizes at the carnival. Anyhow, when he raised that gun I figured it was now or never."

"You should have called me," Sonny repeated.

"Never you mind him, Harry, I'm grateful and so, I know, is Rob. You saved our lives."

"How'd you know to go out there, sheriff?" Kevin asked.

"Got me back three reports this morning. One telling me Pete was the one sent you all them roses and the orchids, Teddy. One from the state's auditor indicating that it was impossible for Ben to have gotten away with it all this time without one or more of the contractors being in on it. One saying the paint on Rene's car matched the sample I got off Dave's pickup." He took a big bite out of his donut, chewed, and swallowed. "So I went out looking for

Dave to have a little chat. His wife said he would be up to Harbor Court."

"Oh my God. Pete," Teddy remembered. "Did you let him loose?"

"Not yet. He's still got a whole lot of explaining to do unless you're going to tell me now his attentions are welcome."

"No, I mean... I mean, no. I'm not interested in Pete that way, he just wouldn't believe me. And I think he needs help. I know he needs to leave me alone."

"Well I think he may have gotten the hint the other night. But just in case, I think we better let this play out through the system. He did admit to making those calls. Even called you twice from jail!" Sonny shook his head sadly. "Harry, you and me are going to have to find a whole new bunch of good ole' boys to play poker with."

"Ain't that the truth," Harry sighed.

CHAPTER 35

Thursday afternoon, from a lounge chair on Teddy's patio, Rob supervised as Kevin and Leroy used shovels to put the finishing touches to the re-covering of Teddy's leach lines. Most of the work had been done the day before by the little dirt mover and the silent man who had operated it.

Rob said the trust was paying for it - the least Ben could do for her under the circumstances. "It's bad enough he was an uninvited guest in your septic tank, his greed caused you a lot of trouble and nearly cost us our lives. You don't really want to move that rock in a wheelbarrow, do you?"

Teddy had given in and was glad she had. "Beer or lemonade?"

"Oh, they'll want beer."

OTHER BOOKS BY AMANDA GLENN

Teddy Books

Pushing Up Purple Daisies
Something In The Corner
Not A Suspicious Death
At The Bottom Of The Garden
Death's Doorbell
They Call It A Murder
Trillium Trouble
Some Body
Tester's Ghost
I Found The Body

Taylor Books

Triangles – Dying In Mexico
Connections – Dead On Arrival
Waves – Dangerous Dancing
Pyramid – Missing In Cancun
Boxes – Death On The Intercoastal
Spirals – Deadly Memories
Kaleidoscope – Warning Lights
Triptych – Little Boy Lost
Tangled – Is She Dead Yet?
Circles – Where The Bodies Are Buried
Focus – Death Scene
Internet – The Glass Globe 2023

GTC – Good 'til Canceled

Fenner Curtis Letters Vol. I 1836-1852
Fenner Curtis Letters Vo. II 1853-1856

Eight Fables And An Essay

Being Of Sound Mind   2022

WRITTEN AS GLENN SPECHT

Darkout
Darkout – JVIII
Darkout – The Moon And Mars
Darkout – A Distant Light
Darkout – Meltdown

Hope you enjoyed the book.
glenn4amanda@gmail.com

Made in the USA
Monee, IL
17 October 2023